INNOCENCE FOR SALE

Confused, Tessa demanded, "What are you talking about?"

"I'm talking about Harley Knox. He's a gentleman, all right, but he also runs one of the most exclusive whorehouses in San Francisco."

Tessa gasped.

"He imports his whores from France and promises the men who patronize his establishment that he affords something *different* that is worth every penny he charges." Lucky's eyes narrowed. "And he's always looking for an *added edge* to increase the patronage of his establishment."

Tessa's eyes widened.

Lucky pressed, "You do understand what I mean by an *added edge*, don't you?"

Tessa swallowed. A single word squeaked through her choked throat. "Me?"

ELAINE BARBIERI

Getting Lucky

LEISURE BOOKS NEW YORK CITY

To my family who makes all things possible.

A LEISURE BOOK®

December 2009

Published by

Dorchester Publishing Co., Inc.
200 Madison Avenue
New York, NY 10016

ISBN 10: 0-8439-6320-4
ISBN 13: 978-0-8439-6320-5
E-ISBN: 978-1-4285-0774-6

The name "Leisure Books" and the stylized "L" with design are trademarks of Dorchester Publishing Co., Inc.

Printed in the United States of America.

10 9 8 7 6 5 4 3 2 1

Visit us online at www.dorchesterpub.com.

Getting Lucky

Chapter One

Tessa White stood in the ring of darkness surrounding the brightly lit city of tents in San Francisco Plaza. Her pale eyes widened. The flickering lights were mesmerizing, causing the interiors to glow like great, golden bursts of welcome. Light streamed through open doorways where roars of laughter, singing, and shouting in different languages could be heard. Her bared feet cooled by the mud that filled the street, her face bathed by the sea breeze wafting across the square, she staggered toward the nearest structure.

Wavering unsteadily, she did not realize that she was a shocking sight to see. Her dress, once a stylish garment she had been proud to wear, was ragged and dirty. Her fair, curling locks were darkened by the grime of the trail and hung in knotted strands. Her formerly well-proportioned figure was skeletal. Black circles ringed her eyes and shadows eclipsed her delicate facial structure. The filth of countless, water-scarce weeks marked her skin, and her feet were bloody from trudging dusty, rock-strewn miles without shoes.

She had arrived a "walker" on a California-bound wagon train that was to deliver its passengers to instant wealth in the gold fields. Yet when the wagons reached their destination, she had been too exhausted to do anything but lie down and close her eyes. She had awakened hours later in a strange, dark field, lying beside a prairie schooner. Still exhausted, almost delirious from hunger, she had wandered toward the sound of music nearby to take in her first glimpse of San Francisco.

It did not occur to her that the frivolity she saw in the tents was more drunken and frantic than joyful, or that the scene was one of the dens of iniquity her mother had warned her against. She knew only that she had slept shivering and alone on the barren ground for too many nights to count, that the few faces she had seen upon awakening had been as frightened and exhausted as her own, and that the music and laughter seemed to draw her in.

Tessa hesitated in the doorway of the closest tent.

Her smile brightened the moment before she suddenly collapsed, unseen by most as the merriment continued.

"Get that walker out of here!"

Lucky Monroe turned toward the gruff command spoken by a drunken fellow at a distant card table. He saw his two muscular hirelings approach the unconscious figure lying in the tent doorway. And when a bearded prospector at his poker table took a concerned step toward her, he ordered, "Sit back down, Buck. You have a hand to play. Jake and Larry will take care of her."

"I ain't about to sit here while your fellas throw that poor girl out of here to get eaten up by some night critters."

Lucky shook his head, a wry smile twisting his lips. "There aren't any night critters close to these tents. It's too noisy for them. Besides, who says my men are going to throw her out to the wolves?"

Buck frowned.

Noting that other men at the table appeared equally disturbed, Lucky ordered, "Just play your hands, fellas. I'm used to handling these things. My men will take the girl to one of those 'bleeding heart stations.' She'll get the attention she needs there."

Buck's frown darkened. "Ain't you heard? Them places are filled up. They ain't taking no more people in."

Lucky noticed that he suddenly had the full attention of the men seated at the poker table. Forgotten were the loose women who hung on their shoulders, the drinks they had been imbibing liberally, and all thoughts of the money they'd won or lost. Sympathy for the plight of the girl was bright in their eyes—sympathy that he had surrendered a long time ago.

Because he had been there.

Lucky glanced around the table to see that most of the men were ready to turn down their cards in order to help the girl. Thinking quickly, he shrugged and said, "Those 'bleeding heart' agencies aren't accepting any more stragglers, huh? Then I guess I'll have to tell my men to take the girl to my hotel room until morning." He turned to wink at the full-blown beauty standing behind him. Delilah's gaze became sultry when he added, "I won't need that bed tonight anyway."

Noting that this alternative seemed to satisfy the men at his card table, Lucky spoke a few words of instruction to Jake and Larry. He then returned to the game without another thought.

Lucky paused as he emerged from the hillside tent that Delilah had temporarily claimed for her use. He stretched a muscular frame tight from sleeping on an uncomfortable cot that was not his own, then lifted his hat from his head to run a hand through the heavy dark hair underneath. He looked around him, breathing deeply, unaware of the picture he made, his deep chest, narrow waist, and slim hips causing women's scrutiny to linger. He knew his rugged features and tall, muscular body made women consider him handsome, but he had earned every bit of his rugged persona the hard way. Good looks hadn't helped him when he was ten years old, abandoned, and forced to make his way in a land where only the strong survived. His broad shoulders and muscular stature were the result of hard labor during those years. He had learned to take nothing for granted and to use every attribute he possessed. He had finally achieved success and wealth with ingenuity, with opportunity grasped in both hands, and with sheer determination.

As a result, he had little sympathy for those who refused to work as hard as he did to survive—no matter their gender.

His thoughts drifting, he gazed out from his position on one of San Francisco's many hills at the gray-green color of the bay. He knew that with the passage of the sun to midafternoon, the color would change to a breathtaking, glittering blue. He also knew that although it was a spectacular sight to see, it was now marred by the abandoned ships anchored in the harbor whose crews had deserted to go hunting for gold. Ironically, the abandoned ships were now being used as shelters where desperate men gladly paid extravagant fees for the luxury of a roof over their heads and a cot to lie on.

He saw the city of tents in San Francisco Plaza, then looked toward Telegraph Hill where Chilean harlots congregated in an unsavory neighborhood. He glimpsed odd-looking, oriental shanties where Chinese immigrants wore strange clothing and braided their hair in a single pigtail hanging down their backs. He glimpsed city activity coming to life in other areas, where men scurried between ramshackle houses, tents, and whatever shelter they could find to lay down their weary heads.

It had not taken him long to assess the opportunity this place presented. He had realized that there was money to be made where the fortunate few successful in the gold fields joined others who had come to San Francisco to drink, whore, and spend recklessly in order to forget their fruitless labor there. Added to the mix were those who had traveled long and hard to reach the city, believing that gold was just waiting for them to find it.

Reality was harsh. Shortages and exorbitant prices made some even more reckless, hoping to earn a good stake at the gambling tables. Monte was the most popular game, but he had become skilled at all of them.

Lucky had had personal experience with all the problems the gold rush presented, including the housing shortage. He had taken whatever privacy he could find until he was able to afford a room of his own. Delilah and her ilk boasted cots that some would find comfortable, and pillows and sheets that were relatively clean. He was a trifle stiff after taking advantage of the comforts she offered, but it had been worth it. And now he could go back to his own room at the lavish Parker House Hotel where clean sheets awaited him and where he—

Lucky's dark brows drew together in a frown as he realized he *couldn't* go back to his own room. The youthful "walker" who had stumbled into his tent the previous night was there. He didn't like the idea of having a dirty, probably disease-laden girl in his bed.

He had earned the right to clean sheets, and he refused to compromise it. It was time to send her to one of the agencies founded for people like her. There had to be room for her somewhere.

His mind made up, Lucky strode toward the hotel with a look of grim determination. He was still wearing that expression when he opened the door to his room to find the girl, as dirty and disheveled as he remembered, sleeping in his bed.

Lucky closed the door noisily behind him. She was obviously exhausted and did not hear him approach the bed. Annoyed by the pang of empathy that struck him, he was about to wake her and order her out when she opened her eyes unexpectedly.

She stared at him with large, bewildered eyes. He forced aside the impact of that gray-eyed gaze and took note that her clothing was stained, that it hung on her emaciated frame, and that her stringy hair overwhelmed her thin face. Yet he could not ignore her small, bare, muddy, and bloodstained feet. They spoke more loudly than words.

Lucky hesitated and then asked gruffly, "What's your name?"

Tessa looked at the big man who stood over her. He was bigger and broader in the shoulder than the men she was used to. She unconsciously noted that although his features were too strong to be called handsome, he was somehow pleasing to the eye. And if he was just now a bit disheveled, with the shadow of a dark beard covering his strong chin and his clothing wrinkled, he was better dressed than she was accustomed to seeing.

She suddenly wondered if Mother would approve of her being alone in a room with a man like him.

But Mother is dead.

Tessa swallowed when sharp memories returned. Her parents and she had started out with such high hopes. Joining the wagon train of prairie schooners on their way to the gold fields had seemed an exciting step for Angus and Marta White. At eighteen years of age, Tessa had turned down an offer of marriage, packed up her belongings, and joined her parents' call to adventure. Neither they nor she had realized, however, that they would see the trail to fortune marked by the discarded furniture, stoves, dishes, and cooking utensils of previous overlanders. They did not expect to cross a wilderness strewn with hasty graves, dying oxen, horses, and abandoned wagons and carts. They did not think their wagon would suffer broken axles that would finally disable it, that they would also abandon their belongings, or that their own oxen would fall prey to lameness. Neither did they take into account the Indian menace or the cholera and scurvy that ended so many lives and left so many shallow graves marked with wooden crosses behind them.

And never—in a million years—did her parents think that their own graves would join that number.

After the loss of her wagon, livestock, and parents, Tessa ended up a "walker," trailing alongside the wagon train, though no longer officially considered a part of it. When she'd started the journey, she'd not imagined that she would be left with no recourse but to go on.

No longer able to cry, she had walked endless, dusty miles. She had trudged the arid, thirty-five miles of Sublette's Cutoff, and had staggered the forty miles of desert between the Humboldt and Truckee rivers. With little water and less help from the people of the wagon train who themselves had so little, she had barely managed to survive on what the countryside had to offer. Yet she had forged on.

Tessa swallowed again and looked up at the man glowering down at her. She then glanced around her. But where was she now? She was lying in a large bed in a light, airy room where the furniture was dust free, the floor was covered with a colorful rug, and the sheets were surprisingly clean. Yet she could not remember how she had gotten there.

Was she dreaming?

"I asked your name."

Reality returned with a snap. Her name. No one had asked her name recently. She had merely been what she was—a hanger-on, a walker, trailing beside a wagon train.

"Your name—do you know it?"

The big man looked so forbidding, so harsh, and so

healthy. He could not possibly comprehend that she had once been the cherished daughter of a loving couple who had started out on a great adventure, or that she had been a young woman who was loved, respected, and valued. He could not comprehend all that because she did not quite understand it herself.

"Your name . . ."

Tessa jumped to her feet, only to sway uncertainly. The big man grasped her arm supportively and ordered, "Sit down."

Refusing to sit, Tessa replied with a touch of her old hauteur, "My na . . . name is Tessa White."

"Where is your family . . . your relatives?"

"Dead."

She saw him glance again at her feet. She raised her chin defensively when he asked, "You walked part of the way to San Francisco?"

She nodded.

The big man nudged her toward the bed and ordered again, "Sit down before you fall down, damn it!"

Lucky studied the girl more closely. She was independent even in her wasted condition. She probably hadn't had a good meal in months.

Walking to the doorway, Lucky picked up the instrument there and blew into it.

"What are you doing?"

She was nosey, too.

"I asked—"

Responding instead to the voice in his ear, Lucky ordered, "Send up two breakfasts."

When he looked back, the girl was frowning. She didn't frown when the food was delivered.

Eating slowly, almost ashamed of his leisurely pace, Lucky watched as the girl sat on the edge of the bed, stuffing fried eggs and bacon into her mouth. With bulging cheeks, she fit a piece of bread into the small space remaining and chewed as best she could.

Lucky ordered gruffly, "Slow down or you'll get sick."

The girl stopped chewing and flushed. She swallowed and said, "I haven't eaten a real . . . I mean, I was hungry."

"So you're a walker."

Lucky was unprepared for the tears that filled the girl's great eyes, or the way she blinked them back when she said, "My parents thought they would strike it rich out here. They were wrong, but they paid a heavy price for their mistake."

"You lost your wagon and your animals?"

"Yes."

"You walked the rest of the way by yourself?"

"I followed the wagon train."

"What are you going to do now?"

The girl took a deep breath. "I don't know."

Her eyes suddenly widened. "I . . . I think I'm going to be sick!"

Lucky scrambled to retrieve the pail in the corner of the room. Returning just in time, he held the girl's head as she purged the contents of her stomach and then closed her eyes. Lucky dropped the pail, suddenly disgusted with his spontaneous actions. When had he sunk to the category of *a bleeding heart*? He knew where that kind of thing could lead and he couldn't afford to go there. Not now. No one had had sympathy for him when he was younger. He'd had to fight every step of the way.

Still—

Lucky watched as the thin, dirty, and bloodied young woman lay back against the bed, exhausted from her ordeal.

Damn it!

There was only one thing he could do.

Tessa walked behind the big man as he strode resolutely up the narrow, winding path toward the outskirts of the city. They had left the hotel as soon as she'd recuperated from her purging. Her ordeal had been embarrassing, especially when she had felt the big man's hand on her forehead as she emptied her stomach. Yet despite it all, she was hungry again, although truly uncertain if she'd ever be able to eat a full meal again.

Tessa's strength lagged. The man's stride was too long, his pace too quick, she was too tired; and the truth was that she wasn't even sure why she was following him.

Breathless, Tessa almost walked into her guide when he turned abruptly toward her.

"Can you make it? It's only a little farther."

"I can make it."

His frown darkened when her instinctive independence surfaced again. He continued on and a question flashed in the back of Tessa's mind: Where were they going and what did he have in mind?

But then she was too tired to think at all.

Lucky paused in front of the dilapidated log cabin atop the desolate hillside. He glanced behind him and frowned at the exhausted girl, who stopped when he did. Well, she had made it. That was good. He would have hated like hell if he'd been forced to carry her up here.

But the girl's eyes were drooping. It had taken all her strength to make the difficult climb on the narrow trail. He took her arm as she swayed, noting that she did not shake off his hand as he called out, "Maggie, are you home?"

He waited. Maggie Windline was the answer to the dilemma he suddenly found himself in. She had the reputation for taking in strays and he figured the girl qualified. He knew, because he had been one of the strays that Maggie had rescued.

Despite himself, Lucky smiled when the door of the cabin opened and three large dogs came galloping out with welcoming barks. He fought off their friendly attentions and patted their heads, remembering that he had personally delivered one of the younger mongrels there. He noted that the girl seemed bewildered again and did not respond when the dogs jumped at her in welcome.

Lucky smiled more broadly at Maggie when the old woman beamed at him and said, "If you ain't a sight for sore eyes! It's been too long since I seen you, Lucky. What are you doing here?"

"I've brought you another stray. Her name's Tessa White."

Motioning toward the girl with his chin, Lucky watched the old woman's reaction.

She briefly scrutinized the girl and replied, "I can see that you did, and just in time, I'd say. This child needs a good meal."

"Not too good a meal . . ." When the girl blushed, Lucky continued. "I'd take it slow feeding her. Anyway, I figure you're the woman for the job of getting her back on her feet."

The girl blinked but she did not speak.

Maggie said, "Well, you know me."

"You can count on me to do my part, too, like always."

The old woman smiled back. "Yeah, like always."

Speaking up unexpectedly, the girl stammered, "I . . . I can take care of myself. I'm ready to work now."

"No, you're not," Lucky countered.

"Yes, I am."

"I say you're not, and I make the decisions here."

"Says who?"

The girl's stubbornness annoyed him. "*I* say so, and you're not in any condition to say otherwise."

"Even if I disagree?"

Damn her independence!

Lucky responded coldly, "Do you really think anybody would hire you now, in your condition?"

The girl considered his question. "Maybe not, but . . . but I'll pay you back for my care."

"Will you?"

Obviously angry at his response, she said unexpectedly, "I'll need to know your name, so I'll know to whom I'm beholden."

"My name's Lucky Monroe."

The girl mumbled.

"What did you say?" he asked suspiciously.

"I said you're lucky all right, running into me."

"Let's get this straight." Lucky stressed, "*You* ran into *me*."

The girl did not respond and Lucky continued. "Maggie knows what she's about, so just do what she says. If you want to pay me back, come to my place of business when you're feeling better. In case you don't remember, that would be the tent where you collapsed last night."

"Collapsed?"

"That's right, collapsed, before my men took you to my hotel room—which I didn't use last night."

Ignoring the girl's obvious confusion, Lucky faced the old woman and said, "I'm going back to my room now, Maggie. I'm tired. I had a hard night."

"I bet you did. Delilah again, huh?"

Lucky's briefly raised brow neither confirmed nor denied Maggie's supposition as he instructed, "Just clean the girl up, and fatten her up, too, while you're at it. I'll take care of the rest. When she's presentable, tell her where my tent is if that's what she wants." He glanced again at Tessa and added, "Although she probably won't remember anything she just said."

"I'll do that." When Lucky tipped his hat and turned away, Maggie called, "Nice seeing you again, Lucky."

Lucky did not bother to smile. He had done what he had to do. He had seen to it that the girl would get back on her feet, although the truth was that he doubted he'd ever see her again. She would get well and go home to Iowa or Illinois, or wherever she came from, as fast as she could. Just another "walker" lucky enough to have made it to San Francisco. She would go on with her life and attempt to forget the past.

It was either that or pursue the only other alternative open to her in a place like San Francisco.

He had seen it all happen before. This girl would be no different.

Tessa looked at the unkempt old woman: long, unbound gray hair that all but obscured her lined face, small brown eyes that seemed to see right through her, a slightly stooped posture, male clothing that did not hide the matronly figure underneath. Maggie Windline's appearance was in direct contrast to Lucky Monroe's fastidious dress.

Tessa did not understand the affection between the old woman and the angry Lucky Monroe, but it had been obvious in the few words they had exchanged. The truth was that she didn't even comprehend what she was doing there.

Giving her a speculative gaze, the old woman said, "You'd better get into the cabin. I'll make you something to eat, and then I'll get the bathtub."

"No, I—"

"Don't give me no back talk, girl! You need a bath, and that's what you're going to get."

"But—"

"You heard him. Lucky's depending on me to do right by you, and I don't intend to let him down."

Tessa was about to respond when one of the hounds jumped up for a friendly pat. Having no choice but to accommodate him, she struggled to maintain her balance while thinking that if the dogs were any judges, the old woman could be trusted.

Her old eyes softening, Maggie suddenly urged, "Come on, Tessa. That's your name, ain't it? You can call me Maggie, and these dogs answer to the names, Blackie, Whitey, and Spot."

Three tails wagged joyfully in response to their

names and Tessa shook her head. Confused, she said, "But their fur . . . all three of them are brown."

"So?"

When Tessa did not answer, Maggie took her arm. "Come on. I'll cook you some breakfast."

Allowing Maggie to lead her into the house with the dogs at their heels, Tessa gave in. She was hungry and weary. She couldn't think anymore, but she knew one thing for sure. She would pay her rescuers back for their unlikely kindnesses if it were the last thing she ever did.

Chapter Two

"You have to eat more."

"I've eaten enough."

"No, you haven't. You're still too skinny. You need some flesh on your bones."

The morning sun shone through the window of the cabin as Tessa regarded Maggie silently. Tessa was wearing one of the nightgowns that the older woman had washed and put away when it no longer fit her, and she was grateful for Maggie's generosity. She was also grateful for Maggie's unrelenting care. During the three weeks that she had resided there, she had grown to love the gray-haired old woman. In that time, she had realized that Maggie wore baggy men's clothing out of convenience—it was less expensive than female clothing and fit her proportions better. She now understood that whatever her appearance, Maggie could be depended upon to keep her word, and that the heart underneath that faded shirt was kind and pure.

Tessa respected her.

She looked at the cleaned breakfast plate in front of her. She had eaten well and with gusto, but she knew that more scrapple still filled Maggie's frying pan. She also knew that the bucket beside the fireplace contained milk that was warm and frothy. Maggie kept a cow hidden behind the cabin. Miraculously it had survived the hunger for good food that plagued the city below, and a few egg-producing chickens pecked at the yard. The cabin's isolation also afforded Maggie the opportunity to raise vegetables in her small garden, and the old woman used them well.

Maggie had set up a cot for Tessa in the corner. Her own larger bed, a simple, wooden table, and two chairs, were the only furniture in the cabin. The fireplace where Maggie cooked was opposite her, and the shelves containing a surprising variety of supplies, as well as the simple housewares with which Maggie conducted her daily life, were nearby.

The dogs that Maggie had adopted, and which seemed to have adopted Tessa as well, slept together near the fireplace. Let out to run in the morning, they traveled into the hills part of the day and returned in the afternoon. Strangely, they never went down into the city. Tessa silently wondered if that behavior was due to Maggie's training, or simply a matter of the dogs not wanting to go where they were not wanted.

Maggie's way of life was adequate and comfortable, and Tessa had grown to appreciate it.

One of the highlights was the view from the hillside just outside the cabin doorway. It was an exquisite sight: blue sky, rolling hills, wildflowers in full bloom. Even the din of the constant construction below was muted. Distance also made less visible the squalor in some areas, and even dulled the din of the nighttime merriment that had originally drawn her to Lucky's tent.

Yet despite her growing understanding of Maggie's life, the old woman's genuine fondness for Lucky Monroe remained a mystery.

Tessa recalled the big man with silent resentment. It galled her that Lucky had dumped her on Maggie, taking advantage of the old woman because no one else in the booming city below would have spent the time or would have had the patience for a sick, indigent young woman with no prospects at all.

Yet she could not seem to make Maggie see things that way, and she had since given up trying. Maggie had explained that she had helped Lucky when he was in need. Her claim that Lucky had not forgotten her had been spoken with obvious pride. Maggie had whispered in confidence that Lucky had left orders at the mercantile that Maggie's supplies were to be charged to his account.

Tessa was not convinced. His actions might make him a hero to Maggie but they required no effort at all, and used funds that he knew he would reclaim at the gaming tables later.

Though she could not bring herself to speak those negative thoughts to Maggie, Tessa could not pretend to feel the same affection for Lucky that Maggie felt. When she mentioned Lucky's gruffness, Maggie merely replied, "That's just his way." When she commented that he had not visited the old woman during the three weeks that she'd been there, that he seemed to remember Maggie only when he needed her, Maggie simply claimed, "He comes when he can."

Excuses!

Maggie would not admit, even to herself, that if Lucky truly cared about her or the "walker" who had stumbled into his life, he would have visited at least once.

Maggie might be forever grateful to him, but Tessa wasn't. Lucky's caustic glance and dismissive shrug when he'd said she could come to him for a job when she recuperated stuck in her memory. He didn't expect to ever see her again; but whether he knew it or not, she *would* pay back every cent he had spent on her.

Noting that Maggie still hoped she would eat more breakfast, Tessa said with a smile, "I'm thin, but I'm healthy now, thanks to your care, Maggie. And I appreciate all you've done for me."

Maggie sighed at her response and put the frying pan down. She knew when she was beaten, which only made Tessa love her more.

"I'm going to see Lucky later this morning for a job," Tessa announced. "I need to work off the debt I owe him."

"I'm sure Lucky doesn't remember what you said about paying him back." Maggie continued more slowly. "Even if he does, he won't really expect you to show up. The truth is that he doesn't have any work to offer that would suit a young woman like you."

Tessa's mouth twitched. "Lucky will remember every word I said when he pays his account."

"You've got him all wrong." Maggie's bleary eyes grew moist. "Lucky's a nice fella. He's much nicer than he wants to be."

"Then he'll give me a job so I can pay him back."

Maggie repeated, "You're not the kind to take any job Lucky is able to offer."

Tessa forced a smile. "I found out the hard way that I can handle anything that comes along. All I have left in this world is my word, and I intend to keep it."

Ignoring Maggie's frown, Tessa turned toward the freshly washed clothing that Maggie had provided. The dress was shabby and a bit too large, but it was clean and as she put it on, Tessa cherished the feel and scent of that cleanliness against her skin. She had known the opposite and she would never forget the memory.

Dressed at last and with her self-imposed chores completed, Tessa smiled at Maggie, patted Blackie, Whitey, and Spot on their heads, and said resolutely, "It's nearly noon. Lucky should be awake by now. I'm going to find him, but I'll be back."

"You do remember where the Parker House Hotel is, don't you?"

"I'll find it." Hesitating, Tessa added, "I'll pay *you* back, too, as soon as I can." She dismissed Maggie's spontaneous retort by saying, "I want to do it. I hope you understand that I *need* to do it."

When Maggie went silent, Tessa turned toward the door.

Lucky walked down the stairs of the Parker House Hotel and glanced at the clock in the lobby. It was just past noon, a reasonable hour to start the day when a man spent the greater portion of the night carefully contemplating his cards. He was still weary but wearing a freshly pressed suit, the brocade vest that had become his trademark, clean linens, a dark, broad-brimmed hat, and his hand-tooled boots. It was easy for a man like him to be well pressed and dressed. Laundries had sprung up with the population explosion in the city, and he had the funds to purchase whatever he needed. He enjoyed that luxury more than anyone realized. Eating and sleeping where he preferred, regardless of the price, never grew old. He had known want. He had wandered aimlessly when he'd lost his parents. He'd been hungry, desperate, uncertain how he would survive. He had no intention of ever going there again.

Lucky had scrutinized his appearance in the washstand mirror a few minutes before and had decided that he needed a haircut. He also needed a shave. A trip to the barber was in order.

Lucky smiled when he touched the few coins the barber would charge. When he'd first reached San Francisco, he would never have parted with those coins for a shave and a haircut. Each one would have represented hours of hard labor. Yet he now earned more money in his tent in one night than he had earned in six months of gold panning.

Lucky . . . well, he supposed that nickname had stuck to him because it was appropriate in a way, but he would never forget—

Startled by the appearance of the thin young woman entering the hotel lobby, Lucky frowned. Her dress was faded and a bit too large. However, it did not conceal the slender, female proportions underneath, or detract from the long, platinum hair that was a burst of sunshine in the shadowed lobby. It was obvious by the way she approached Harley Knox, a well-dressed but questionable character, that she was as inexperienced and as innocent as she appeared to be. He wondered why someone like her would walk into a place like this hotel lobby unescorted—and why Harley Knox had directed her toward him!

Lucky frowned more darkly as the young woman came closer. The activity in the hotel lobby had come to a standstill at her entrance, and he knew why. Although he was certain that hardly a man in the place had ever seen hair the color of hers, he was sure they were all familiar with the way she had secured the front strands back from her face, leaving the remainder loose to stream onto her narrow shoulders. It was a simple and practical hairstyle—reminding them of home. Yet he supposed those same men had never seen anyone like her at home, with features so delicate and cheekbones so unexpectedly elegant, or with full lips so soberly composed. And he doubted that they had ever seen skin so smooth and clear, or eyes so wide and light.

What color were her eyes anyway? Gray?

Gray.

With dawning realization, Lucky looked at the young woman's feet. She wore makeshift sandals that were muddied from the streets and also too large, but they allowed anyone to see the scars of her shoeless journey to San Francisco.

Glancing up again, Lucky caught the gaze of those large gray eyes, and he knew.

Halting in front of him, the young woman said simply, "I'm here, just as I promised I would be. I'm ready to work off my debt any way you ask."

Hell, did she know what she was saying?

"You do know who I am, don't you?" Lucky saw uncertainty enter the young woman's expression for the first time as she continued. "I realize I look different from the last time you saw me." She added, "My name is Tessa White."

She looked more different than she realized.

His gruff tone concealing his momentary surprise, Lucky replied, "You're the 'walker.'"

The young woman grimaced. "If that's what you want to call me."

"So what are you doing here?" Lucky glanced around him before she could respond. He saw the continued attention she was attracting, as well as the interest in Harley Knox's eyes. He took her arm and ushered her out the doorway. "I left you with Maggie. She was supposed to take care of you."

"She did and I've recuperated. It's time to pay back what I owe you."

Lucky nodded, noting her determined expression. He asked unexpectedly, "What are your long-range plans?"

"Long range?" She obviously had not anticipated that question. Shrugging, she hesitated before continuing. "I haven't thought that far ahead, but I suppose I intend to go home to my aunt's farm in Iowa once my debts are paid and I can earn enough money not to be a burden there."

So he was right. She was an innocent from Iowa.

Lucky noted the attention they drew when they reached the street. He looked around for a spot where they could continue their conversation in privacy. It wouldn't do for a young woman like her to be seen consorting with a gambler like him. As a result of his chosen profession, he now needed to be content with women like Delilah and possibly Marisa, the brunette who stood waiting in the wings for him to become tired of the red-haired beauty. He did not complain. Those women served his purpose very well and he was satisfied with his life. The last thing he needed were the complications that a young woman like Tessa White could add.

With those thoughts in mind, Lucky said simply,

"If you need money to go home, I'll give it to you, but if you stay in this town alone, you won't remain the person you were when you first came."

"I'm not that person anyway."

Lucky's eyes narrowed. "You're not, huh?"

"The person who 'walked' to San Francisco was destitute, helpless, and sick. The person I am now is well and strong, and willing to earn her way home."

He shook his head.

"What is that supposed to mean?" Suddenly angry, the young woman insisted, "You promised that if I came to see you, you'd give me a job."

"I'll give you the money to go home, instead."

Tessa grated, "I don't want your money. I want a job."

His hand tightening on her arm, Lucky dragged Tessa along beside him as he continued. "You wouldn't want any job available for you in my tent."

"I'll do anything. I'll clean . . . scrub . . . prepare the tables for the night."

"I have hired men who do that."

"I'll provide change for your customers."

"Change . . ." Lucky almost laughed. "You're not in Iowa anymore, Tessa."

Blinking at his use of her name, Tessa said, "All right, I'll . . . I'll weigh out the gold dust."

"You know how to do that?"

"No, but I can learn."

"I don't run a school."

Tessa's jaw locked tight as Lucky shoved her into an

alleyway between two buildings. She insisted coldly, "I said I'd do anything."

"All right," Lucky challenged. "Just what *can* you do?"

Tessa raised her chin. "I can cook, clean, sew."

"Wonderful."

"I can read and cipher, too."

"Admirable."

Smarting at his sarcastic tone, Tessa replied, "I said I'd do anything."

No, she doesn't realize what she's saying.

At his continued silence, Tessa retorted, "So maybe the men who come to your tent don't care about cleaning or sewing, or even ciphering or reading, but they all *eat*. I can cook, and Maggie said that men in San Francisco are willing to pay just about anything for a good, home-cooked meal."

"I serve whiskey in my tent. I don't serve food."

"Well, maybe you should serve food!"

Lucky stared at the slight young woman standing in front of him. The sun slanting through the alley played over her hair, highlighting its brilliance in the flickering rays. Her skin seemed to glow in the semi-light, but her expression remained tightly drawn, and her light eyes snapped with anger. She had no fear of challenging him, which revealed her inexperience with men like him. She was determined.

Lucky's grim expression did not change. No, he didn't need the trouble that would come with this determined young woman. Innocent as she was, she was prime fare for the vultures that flocked to San Francisco.

"Well?"

"Well, what?"

"Are you going to hire me or will I have to find a job elsewhere?"

Lucky reiterated slowly, "I don't have a job for you, not a job that you'd want to do anyway."

Tessa turned on her heel. She was about to walk past him when he grabbed her arm.

"Let me go." Her light eyes scorched him. "I'll find a job and I'll pay you back every penny you spent on me. You'll see, I'll—"

"I'll try you out tonight."

"Wh . . . what?"

"I'll put up a table in my tent where you can set your food. We'll see if you bring in any money."

The young woman took a breath, suspicious at his sudden change of mind. She nodded. "That's fair."

"But there's a catch."

Tessa's eyes narrowed. "I thought so."

Ignoring her response, Lucky said resolutely, "If it doesn't work out, I expect to lend you the amount you'll need for transportation home." At her instantaneous protest, he stressed, "I said *lend*. You can pay me back."

"I won't go home in debt."

"That's the deal. Take it or leave it."

The young woman's chin rose a notch. She hesitated, and then said, "All right, I'll take it. But you'll see. The men in your tent will love my food—if you don't put too high a price on it, that is."

"The price will be up to me."

Tessa mumbled.

He snapped, "What did you say?"

"I said I expected as much!"

"Take it or leave it."

"I said I'd take it. When do you want me to come?"

Lucky shrugged. "Eight o'clock is good enough."

"I'll be there."

Lucky watched as Tessa strode resolutely out into the sunshine. When she stepped out of sight, he mumbled under his breath, "Damn, what have I gotten myself into?"

What had she gotten herself into?

That question rang over and over again in her mind as Tessa strode down the busy street. She realized she was quite lost.

Tessa turned the corner, her stride slowing at the unexpected sight that met her eyes. Stunned, she walked a little farther to view more closely the unpainted shanties that abounded on the wharves, and the abandoned ships in the harbor that she had noticed from a distance. She bit her lips, frightened by the sordid scene. The area was dirty and unkempt, with garbage floating in water that had formerly appeared to glitter a clear, faultless blue in the afternoon sun. The wharves teemed with frenzied, foreign-looking men alighting in a steady stream from ships that must be the Panama steamers she had read about. The crowds moved rapidly in all directions, filling the street, pushing and shoving while shouting out in various languages. In their midst workers pushed baggage carts, soiled doves plied their trade, and a few old-time settlers sauntered casually, appearing almost amused by the antics of the newcomers.

She saw another ship maneuvering its way into port, hoping to squeeze into the last remaining dock space there. The arrivals were endless, depositing gold seekers of all types and classes on the shore to begin their quest for the instant wealth that would not come to many.

Tessa had the disturbing realization that in this vast, unlikely place, she was totally alone.

She suffered a moment's panic. She had agreed to a deal that was unlikely to end in her favor. She did not doubt her culinary talent. Her mother had taught her to cook good, hearty meals that would satisfy the workers on their farm at harvesttime. That was not the problem. Her lack of equipment and foodstuffs was. She had no stove, no pots or pans, no spices, no place to put supplies, and most importantly, no idea what was available to her in this city where shortages of basic staples were common. Yet she needed to put it all together by eight o'clock, when Lucky Monroe would be waiting for her to produce a meal that would determine her future.

About to despair, Tessa heard a voice at her elbow. She turned to see the same fellow who had directed her toward Lucky in the hotel lobby. He was smiling a warm, comforting smile as he said, "You look like you could use some help."

Tessa scrutinized the stranger. He was young, probably no older than his late twenties. Clean-shaven, with light brown hair and eyes, he seemed pleasant enough. His suit was clean, fashionable, of good quality, and obviously hand-tailored; and he seemed interested in a friendly way. She realized that she had probably sensed that quality in him, which had caused her to approach him in the hotel lobby even though he was a stranger. In any case, he had helped her once. She hoped he could help her again.

She ventured, "I seem to be lost at present. I . . . I would appreciate it if you could direct me to the mercantile store."

"Gladly, but I would like to introduce myself first. My name is Harley Knox. And you are?"

"Tessa White. I'm going to cook for the men in Lucky Monroe's tent tonight, but I need to find the mercantile first."

"Of course. I'll take you there."

Harley took her arm. Gently freeing herself, she said with a smile, "Directions will suffice."

Harley's smile broadened. "It's obvious from your speech that you're well educated, Tessa. I admit to surprise at seeing you here alone."

"I didn't start out alone. I ended up that way when my parents died on the way west."

"Oh, I'm sorry."

Tessa took a breath. "I am, too. But they would want me to go on, and that's what I'm doing."

"What made you go to Lucky Monroe?"

"It worked out that way." Unwilling to volunteer any further information, Tessa pressed, "The mercantile?"

"It's just a few blocks over. I'd be glad to show you the way if you'll agree."

He is pleasant, with good manners, a gentleman.

Making a snap judgment, Tessa nodded. Again taking her arm, Harley urged her forward as he said with obvious regret, "I just wish you had come to me first, Tessa. Lucky Monroe is a gambler. He doesn't have the best reputation around here."

"Maggie Windline seems to think well of him."

"Oh, that old crazy."

Tessa went abruptly still. Shaking loose his grip on her arm, she said stiffly, "I think I can find my way from here, Mr. Knox. The mercantile can't be much farther."

"I'm sorry. I didn't mean to offend you."

"But you did. Maggie is my friend."

"Then she is my friend, too." Appearing contrite, Harley said, "Please accept my apology. I suppose I shouldn't listen to what others say about her."

"I don't care what anyone else says. Nor do I care what you say any longer. Thank you for your help, Mr. Knox."

Tessa was about to turn away when Harley gripped

her arm again and repeated, "I'm sorry. I didn't realize . . . I mean . . ."

"I accept your apology. Now I must go."

Striding away when Harley dropped her arm, Tessa turned the corner. She saw the mercantile store then. Her mind emptying of all other thoughts, she remembered that Maggie said Lucky had established an account for her there. She hoped Maggie wouldn't mind a few extra charges as long as she paid Lucky back.

Bravely, her heart pounding, Tessa entered the store. Noel Richman, the proprietor of the mercantile, was overweight and balding, a man whose assessing glances she did not particularly like. Yet she emerged a short time later with a workman walking behind who carried her supplies to a wagon that the proprietor had provided for transportation back to Maggie's cabin. Aware of that necessity despite her uncertain feelings about the man's knowing stare, Tessa forced an absentminded smile when the old fellow at the reins headed the wagon toward the trail she had descended that morning. Her thoughts were racing ahead to the meal she was planning.

It was now or never.

In lesser spirits as the sun set on the horizon, Tessa sat stiffly in another wagon as it drew up to Lucky's tent. She was arriving earlier than the last time she had approached his tent, but lights blazed from within the canvas structure nevertheless. A buzz of voices punctuated by sharp laughter and the slap of cards could be heard. Her memory of her first night in San Francisco was poor, but she remembered that the glow from within the tent had seemed to call out in welcome, and that she had staggered toward it. The laughter, singing, and joking seemed more shrill tonight.

Tessa signaled the driver to halt. To his credit, Lucky had arranged for a wagon to transport her offerings to his customers that evening. She hadn't thought of that problem, and Lucky had saved the day once again. The realization that she was further indebted to him annoyed her.

Tessa jumped down from the wagon when it halted. She entered the tent cautiously. Forcing a smile at the surprised glances that turned her way, Tessa turned toward Lucky as he approached. Strangely, her heart leaped at seeing him. She corrected a prior thought. He was indeed handsome despite his sharp features and intense stare. Taller than the average male, he walked with a resolute but easy step, indicating an air of authority. His muscular stature was not missed by the many heavily painted female eyes turning covetously his way. Yet with her first glimpse of his harsh expression, reality returned. No matter how different he now appeared to her, Lucky was the same man—callous, demanding, and determined to be rid of her.

Halting to tower over her when he reached her side,

he drilled her with his dark-eyed gaze as he growled, "So you showed up."

"I told you I would. Where should I put the food?"

"I had my men set up a table over there." Indicating a dark corner, he mumbled, "It's as good a spot as any."

Turning away from her, he ordered, "Pedro, help the lady with her things."

Short, with graying hair, a dark complexion, and a ready smile, Pedro appeared as if by magic at the summons. The man said courteously in heavily accented English, "How would you have me place the food, *senorita*?"

"Simply, if you please, with the flatware at one end of the table and the dishes and bread at the other."

"*Sí, senorita.*" He whispered when he placed the heavy pots on the table minutes later, "The stew smells very good, almost like home."

"That's what I'm counting on, Pedro," she commented. But she gasped when she saw the hand-lettered sign that declared the outrageous cost of a simple plate of her mother's favorite stew. She glanced back at Lucky, who didn't even blink.

He *wanted* her to fail!

Suddenly angrier than she had ever been, Tessa took her place behind the prepared table with a stiff smile.

She waited.

Lucky inwardly winced and threw his cards down on the table in front of him. To the amusement of the bearded prospectors sitting across from him, he had lost another hand and he knew it was his fault. He wasn't concentrating. He *couldn't* concentrate with Tessa standing there with a smile plastered on her face for the better part of a half hour, while his customers resisted the rapidly congealing stew she offered.

Oh, they had looked at her, all right. What man wouldn't? She stood like a beacon, simple and fair in a sea of overblown and overpainted, overly accommodating beauties. But he knew what those fellas were thinking. What was she doing there? She shouldn't be in a place where men dispensed with their inhibitions after long months of hard work that had netted only a few rewards.

And why did he care about her predicament? Why had the gaze of those great gray eyes remained in his memory so clearly that he had been unable to get the scruffy, dirty little urchin he'd first seen out of his mind? Each wagon train delivered more orphans to San Francisco than he cared to count. One agency or another eventually took them all in, and he felt no sense of responsibility toward them. Someone had said those agencies couldn't handle anyone else. He had his doubts about that, but somewhere in the back of his mind was the realization that he had been reluctant to turn that particular girl over to them. Once he had settled her in Maggie's cabin, he had been so determined to forget her that he had deliberately avoided visiting while she was there. He had told himself that he didn't care how she was faring; yet every glance of her eyes now played on his senses.

Why?

In truth, the answers were simple:

Because she was *an innocent*.

Because the day she lost her innocence would be a day she would not forget.

Because to lose her innocence would be to stop trusting others as well as herself, and for some reason he didn't want that to happen to her.

Because once she took that step, she could not go back.

Because all the aforementioned was inevitable if she remained alone in San Francisco much longer. He wanted to protect her from her own determination to do what he did not believe she could accomplish.

Somehow she disliked him for his concern. She had made that evident, but he had already decided that he didn't need her friendship. Most important to him was to get her out of harm's way, for her own sake.

And possibly for his own.

"Come on, Lucky, stop shuffling those cards and deal."

Lucky's attention snapped toward the grubby fellow who had spoken so impatiently. The man's hair was too long, his beard was too straggly, and his clothes—well, he had become accustomed to the smell.

Lucky's mouth twitched as he struggled against the emotions overwhelming him. He didn't care about that prospector. He only cared about the young woman who stood there alone, awaiting cruel disappointment.

The funny thing was that he didn't want Tessa to succeed, yet he couldn't bear for her to fail, either.

Agitated, he took a breath. He didn't know what he wanted, damn it!

"Are you going to deal or not?"

His mind returning to the game in front of him, Lucky dealt the cards and picked up his hand. His glance moved to the table where Tessa still stood motionless, and his stomach clenched. His only consolation was that in a few hours it would be over and Tessa would have no choice but to agree to the deal they had struck. She'd go home and that would be the last he would see of her.

That was good.

So why did it make him feel so damned bad?

Tessa resisted asking Pedro how long she had been standing there in Lucky's crowded tent with pots of stew growing cold in front of her. She was sure he knew because he had been standing at the opposite end of the table, waiting for a rush that did not come.

She glanced at the old Mexican and shot him a shaky smile. Pedro did not smile in return. He had briefly whispered his background to her, that he was a family man with three young daughters to support, and that Lucky was making it possible for him to do that comfortably for the first time in his life. He wore his emotions on his face, and it was clear to see that he was upset at her embarrassment.

Tears filled Tessa's eyes, but she blinked them back. She would not fail. She would not allow it! She would go out on the street to sell her wares if she needed to. She would—

"Nice to see you again, Tessa."

Tessa blinked at Harley Knox, who had appeared unexpectedly in front of her table. She nodded but was unable to return his greeting before he spoke again.

"I thought I'd try to apologize one more time."

"I accepted your apology already, Mr. Knox."

"Yes, but you didn't mean it."

Tessa admitted slowly, "No, I didn't."

A smile broke unexpectedly across Harley's pleasant face. "An honest answer. Now will you say you forgive me like you mean it?"

Tessa replied reluctantly, "I suppose I should. It wouldn't take much to think that Maggie is a foolish hermit and to believe whatever people say about her if you didn't know her. But I do, and she isn't. I also know, however, that a person shouldn't condemn anyone on someone else's word."

"I have been properly chastised." Harley looked down unexpectedly at the pot in front of her. He said, "Is that beef stew I see there . . . *real beef stew*?"

Tessa's face flushed. "You don't have to—"

Ignoring her interruption, Harley said, "Fill a dish

for me, if you please. I didn't have time to eat this evening, and I expect it's going to be a long night."

Uncertain what he meant by "a long night," Tessa dutifully dished up the stew.

Tessa smiled when Harley rolled his eyes approvingly after his first taste and disappeared into the crowd. Her first sale, but it also appeared to be her last. Still standing there, waiting for a rush that did not come, she did not notice when an old fellow who had been playing poker at a nearby table threw down his cards and stood up unexpectedly. She only noticed him when he limped toward her and said, "My name's Strike Walker, ma'am. I've been losing at cards, and I think it's because I'm damned hungry and I can't think about anything else. I figure the best thing to do is to stop smelling that stew you got there, and try putting some of it in my stomach. If it's as good as the aroma it's giving off, I figure I'll be doing myself a favor."

Wizened, with bowed legs, the prospector was short, his beard and eyebrows were gray, and his face was hardened from long days in the sun. Yet his rheumy gaze was direct as he waited for her reply. Finding it hard to speak past the lump in her throat, Tessa simply filled the plate that Pedro handed her and squeaked, "I hope you like it."

"I'm sure I will, ma'am."

She whispered, "You did look at the sign on the table, didn't you? You know how much this meal will cost you?"

"I did, and I'm sure it'll be worth every penny."

Tessa's throat choked tight again. She waited until he dipped his spoon into the rich gravy. She released a relieved breath when he commented, "Just like I said, it's worth every penny."

She could have kissed him.

Tessa's eyes widened at the line that rapidly formed before her table when he walked away. She shot Pedro an appreciative glance when he cut the loaves of bread she had so carefully baked and placed a thick slice on the side of each plate. She could not believe it when she scraped the bottom of the last pot and was forced to apologize to the next man in line for running out of food.

Tessa stood still for a few moments with the empty pot in front of her and an unhappy line dispersing. She had sold out without a single complaint about the price!

Her mind flew ahead to the next night when she would offer the same menu, but with a dessert of apple pie made from the dried applies she had seen at the mercantile. She was sure the men would love it and she—

"You can get your things out of here now. We have some serious gambling to do."

Tessa blinked when Lucky's voice sounded beside her. She started to reply but saw that he was already issuing instructions to the accommodating Pedro. Within minutes, the table was cleared, the wagon loaded, and the tent had been restored to its original appearance.

She glared at Lucky as he rushed her outside and then left her to speak quietly to Pedro beside the wagon.

"You look angry, Tessa."

She turned toward the tent as Harley Knox emerged. She had not seen where the man had gone once he stepped away from her table. In the ensuing rush, she had forgotten all about him.

Harley laughed. "You look surprised to see me."

"I'm sorry. I didn't know you were still here."

"I told you that it would be a long night. Waiting is never easy." Sobering, he said, "May I see you home, Tessa?"

Surprised, Tessa asked candidly, "Why would you want to do that?"

"Why?" Harley shook his head. "I suppose because I've been thinking about you all day and I've decided that I'd like to know you better."

"Why?"

"Because . . . because you're beautiful, honest, and you remind me of home."

"Too bad you're going to be disappointed, Knox, because *I'm* going to see Miss White home tonight."

Tessa's mouth dropped open when Lucky appeared suddenly behind Harley and added, "We have business to discuss. Isn't that right, Tessa?"

Speechless, Tessa nodded. She muttered a good-bye to Harley and followed Lucky to the wagon. She caught her breath when he swung her up onto the wagon seat without another word and then took his place beside her and clucked the horse into motion.

Delilah watched from the doorway of the tent as the wagon carrying Lucky and Tessa White snapped into motion. She ran a hand over the upward sweep of hair that was too bright a red to be natural, then moved the revealing neckline of her dress a bit lower. She was amply endowed in that area and the white flesh bulging above the beaded bodice was soft and appealing. She counted on that. She did not doubt that it was the womanly proportions she so generously displayed that had first drawn Lucky to her. She had made sure that the expression he saw when he looked up at her face for the first time was warm, inviting, seductive, and above all, *willing*. She'd had no fear that he would lose interest in her, or that he'd turn to Marisa, who had been waiting unsuccessfully in that hope. She had worked hard at keeping Lucky's attention and she had seen to it that he would not grow tired of her. Her reasoning was simple. Lucky was everything she wanted in a man. He was wealthy, had a tent of his own, was a true hand at cards; but most of all, he was handsome and manly—more so than any other fellow she'd had before. And he was clean. He smelled good. She had never become accustomed to odors as some of the other women in the tent had.

In addition to everything else, she loved him as much as it was possible for her to love. She knew that

Lucky did not love her in return, but he *liked* her, which was good enough for the time being. She had figured she had time to build on his affection until Tessa White walked onto the scene.

Delilah snorted. She knew the darling Miss White's type: innocent, needy, and sweet. She would draw Lucky relentlessly into her web with her innocence before becoming willing. Then she would trap him and offer no means of escape. No, Delilah did not intend to allow Lucky to become ensnared by that clever woman or anyone else.

But for the moment, she'd bide her time. There were other fish in the sea that would enable her to earn a living until she snagged *the big one.*

Harley stood unseen outside the doorway of Lucky's tent. He had seen Delilah's face just before she walked back inside. She didn't like what she saw and she was experienced enough to be dangerous. She did not intend to lose Lucky to the innocent upstart with whom he seemed so engrossed at present. Harley wondered if Delilah would recognize that same expression on his own face if she saw it, and if she would realize that he did not intend to allow Tessa to get away from him, either.

Delilah disappeared within and Harley turned back toward the wagon carrying Lucky and Tessa as it slipped out of sight on the trail. His plans had been circumvented that evening, but the situation was only temporary. The evening had been long and the waiting tedious, but he was doing extraordinarily well with Tessa White. His efforts would be worth the trouble in the end because the proceeds would be enormous. Tessa was inexperienced, which was a point in his favor if he acted swiftly. She would not listen to any of the talk about him, either. She would make her own judgment, which he fully intended to influence with faultless behavior until he was ready. Lucky knew him well, but he did not know him well enough to comprehend how determined he could be.

Harley smiled, recalling the reaction of everyone in the hotel lobby when Tessa had walked in. She had had the same reaction on the crowd in Lucky's tent. Every man there had been fascinated, struck silent at the first sight of her. He knew they had seldom seen a young woman like Tessa. Her features were so refined, her air so unconsciously genteel, and her hair so light as to make her appear the personification of a storybook princess despite her cheap clothing. Dressed properly, she would be an instant draw for any man who chose to spend the fee Harley's house would charge for her services. He had found it extremely profitable to cater to those chosen few. He expected that number to rise when Tessa White was added to his stable.

And if he knew human nature as well as he thought he did, that wouldn't take long, especially with the help of the chemical sources at his disposal. Happily, there appeared to be no love lost between Tessa and Lucky. If

Harley played his cards right, Tessa would not listen to a negative word that Lucky said about him.

He'd wait until tomorrow before making any definite plans. He was sure of one thing: eventually he'd get Tessa to see things his way. If he didn't miss his guess, Lucky was playing into his hands right now.

"Don't come back to my tent tomorrow night, or any night for that matter. I run that tent to make money, and the price of the meal you cooked didn't make up for what I lost while the men were lined up to eat."

Lucky's shocking statement broke the unnatural silence that had reigned between Tessa and him for the greater portion of their drive back to Maggie's cabin. The wagon rocked and swayed uncomfortably, with only the moon's brilliant rays to light the trail while Tessa stared at him.

When she remained speechless, Lucky continued. "I'll get your tickets for transportation back to Iowa tomorrow, just as we agreed."

Stunned, Tessa muttered, "But . . . but I sold out. All the men asked me what I was cooking tomorrow. I have a menu already planned!"

His features tight, Lucky repeated, "I'll have your tickets ready for you tomorrow." He added with the same intensity, "And don't have anything to do with Harley Knox, either. He's bad news."

"And you're not?"

When Lucky did not reply, Tessa regained a semblance of control and continued bravely. "I'm afraid I'll need a clearer explanation than you've given for firing me."

"Really?" Lucky allowed the reins to fall lax while he pinned her with his gaze. She had no idea of the depth of appeal she'd had for the men in his tent that night. Nor did she realize that however good her stew tasted, those men would have lined up for whatever she had to offer, and at any price. Nor did she realize that with the moonlight turning her hair to pure silver, with her features too perfect to be real, he ached to curl his arms around her and keep her safe from whatever other heartbreaks were to come her way.

He could not deny his pangs of envy when she laughingly responded to the prospectors whose plates she filled. He was intensely aware that she had never been so relaxed with him. Yet even though she now sat so close to him on the hard wagon seat that he could feel her thigh pressed against his, could hear her breathing, and could almost taste the distinctive, appealing scent of her body, her innocence remained a rigid barrier between them.

Nearing panic, Lucky realized he needed to be certain that Tessa left San Francisco soon, before it was too late.

Lucky made a sudden decision and grasped her suddenly tight against the muscular wall of his body. He kissed her with cruel, lingering intensity. She was so slender in his arms as he held her. She was so warm, so real. He wanted . . . he needed—

Realizing abruptly that Tessa was more dangerous than even he had realized, Lucky thrust her away from him and said with sudden fierceness, "That's what you can expect from those men if you stay."

Tessa struggled to catch her breath. "I don't believe you!"

"That's your mistake."

His anger rose a notch higher by her naivety and by the desire still surging through his veins. Lucky continued hotly. "You'll be better off in Iowa, and I'll be better off without a woman like you distracting my customers."

Tessa ignored the inference in his tone and responded stubbornly, "The night isn't over yet. You may still make plenty of money now that the men are gambling again."

"Those few hours were all the proof I need."

"You're jumping to conclusions."

"No, I'm not."

"You're not giving those men any consideration."

"I sure enough am. You made them comfortable, all right—comfortable enough for some of them to sit back with a full belly and fanaticize—which translates into wasted time."

"What did you expect them to do instead of *wasting time*?"

"I expected them to spend money. I also expect them to go other places to fulfill their sexual fantasies when necessary. They come to my tent to spend money gambling."

"You mean lose money."

Lucky's brow tightened as he repeated, "Those prospectors come to my tent because they're looking for an honest game, and that's what I give them. They want to forget their troubles for a night and have some female company—without ties—and I give them that, too."

"With whiskey alongside."

"They drink, which does not interfere with either of those pastimes."

"If they have full stomachs to start with."

"I'm not responsible for their 'full stomachs'!"

"I don't expect you to be. *I* can fill that need."

"No."

"But—"

"I said no. I gave you a chance, but you interfered with my profits."

"I didn't."

"It's my tent, and *I* say you did! I'll have your tickets ready tomorrow."

"I'm not going anywhere."

"That was our agreement."

"The terms of our agreement were that you would provide the tickets if I failed. I did not fail."

"As far as I'm concerned, you did."

"I don't agree."

Drawing the wagon up in front of Maggie's cabin at last, Lucky turned fully toward Tessa, but his throat went suddenly tight. She was so damned beautiful in her fury, so appealing, and so damned vulnerable—more than she knew. He could not bear the thought that men gripped by San Francisco's gold mania might change her.

Those thoughts weighed heavily on his mind as he said gruffly, "Get out of the wagon. I'll take your things into the cabin."

"I'll take them in myself."

"I said I'd do it."

Tessa's eyes narrowed but she jumped down from the wagon, stomped into the cabin, and slammed the door closed behind her. Her back was turned toward him when he carried in her supplies, and Lucky was glad. He was uncertain what would happen if she looked at him just then.

Maggie glanced between them without saying a word. Lucky slammed the door behind him when he was done, and left without breaking either his stride or the silence.

His anger soared as the wagon rattled back down the trail. He remembered seeing Harley Knox walk toward Tessa outside the tent that evening. Rage had twisted tight inside him at the easy way they conversed. He had decided then and there that he'd never let a smooth-talking weasel like Harley Knox pull the wool over Tessa's eyes.

Lucky's lips twisted at the thought. All San Francisco knew what Harley Knox was. It wasn't hard to see that Harley had recognized Tessa's potential. Even poorly dressed and coiffed, she seemed to mesmerize men. Harley obviously also realized that her innocence would draw countless customers—until it was destroyed.

Lucky shook his head. He needed to make sure that didn't happen. He needed to make certain that Tessa did not fall for the sweet talk of a man who pretended to be what he wasn't. He needed to get her out of the unnatural environment that the gold fields created, where a young woman like her had nowhere to go but down.

Lucky took a determined breath. He would get her tickets tomorrow morning.

Chapter Three

Tessa had been walking the San Francisco streets since early morning. During the long and sleepless night, she had determined that when Lucky Monroe brought her tickets to Iowa, she would tell him that she had another job, and that she would earn her own way home.

That had been her plan, anyway.

Tessa shook her head at the numbing realization of how few places a young woman could find work in San Francisco. She had walked from the crowded waterfront to the rocky hills, through filthy, muddy streets where boxes, bags, and crates were piled in stagnant water awaiting distribution by men who were otherwise occupied. She had wandered among tents and had covered her ears against the din as auctioneers fought to be heard over the chaos of flapping canvas, but she had found no positions for women. She had visited hotels to find no work for her there; she had even applied at the attached bathhouses, where only the most humiliating jobs were available. She had taken a breath and steeled her nerves in billiard rooms, boardinghouses, and saloons.

Out of desperation, she had suffered the embarrassment of going to the mercantile where she had bought supplies the previous day. She remembered only too clearly Noel Richman's welcome when she walked through the doorway, then the aging proprietor's surprise when she said she was not working for Lucky any longer, and finally his annoyed frown when she turned down a lurid suggestion that he could find work for her if she'd be willing to perform certain intimate duties.

Tessa's steps faltered at the realization that the only positions she had been offered during the long hours spent combing the streets of the city had been those that would have made her mother blush. She was hungry and tired, but too proud to return to Maggie's cabin, especially without a positive report.

Tessa sighed.

"So, we meet again!"

Tessa did her best to smile at Harley Knox when he appeared unexpectedly at her side. He commented, "You look dispirited. Is something wrong?"

"Nothing is wrong. I've just had a difficult day trying to find a position so I can earn my fare back home."

"A position?" Harley's brows drew together in a frown. "You won't be serving dinner at Lucky's tent?"

"No. It . . . it didn't work out."

"Didn't work out." Harley's expression stiffened as he paused for a breath and asked bluntly, "Did he act improperly on the way back to Maggie's cabin last night?"

"Of course not!"

"Oh, that's a relief."

Tessa stared at him. Strangely, she could not discern whether her reply pleased or displeased him.

"Have you eaten yet this afternoon, Tessa?" he asked.

"No, not yet."

"In that case, I hope you will share a meal with me. I admit to being tired of my own company and having the company of a young woman like you will be an unexpected pleasure."

"No." Tessa smiled and shook her head. "I think not."

"Please."

Her stomach took that moment to growl loudly, and Harley laughed. "I think that is my response."

Unable to deny her hunger, Tessa hesitated a moment before allowing Harley to tuck her arm under his. Within minutes they had entered a hotel and were seated at a table. When the waiter delivered a filled plate without consulting them first, Harley merely laughed. "One can fill one's stomach here, but unfortunately, the food isn't up to the quality you served last night."

Tessa looked down at the sliced meat and the lumpy gravy congealing beside it. She could not disagree, but she was hungry. Consuming every bite while Harley ate in a leisurely fashion and maintained a one-sided conversation, Tessa raised her head only when her plate was emptied at last. Embarrassed to see that Harley's plate was still half-full, she was determined to join the conversation so he would have time to eat.

"What exactly is it that you do in San Francisco, Mr. Knox?" she began.

"Please, call me Harley. I already call you Tessa. It seems only right."

Tessa repeated with a smile, "What is it that you do here, Harley? You don't seem to have an interest in the gold fields."

"So few return from the gold fields with something to show for all the backbreaking labor involved. I prefer to use my talents in San Francisco."

"Meaning?" Her expression quizzical, Tessa awaited his reply.

"I'm a true entrepreneur, Tessa."

"What does that mean?" she asked.

"This is a growing city with opportunities galore. I have been successful in seeing where opportunity awaits and in capitalizing on it."

"Oh." Still confused, Tessa was about to reply when Harley leaned toward her, took her hand, and said, "But let's not talk about me. Let's talk about you."

"About me?"

Unsuccessful in freeing her hand from Harley's grip, Tessa was about to reply when a voice said from behind, "No, let's not discuss Tessa. She won't be in San Francisco very long, anyway."

Tessa turned toward the familiar voice to see Lucky glowering. Her relief at his appearance surprised her. It changed to more familiar anger when he ordered gruffly, "Get up, Tessa. We have business to discuss."

"I beg your pardon!"

Awaiting an apology that did not come, Tessa did not comply. But Lucky pulled her up to a standing position and locked his arm around her waist, holding her there as he looked at Harley and said coldly, "Thank you for looking after Tessa until I could find her, but you can be sure that I won't let that happen again."

Tessa's eyes widened at Lucky's proprietary tone. She was about to reply when he urged with an iron grip, "Let's go."

Tessa realized her choices were simple—either comply or make a scene.

She chose the former.

Turning on Lucky abruptly when they were out on the crowded street, Tessa asked haughtily, "How dare you?"

"How dare I?" Annoyed at having missed her at Maggie's cabin earlier, angry after searching the city all morning, furious to see her holding Harley Knox's hand, Lucky shook his head disbelievingly.

Aware that they were drawing curious stares from passersby, Lucky pulled her into an alleyway where they would have a semblance of privacy and demanded, "How dare I? Isn't that question better directed at you?"

"You're the one who acted like . . . like a madman just now!"

"I'm a madman, huh? What would you call Harley Knox, then?"

"Unlike you, he's a gentleman."

"Unlike me." Lucky nodded. "Perhaps you're right. I'm not a gentleman. I never claimed to be one. I've been too busy earning my way."

"Oh, is that what you call it?"

"At least I earn my way with games that are honest. And I don't use women."

"Oh, really?" Tessa flushed as she continued. "You forget that I saw the painted women in your tent encouraging drunken prospectors to part with their money, and then sauntering out the doorway with them later. I even saw a particular redhead who seemed to think she had some claim on you."

"No one has a claim on me."

"You'll have to tell the redhead that."

"Whatever Delilah does on her own time is *her* business. But like the other women who work for me, she is not required to take that walk outside. Unlike some others, I don't run a brothel."

Confused, Tessa demanded, "What are you talking about?"

"I'm talking about Harley Knox. He's a gentleman, all right, but he also runs one of the most exclusive whorehouses in San Francisco."

Tessa gasped.

"He imports his whores from France and promises the men who patronize his establishment that he offers something *different* that is worth every penny he

charges." Lucky's eyes narrowed. "And he's always looking for an added edge to increase the patronage of his
establishment."

Tessa's eyes widened.

Lucky pressed, "You do understand what I mean by
an *added edge,* don't you?"

Tessa swallowed. A single word squeaked through
her choked throat. "Me?"

Lucky did not bother to reply. Instead, he looked at
Tessa's stunned expression. Damn, what was wrong
with him? Why did he feel so responsible for Tessa? She
had told him clearly enough that she intended to
take care of herself.

Regaining her composure, Tessa said, "I don't believe
you."

"What?" Lucky was incredulous. "Why would I lie to
you?"

"I don't know. Because I make you uncomfortable
and you want to get rid of me? Whatever the case, Harley
has always been a complete gentleman with me."

"He knows an inexperienced woman when he sees
one. He figures if he plays it right, he can talk you into
joining his stable."

"I'm inexperienced? After all that has happened to
me since I left home with my parents? And you called
Harley's workforce his *stable*? As if the women he
hires—if he is indeed what you say he is—are horses?"

"He treats them all well enough, like Thorough-
breds, as long as they suit him. If they have some hesi-

tation about their duties, he provides aids to relax them. When they cease to perform to the satisfaction of his customers, he throws them out on the street like used-up nags."

"Aids?"

"Laudanum."

"Laudanum?"

"Laudanum is—"

"I know what laudanum is! It's a medicine."

"For some. For others it's an addiction."

"No."

"Yes."

"I . . . I don't believe you."

"Tessa, damn it, what do I have to do to convince you that Harley isn't the man you think he is?"

"B . . . but why would he be so determined to add me to his 'stable'?"

Lucky shook his head, and then said helplessly, "Have you ever looked in the mirror?"

"Yes, I have. I know that I do not look my best now, but even at my best, I have never seen anything special."

When Lucky was at a loss for a reply, Tessa attempted to walk past him. Grasping her arm, he asked, "Where are you going?"

"I don't know." She glanced up. "But I do know that I'm not going back to Iowa with those tickets you bought, no matter what you say. The smartest thing for you to do would be to get your money back."

"If you stay in San Francisco, either Harley, someone

like him, or desperation will force you to take a path you won't even consider now."

"That's not true!"

"It's more true than you realize."

"You don't have the slightest confidence in me, do you?" Tessa's eyes narrowed even as they filled with tears. "Well, I'm going to prove you wrong. I'm going to make it here. I'm going to earn enough money to go back to my aunt and uncle without becoming a financial burden. And then I'm going to go on with my life—with no regrets. Do you understand? With no regrets!"

Shaking her arm free, Tessa rasped, "Now let me go!"

Unwilling to let her go but unable to stop her, Lucky watched as Tessa left him where he was standing and walked out into the crowded San Francisco street. Suddenly possessed with frustrated fury, Lucky pulled the tickets from his pocket and ripped them into shreds. He then tossed them onto the wet ground without a word and stepped out into the sunlight.

This was going to be harder than he'd thought.

Through the window opposite his table, Harley watched Tessa emerge from the narrow alleyway that Lucky had pulled her into. Her head was high and her narrow shoulders were stiff. It was obvious that Lucky and she had had an argument. He suspected that the argument had been about him. It was apparent that

Lucky had appointed himself Tessa's guardian for some reason. Harley wasn't certain how or why that had happened. Lucky was a man of the world with a woman to satisfy his every need. He had heard the talk about Tessa collapsing in Lucky's doorway weeks earlier, but that circumstance didn't demand any responsibility for the young woman afterward.

But of course, Tessa wasn't just *any* woman.

Harley's mouth twitched at the thought. She was young, proud, and totally innocent in the ways of men. He had felt the power of her wide, gray-eyed gaze himself. He was well aware of the effect she would have on patrons of his house who were looking for something other than the usual practiced French whore. He didn't pretend that Tessa hadn't affected him or that he would be beyond sampling what she had to offer when the right time presented itself. If she were good enough, he might even consider keeping her for himself temporarily while the prominent men who patronized his establishment salivated.

He laughed, suddenly amused at the thought.

His smile gradually faded with the realization that like all the others before her, Tessa would soon lose her freshness, her sweet innocence. Within two or three years at the most, he'd be forced to put her out on the street to find work in a lower-class brothel. But that was the way of the world in which they lived. Only the bold survived, and only the ruthless grew rich.

Harley slapped the price of the meals they had eaten down on the table as he stood. He had made a mistake sitting where Tessa and he might be seen from the street. He had just been beginning to make progress with her. But he had time. Tessa wasn't going anywhere, and from the look of things, the relationship between Lucky and her wasn't even civil. It appeared Lucky didn't realize that Tessa would not be told what to do, or that she considered herself mistress of her own fate.

Harley chuckled again, ran his hand through his thinning brown hair, and reached for his hat. In his favor was the fact that he had become a student of human nature. He knew exactly how to handle a stubborn young woman like Tessa. Achieving his end would only take a little longer than he had originally thought.

"I'm sorry, Maggie. I couldn't find work today, but I will. I promise you that."

Maggie looked at Tessa, aware that she was despondent after a long round of refusals and leering glances. She had watched from her cabin as Tessa climbed the uneven trail back to her cabin as daylight waned. Aware of the difficulty Tessa would face despite her determination to find work, Maggie had been waiting for her with a warm meal and a tender heart. She loved the dear girl, even if she didn't understand why Tessa was so determined to dislike Lucky.

As Maggie looked at Tessa, she recalled happier days when Wally was still alive and working his claim, and when Elise—dear Elise—was the light of her life. She had not realized how privileged she was then, despite the heavy workload a husband and daughter demanded. A sunny, busy life had been her lot, with days filled with satisfying work and simple happiness. Elise had turned eighteen so quickly, almost before Wally and she were ready for her to grow up. She had been planning Elise's future when cholera ended it all so swiftly. Why she had survived when Wally and Elise did not was a question that still plagued her. Left middle-aged and bewildered, she had lost all sense of self, becoming a hermit in her simple cabin. It wasn't until Lucky stumbled into her life that everything changed.

Maggie's heart warmed. Lucky had been younger then. Separated somehow from his parents on the way west, he had never found them again. He had made his own way while attempting to find them, sleeping and eating where he could. She had met him when he was in his late teens by then, he had given up that hope and had already been hardened by his fate. She knew he had come to the devastating conclusion that his parents had simply abandoned him. She had been unable to convince him otherwise; yet their meeting had changed both their lives.

Maggie grew teary eyed. Lucky had not forgotten her when San Francisco became a mecca for gold seekers and his gambling tent began to make him a wealthy man. She was as proud of his fidelity as she was of his success. She wished others besides her could see past his hard exterior to the man underneath. She had believed for a moment that Tessa would understand his true worth, but she was wrong. Tessa resented Lucky's occasionally high-handed attitude. She refused to acknowledge that it was the result of a determination similar to her own.

Returning to the present with a frown, Maggie searched for something encouraging to say, but she knew that anything she could offer then would be a lie. There was simply no work for Tessa in San Francisco—at least not work that a young woman like her would want.

Maggie's face was lined and weary as Tessa awaited a response to her adamant assertion. She sensed that Maggie did not believe she would find work that suited her, but Tessa knew she had no other choice. She could not remain dependent on the old woman's goodwill, and she refused to accept Lucky Monroe's charity.

"I knew it wouldn't be easy for you to find work," Maggie said at last. "San Francisco isn't what it used to be. It is now merely a gateway to the gold fields, where everyone believes fast fortunes are to be found."

Tessa shrugged. "I guess that's true. My parents and I were caught up in that dream. And that's what it was, a dream that faded into harsh reality along the way."

"That dream hasn't faded yet for some."

"It has for me. It's time to go home, but getting there on my own is the problem."

Maggie paused and then said, "Lucky was here looking for you."

Tessa tensed. "He found me." When Maggie waited for her to say more, Tessa continued. "He had the tickets for my transportation home. He doesn't believe me when I say I want to pay him back first for the expenses related to my care. He just wants me to leave San Francisco. I guess it would be easier for him that way, but it wouldn't be for me."

Gray strands of hair escaped Maggie's feeble attempt at a bun when she shook her head and replied, "That's not really true, Tessa. Lucky's been through it all. He knows what's out there for women, and he doesn't want you to get caught up in it."

"Then why did he say that he lost money last night?"

"Because he probably did."

"I don't believe that! I sold everything I cooked. Some fellas returned for seconds, but I had to turn them down. They made me promise to come back tonight. I don't like it when someone forces me to break my word."

"Maybe you shouldn't have given your word without checking with Lucky first."

Maggie's response made Tessa frown. "I can see it's useless to say anything against Lucky to you."

"That's not true, either." Maggie sat abruptly on a nearby chair. Appearing suddenly exhausted, she said, "I'd be the first to agree if I thought Lucky was wrong. I'm just trying to make you see Lucky's side of things."

"He doesn't have a right to his 'side of things.' This is my problem, not his!"

"Tessa, don't you understand? This all became Lucky's problem the minute you collapsed in the door-way of his tent."

"I was sick and exhausted. I was drawn to his tent by the light and the music. I didn't go there purposely, and I certainly never wanted to make Lucky feel re-sponsible for me."

"I know, I know. But you could have been drawn to any of the other tents, where you might have been tossed out without another thought."

"So you're saying?"

"I'm saying that Lucky feels responsible for you whether he wants to or not. What you intend to do about it is your business, but Lucky isn't the bad per-son you make him out to be."

Speaking of bad people.

Tessa asked abruptly, "Have you ever heard of Harley Knox?"

"Oh, *him.*"

"Which means?"

"He's not a nice man."

"And you say Lucky is?"

"Lucky doesn't take advantage of women, but Harley Knox does. His whorehouse is known for miles around."

"Are you just saying that? I mean, are you preju-diced because Harley doesn't have anything nice to say about you or Lucky?"

Maggie's gaze sharpened. "You talk about him as if you've met him. Did Harley Knox approach you?"

"He . . . he's been very kind."

"He's never kind without a reason."

"Maggie—"

"Stay away from him, Tessa. He's not someone you should be friendly with."

"But—"

Standing, Maggie turned abruptly toward the fireplace. "I'm done talking about it," she said angrily. "Do what you want to do. You will, anyway." Pausing, Maggie looked back at her, suddenly dismissing their former conversation with an unexpected smile. "Do you want to eat now? I made chicken soup."

"Chicken soup?" Tessa gulped at the memory of the old hen she had seen in the yard that morning. She had not seen it there when she returned.

As if reading her mind, Maggie responded, "That old bird wasn't good for anything. I did her a favor. Besides, I still have a few good egg producers left."

Tessa's smile was weak.

"Get accustomed to it, Tessa." Maggie responded with unexpected harshness. "This is San Francisco. We do what we have to do to survive."

Maggie turned back to the fireplace with that last sentence lingering behind her like a proclamation of doom.

"Desperation might force you onto a path you won't even consider now."

Not her! Not ever! She wouldn't be like the rest of the women who had faced difficulty in San Francisco with a faint heart! She would find a decent job tomorrow. She'd get up first thing, and she'd scour the city again. Someone would give her work. They'd just have to.

"I came here early especially. I was hoping to be first in line so I could go back for seconds before Tessa ran out of food."

Lucky frowned when Strike Wilson made that declaration. The setting sun shone brightly on the faded exterior of the tent as the heavy canvas overhead fluttered and shook in the steady breeze. Employees worked noisily between the tables, cleaning and washing glasses. It was still too early for the tent to be crowded.

Lucky scrutinized the grisly old prospector who had started the rush toward Tessa the previous evening. He saw a beard and gray hair, a wrinkled face, faded clothing, and old boots streaked with mud from standing for hours in running water while panning for gold. His nose twitched. Strike couldn't possibly be interested in Tessa for anything other than her cooking. He was too old.

"Where is she?" asked a younger fellow who had appeared behind Strike. "I ain't ever et nothing as good as that stew last night, and I figured it was worth getting here early to get some. Besides," he said to Lucky in a more confidential tone, "that young lady said something about making a dessert that might bring back a taste of home. I was looking forward to it."

"Me, too."

Lucky looked at the two men standing behind Strike in the beginning of an irregular line. They were both younger than Strike, though they wore heavy beards and hair too long to be fashionable. Their faded clothing and muddy boots attested to their occupations in the gold fields, but Lucky knew that one of them had been back from his claim for a fortnight, during which he'd frequented all the tents in the square. When Tessa brought her food, however, he had lingered in Lucky's tent all night to gamble.

He was one of many who had done the same, and Lucky wasn't sure of the reason.

His frown darkened with annoyance at the size of the expectant line rapidly building behind Strike. Those men weren't the first to inquire about Tessa since he had walked through the doorway of the tent an hour earlier. He had the feeling that they wouldn't be the last.

Squinting, determined to end it then and there, Lucky said, "Tessa isn't coming back, tonight or ever."

"What?"

Noting that the fellows at nearby tables looked up at his response, Lucky announced in general, "I said Tessa's not coming back."

"What tent is she going to be in, then? Somebody must've snatched her up."

Lucky frowned at that question. He responded, "She's not going to any other tent. She's going home."

"No, she ain't!" a middle-aged fellow challenged from his place in line. "She said she'd be around for a while, until she earned enough money to go home."

"She doesn't have to earn the money," Lucky growled. "I'm giving it to her."

"She don't want your money, except if she earns it. She's that kind."

Strike Williams spoke those words, turning Lucky back to the old man as he continued. "I talked to her for a while. She's a real nice girl, a real lady with the good sense her mama taught her. Them kind is hard to come by in this town."

"And she can cook, too."

Lucky felt a flush rising. He said gruffly, "I'm through talking." Facing the old man in front of him again, he added, "Are you going to play cards, Strike, or are you just going to stand there?"

"So you're through talking about it all, huh?"

When Lucky did not reply, Strike waited a minute before pulling out a chair. The men behind him lingered as he sat down across from Lucky and said with an assessing gaze, "I figure I should play, because this is the night your luck is going to run out."

"What makes you think that?" Scowling as he dealt the cards around the table, Lucky watched as some of the men grumbled and walked out the tent doorway.

"I can think of three reasons: one, because that

young lady ain't here to bring the crowds into this tent; two, because some of them fellas are going elsewhere to look for her; and three, because I figure this ain't your lucky night."

"I never needed Tessa to bring in a crowd before."

Strike replied simply, "Like you said, that was *before*." He looked at the cards Lucky had dealt him and smiled.

Lucky glanced at his own cards, refusing to allow his expression to reflect his disgust. Maybe Strike was right. Maybe his luck had run out.

In any case, he was done with Tessa.

Done.

Delilah smiled when the din inside the tent accelerated as the night progressed, growing louder with each bottle of whiskey that was consumed. She fended off another searching hand and smiled at the offender, knowing that she could not afford to make enemies of men who were poor one day and rich the next, with never a warning in between. She silently admitted to herself that the noise was not as overwhelming as usual because the crowd was more sparse, but Lucky had hired her to amuse the men and keep them happy while they drank and played cards. She did not intend to let him down.

Delilah glanced again at Lucky's table and resisted a frown as she slid a hand against the upward sweep of her hair. She had donned a gold satin gown that was one of Lucky's favorites because the neckline left little to the imagination. She had also taken special pains with her hair and the heavy makeup that concealed the fatigue of long, tiring hours. As yet, all her efforts had been in vain. Lucky was too busy at his table to notice. He was losing.

Delilah batted her heavily kohled eyes at the nearby cowboy whose name she could not remember and leaned closer so he would be distracted momentarily by her bulging neckline. When Lucky threw down another hand, signaling another loss, Delilah could stand no more.

Beckoning to one of the other women to take her place, she sauntered toward the table where Lucky sat and slid her arms around his neck from behind. She whispered into his ear, "It doesn't look like you're earning your nickname tonight. Not so far, anyway. I'm hoping I can change that situation if we get together later."

Lucky looked at Delilah and her heart thudded momentarily in her breast. He was so damned handsome, but it was more than his size and strength that attracted her. When he glanced up at her through that fringe of thick, short lashes and regarded her with his dark-eyed, unconsciously sensual gaze, she felt a thrill down to her toes. She longed for intimate times between them when she could run her fingers through his heavy black hair and press him close, knowing that—however briefly—he was hers alone. The thought of his naked body lying against hers brought a heat that no other man stirred inside her, and the sound of his uneven breathing in the aftermath of their lovemaking sent tremors of desire shooting up her spine. And at times like the present when a smile lifted his lips, her heart actually thundered. She knew Lucky felt only the satisfaction of physical need during their lovemaking, but it was much more for her. She knew the difference, and she was determined to make him feel the same as she did.

"Your suggestion would be my first strike of good luck this evening," he replied.

She smiled warmly at his response.

"But right now I'm busy, darlin'."

Delilah's smile dulled at his dismissal, but she refused to take offense. She was accustomed to making her presence felt, even if it didn't net immediate results. This would be another one of those nights when Lucky would dwell on what she had to offer, and when she would prove to him that it would be well worth his while to accept.

Wrapping her arms more warmly around Lucky's neck, she pressed herself against his back and whispered that thought suggestively into his ear before sauntering off. She glanced back at Lucky to see his responsive smile, and that was all she needed. She would never put Lucky in a position where he would lose at cards because he was thinking of her. But one thing was certain. Neither would she let a tenderfoot like Tessa White steal her man. Lucky didn't know it yet, but he *was* her man, and she'd do what she needed to do to keep him.

"All right, why did you summon me here?"

Harley stood impatiently in his luxurious brothel office. The heavy paneling was hand-carved, the drapes were a deep burgundy satin, and the rug under his feet was Persian. In the center of the large room stood a desk and chair that had been hand-carved especially for him, a leather couch and matching chair, strategically placed cigar humidors, brass ashtrays and spittoons to impress his wealthy clients, and fresh flowers delivered expressly for him. But it was all show. He seldom used the space except for entertaining wealthy customers.

He had known from the first, of course, that he needed the right setting for the buxom, daring French beauties whose accents as well as their sumptuous wardrobes already set them apart from the ordinary whores in that primitive area. The building that he had chosen to showcase his girls had been recently constructed specifically for him. In addition to numerous, large bedrooms, it also contained sitting and gaming rooms, a reception area, and a large kitchen—all of which he had decorated lushly. Blinds and velvet curtains covered the windows when privacy was needed; the furniture was like the women of the house, imported and exotic. The floors were deeply carpeted, and the food served to the chosen few was also French. He, personally, did not care for it, but the cuisine obviously tickled the taste buds of those who insisted upon something unusual. He ordered that the women keep their attire faultlessly clean and that their gowns be constructed of only European-made materials. All was reflected in the prices he charged for the services of the women, and he'd had no complaints at all from his satisfied customers.

But recently he'd noticed that the novelty of his French whores was fading. He had been seeking something new and even more exciting for his clients. The moment he had seen Tessa, he had known she would be his latest innovation. He planned on presenting her, carefully groomed and clothed in the very latest gowns. He would allow customers only a peek at her slender attributes. He also planned on allowing her only limited exposure, claiming that she was an innocent who demanded careful handling. With her startling, natural beauty shining through, she would bring in even the most jaded of men, and each would pay any price he asked for her services.

His plans would make him wealthier than he had ever dreamed, but unfortunately, his house was not without problems.

Harley eyed the older, overweight, elaborately dressed, blonde madam of the house as she stood in front of him. Madame LeFleur spoke her native French tongue, but usually addressed him in highly accented English. Her reputation and experience as a madam were well known, but just now she was upset and agitated, and was sweating profusely. Long, errant strands hung limply from her formerly sophisticated hairstyle, and her thick makeup had begun caking in the many lines around her mouth and eyes. Her age and misspent youth were all too apparent in her face.

Harley knew she did not ordinarily complain because she was afraid of him. He had gone to great pains to establish that fear, and for that reason he knew she was desperate now.

He eyed the nervous woman and urged with growing impatience, "Speak up! I don't have time to waste."

"It . . . it is Clarice, Monsieur Knox. She has slipped out of control. Her use of the medication you gave her has become so important to her that she cares little for the work she is asked to perform."

"Is that all? Do you want me to clarify the situation for her?"

"No, monsieur, the situation is more dire than that." Beads of perspiration appeared on the madam's forehead and upper lip as she continued. "Clarice no longer washes as fastidiously as the other women in the house. Her clothes and her hairstyle reflect that same lack of attention. She has come down to meet her patrons in a state of dishabille which is not permitted in this house."

"And you can do nothing about that?"

"I fear I cannot. I have spoken to her about her patrons' complaints. I have told her that they now visit others, but she only shouts at them and attacks the other girls. I have just experienced another of her episodes and am afraid there is nothing more I can do."

"Let me get this straight, Madame LeFleur. You want me to get rid of Clarice?"

"I ask that you send her back to France. Perhaps there she will come to herself."

"I don't run a charitable organization, Madame."

"But Clarice has served you well and most eagerly, especially since you allowed her to avail herself of medication to soothe the erratic behavior she exhibited when she arrived."

"Do not blame the medication for her actions."

"I do not, but—"

"Send her to me."

"Monsieur, I beg you to be kind."

"I do not waste unnecessary words or actions, Madame. I tell you this because now that you have brought this behavior to my attention, it can only be either Clarice *or you*."

"Monsieur!" Fear shone in the elderly woman's eyes. "I am not capable of making my way in a strange city. I am too old!"

Harley said resolutely, "It's either you or her."

Madame LeFleur hesitated, and then raised a trembling chin to respond, "I suppose it must be Clarice, then, for I would not survive."

Turning without another word, the older woman left and Harley smiled. Placing the disposition of the matter on her had been a brilliant tactic. The older woman would not hold his actions against him. Rather, she would end up blaming herself! It amused him to think that she would suffer for it, while he would not spend a moment thinking about the situation once it had been handled.

Harley walked to the door. *There is no time like the present* was his motto, and it had served him well.

Reaching the heavily carved, mahogany door, he jerked it open and called out in a voice that rang through the corridors of the silent house, "Clarice, come here. Now!"

Within moments, Clarice was walking toward him.

Dawn was breaking through the clouds when Lucky threw his cards down on the table and said disgustedly, "That's it, boys. I'm closing the tent for the night."

"You sure you don't want to play a little longer?" Strike shook his hoary head. "I'm wide awake after sleeping those few hours in the corner and I figure you'll want to make up a part of your losses tonight."

Lucky smiled caustically. "You can come back tomorrow and give me that chance."

"I'll be here." Strike paused, and then added, "About Tessa—"

Lucky looked up. His gaze narrowed, he warned, "I've had all the advice I can take about her, Strike."

"Well, just keep it in mind, especially if you want to stay lucky." Standing up, Strike smiled, waved his bulging money pouch, and said, "Thanks, Lucky. Or should I call you Unlucky?"

Lucky managed another caustic smile, and then turned at a light touch on his shoulder. He frowned into Delilah's sultry gaze.

"I've been waiting for you to finish for the night, Lucky," she said.

Lucky's spontaneous frown was revealing.

Momentarily taken aback, Delilah went on. "Tell me if I'm wrong, but it looks like you aren't too happy to hear me say that."

"I forgot. I mean, it's been a long, hard night."

"You're tired, is that what you're saying?"

Hesitating, Lucky replied, "Yeah, that's what I'm saying."

"Too tired for what I have planned for you?" Delilah raised her brow.

Lucky hesitated and then responded simply, "I'm sorry, Delilah."

"I'm sorry, too, Lucky."

"Another time, when I have less on my mind?"

Delilah shrugged. "We'll see."

Lucky watched as Delilah turned with a deliberate dip of her full bosom and walked out of the tent. Silently cursing his own strange behavior, Lucky stood staring after her for long moments before he thrust his chair under the poker table and headed for the exit as well.

Damn it all! The hard truth was that he knew what he had to do, and he had to do it now, before he changed his mind.

The advent of morning outside the cabin window appeared in brilliant streaks across the deep black of the night sky. It lightened the expanse to a brief, glowing hue so breathtaking that Tessa knew she would never become accustomed to its beauty. But she watched only briefly before rising from her cot, noting that Maggie had already risen for the day.

As she dressed, Tessa moved quickly in the cabin's semidarkness. She would find work somewhere in the city below. She would labor hard and consistently at whatever job she found, however menial, until she was able to do what she intended.

A knock on the door interrupted her thoughts. Tessa turned as Maggie made her way toward the entrance with a frown. Maggie's sudden smile told Tessa who their visitor was. Yet she was unprepared when Lucky looked at her directly.

"I want to talk to you

His tone raised Tessa's hackles. Replying with a feigned excuse, she said, "I'm not fully dressed yet. You'll have to wait."

"I didn't come to assess your wardrobe. I need to talk to you now."

Seething, but aware of Maggie's scrutiny, Tessa reluctantly complied. She waited only until the door of the cabin closed behind her before rounding on Lucky with an intended retort, which ended before it could begin.

"I want you to cook for the tent tonight, but I want you to come early, about five o'clock, so the men will have time to digest before spending a full night at the tables."

"Wh . . . what?"

"You heard me."

Recovering, Tessa looked at Lucky more closely. He looked tired, harassed, out of sorts. He had probably come to the cabin straight from the tent without sleeping, which made his statement all the more confusing. Narrowing her gaze, she responded, "But you said I made you lose money."

"The timing was wrong. If you get there earlier, it should work."

"What should work? I should bring in extra funds?"

"Maybe. Or maybe you won't, but at least the fellas who complain about your not being there will get off my back." Delivering that response without apology, Lucky continued. "I'll give it another try."

Tessa raised her chin. "You're doing me a favor, then?"

"Under the present circumstances, I'm doing both of us a favor."

"Both of us?"

Lucky took an aggressive step toward her. Halting only a hairbreath away, he looked down into her tight expression without blinking and said, "Look, you need a job and I'm offering one to you. It's up to you to make it permanent."

"It's up to me. Again."

"That's right. Take it or leave it."

"You said that before."

"And I'm repeating it."

Lucky saw resolution enter Tessa's angry gaze. He remembered her statement that she was not at her best right now, and he wondered how she could ever be more beautiful or desirable than at that moment. The silver light of approaching morning glinted on her hair, and her gray eyes reflected that glow. His desire for her was an aching hunger inside him that he did not choose to admit.

Lucky stared more intently, and then shook his head with silent incredulity. Why did he even bother to argue when he had a woman who had gone to great lengths to let him know that she would keep him happy for as long as he wanted her?

For as long as he wanted her.

That thought lingered as Lucky grated, "Well, what's your answer?"

The fine line of Tessa's lips compressed, but her gaze did not falter as she responded resolutely, "I'll be there."

He prompted sarcastically, "And don't forget the *apple pie.* I'm tired of hearing about that promise you made to some of the men."

"I didn't promise. I just mentioned—"

Interrupting, Lucky said, "You just mentioned? Then that's another thing you're going to have to learn. Don't speak unless you're sure you can deliver." When Tessa did not respond, he said, "It's settled, then."

Turning, Lucky started down the trail without another word. He knew his actions were abrupt. He also knew he had left Tessa with many questions unanswered, but he was weary to the bone.

And it was safer that way because—

He silently cursed again.

Because he wanted her.

Chapter Four

Clarice was sweating profusely, but she was cold even though the sky was blue, the sun was shining, and the air was warm. Monsieur Knox had cast her out of the only home she knew in this strange country and she had spent the night sleeping in a hotel doorway because she'd had nowhere else to go. She had wandered the city aimlessly since awakening. She had not bothered to eat, but had searched her unclear mind as to the next step to take.

Blinking away tears, she walked along the muddy street. She had not known what to expect when Monsieur Knox called her into his office the previous day. She had never imagined that he would announce she would no longer be tolerated in his house. Neither had she expected him to warn her that if she did not leave immediately, *he* would see to it that she departed. He had not allowed her to defend herself and had shown no remorse for his cruel dismissal. Without providing any funds, or showing any concern at all, he had simply turned her out onto the street in a city where even her friends seemed to have become her enemies.

Clarice brushed away a tear that had slipped down her cheek. Monsieur Knox's behavior was startling and so contrary to his warm welcome when she and the other women of the house arrived from France. He had appeared delighted to see them then, and willing to do anything to make them comfortable. He had been so understanding when she told him about the nervousness she felt in this new country where everything was so different from home. In that last interview, however, he'd revealed an entirely different side of himself. He was no longer the friendly adviser who had supplied the "medicine" to relax her, the drug that had finally assumed control of her actions.

Laudanum.

She had been uncertain about accepting it when Monsieur Knox first offered it to her. She had heard whispers about its effects, but the laudanum had soothed her fears. It had put her into a world where she was relaxed and displaced, and able to perform acts more outrageous than she had ever dreamed. She had not anticipated that she would be unable to control her growing hunger for the medicine, that the hunger would begin taking precedence over all her other duties, or—worst of all—that it would eventually drive away those same men who had formerly craved her services. She recalled her resentment when they turned to other women in the house instead of her. In more rational moments, even she was startled by her bizarre reaction to those desertions.

But by then, the men did not really matter to her. Nor did the fact that her formerly thick, glossy hair had lost some of its sheen and vibrancy, or that the dark strands sometimes came out in handfuls that left ugly marks on her white scalp. Even her pallor did not seem to matter, or the confusion that was often revealed in her dark eyes. She found excuses for the extreme weight loss that left her formerly voluptuous proportions scrawny, for the spots that her shaky hands had left on her elaborate gowns, and even for her lack of attention to personal cleanliness. Nothing seemed to matter. After a while, she did not even bother to dress or bathe when greeting the faithful few who visited her.

Clarice recalled that the look in Monsieur Knox's eyes had been so frightening, she had run upstairs to dress so that she might leave the house within minutes. Out on the street without clothes or money, she became uncertain where to turn but was too terrified to go back.

Yet she had made certain to take her medicine with her. With the large dose that she had consumed that morning, she felt no hunger. Nor did her disheveled appearance concern her, or the fact that her words were so slurred, no decent man wanted anything to do with her. When she finally reached the tents in the square, she bolstered her confidence with another dose of medicine. Despite the weariness and sluggishness that the laudanum produced, she was still French and would be much desired. The proprietors of the tents would argue over who would hire her, and she would accept the best offer. She would then save the money she earned and would return to the land of her birth in style.

Before she left, she would go to Monsieur Knox and tell him that he had made a mistake in casting her aside.

Oui, he would be sorry!

Arriving in San Francisco Plaza at last, Clarice cast all thought of her appearance aside and approached the first tent she saw. She laughed before entering, quite certain of her success.

It was early afternoon. The sunlight outside Lucky's tent doorway was bright and relentless. He knew it would gradually elevate the heat within, but he also knew that the constant sea breeze would cool the canvas so that it would not be uncomfortable when Tessa arrived at five o'clock.

Lucky frowned at that thought. Truthfully, he didn't want her there. She was out of place in his gambling tent, where deprived men shed their inhibitions for a night of revelry. Delilah and the other women knew how to handle anything that came their way, but Tessa was different.

Admittedly, however, even his roughest patrons had been well behaved when Tessa was there—except for assessing glances they cast her way. He was uncertain why he had resented those glances so deeply or when he became determined that if even one of those men stepped out of line, he would take care of it personally.

It was not his usual practice to get his hands dirty. He had hired Jake and Larry for that, the same two fellows who had first delivered Tessa to his hotel room.

Lucky forced that uncomfortable thought aside. Actually, his customers' reaction to Tessa surprised him. Aside from acting polite and ingratiating, they even praised her! He had not expected that they would press him about *when* she would return. He had noted that not one of them had entertained the word *if.* Well, tonight he would discover whether he had taken the right step or not, and he—

Lucky looked at the woman who had just entered the tent. The day's first influx of prospectors had begun, but he noted that even the most trail weary of those men skirted the unknown woman as she approached him. He did not wonder at the reason. She was thin, disheveled, and unclean. Dark, straggly, lifeless hair hung on her shoulders from a scalp that was obviously diseased, and her clothing, although of elaborate construction and richly adorned, was spotted and wrinkled. Yet she walked arrogantly, if a bit unsteadily. When she stopped in front of him, her clothes smelled as if she had slept in them and her eyes had a faraway look that suggested she was drugged. She spoke in a slurred voice that bore an imperious tone as she said, "I have come to offer my services here, and to inquire what the payment would be so that I may consider whether the amount is suitable."

Really?

Lucky did not immediately respond.

"Come, come, monsieur, speak up. I must become settled and I do not have time to waste."

Her accent declared a French background, but Lucky still could not believe—

"Monsieur!" Lucky had little time to consider the woman's background as she demanded, "I would have your answer now. I assure you that my patrons will be very loyal to my services."

"Miss, I—"

"You will please refer to me as Mademoiselle Le-Blanc."

Lucky hesitated, then began again, "Mademoiselle, this is not the kind of establishment you are seeking."

The newcomer scrutinized his hired women, who were grouped in the rear of the tent. "If those women are the best you offer, I assure you that I will prove more profitable to you than they. In addition . . ." Lucky was startled when the woman batted sparse eyelashes at him. "You never have enough women to entertain your patrons. And you must remember that I am greatly desired by many."

Lucky swept the woman with his gaze and realized she truly believed what she was saying. He said coldly, "We're not hiring at present." The young woman's pathetic blink made him regret his response. Reaching for his money pouch, he added more softly, "It looks to me that you're tired and could probably do with a room where you can clean up a bit and—"

"Monsieur, I do not care to hear your opinion of my needs! I warn you, if you do not hire me, another will, and you will be sorry."

Lucky's hand fell back to his side as he repeated, "I have no positions open in this tent, mademoiselle."

"Very well." Her pale face haughty, she said, "I bid you adieu."

Turning unsteadily on her heel, the woman walked toward the exit in an uncertain line. Lucky watched as she stepped out of sight. He had his suspicions where she had come from. Was she one of Knox's discarded girls?

His thoughts drifted as he glanced at the tables surrounding him. For a reason he did not care to explore, there were many more empty seats than he was accustomed to seeing.

He checked his pocket watch. He had set the hour for Pedro to pick up Tessa and her nightly offerings. She was due to arrive soon. Her appearance in the tent would be a surprise to many. He guessed she would also be warmly welcomed. Most of the men arrived in his tent hungry for more than entertainment. Tessa would fill their appetite for food as well as for a taste of home.

Yet even sweet, beautiful, innocent Tessa was no match for gold fever when drink and reckless spending increased as the night lengthened. He had become as impervious to the prospectors' antics as his employees— but Tessa had not. She still believed in integrity and in the innate goodness within the average man.

She had a lot to learn.

And he did not want to see her learn it there.

"I don't want her kind in this tent. Neither do any of the other girls."

Lucky looked at Delilah and noted the tight expression that accompanied her unexpected demand. Mademoiselle LeBlanc had just staggered back through the entranceway, and he had turned back toward the gaming table. Ordinarily, Delilah and the rest of the women he employed would be at the doorway to greet the men when they entered, but this time they had gathered in a tight, angry circle. The day had barely begun and unexpected problems had already developed.

He asked tightly, "What did you say?"

Delilah raised her delicately pointed chin. "That was Clarice LeBlanc, one of Harley Knox's French whores, wasn't it?"

"She's obviously not one of Harley Knox's women now."

"So he threw her out." Delilah nodded as if she'd expected as much. "I knew he would as soon as he found out."

Lucky's eyes narrowed and Delilah continued. "The truth is that she can't be trusted anymore. You saw what she looked like. Word has gotten around that she isn't worth the price Harley Knox was putting on her. As a matter of fact, she was more of a hindrance to him than an asset."

"That doesn't concern me."

Delilah continued despite his response. "She wasn't as high class as she was supposed to be after all, and dosing her with laudanum made her too volatile." She paused, and then said, "But you knew that already, didn't you?"

"I figured she was from Harley's house and there had to be something wrong if one of Harley's women was coming here for work after the luxury she was accustomed to there. But it wasn't my business and I didn't really care."

Delilah raised her chin higher. "She's on her way down. She had it real soft with that fancy accent and the fine wardrobe he provided, but she wasted it all." Delilah unconsciously touched the bodice of her dress. "She let it all go to her head."

"To her head? She came from France, probably from an area where accepting Harley's offer was a step up."

"Yeah, but good old American women weren't good enough for Harley Knox. He brought her over just because she was foreign. He kicked her out when he discovered she's no better than us; now she's looking around for an easy way out."

"Are you saying that's the reason she came here?"

"I'm saying that I saw the way she looked at us. She came here to criticize us as if she's better than we are. She probably thinks that French accent of hers can get some poor fella to set her up if she takes care of him well enough."

Lucky said abruptly, "Just to set things straight, I didn't hire Clarice LeBlanc just now. I don't run that kind of place, and I told her so. I'm telling you, too, because I don't want you to think that anything you said about her influenced my decision. And for the record, I don't pay attention to rumors."

"What I said isn't a rumor."

"Isn't it?"

"She didn't deserve a chance here."

Scrutinizing her more closely, Lucky said, "You make it sound like this is all personal with you, Delilah. I've never seen you act this way before."

Lucky's expression sent a sudden chill down Delilah's spine. She knew she had made an error in judgment. He couldn't possibly understand that although the other women he employed felt threatened by the Frenchwoman in one way, she felt threatened in another. Unfortunately, she'd learned too late that everything she had said was unnecessary because Lucky had already turned the woman down; yet instead of backing off, she had attempted to excuse her protest. It frightened her to realize that as a result, Lucky was looking at her as if he had never seen her before.

Regretting their whole conversation, Delilah attempted to compensate for her viciousness by adding, "You never saw me this way before, and since you didn't hire her, you'll never see me this way again."

Unexpected anger tightened Lucky's mouth. "I hope that's not a threat, because I don't take to threats well."

"It wasn't a threat. It was just a statement."

"I guess this conversation is over, then."

"Yes, I guess it is." Delilah nodded, making an effort to control her emotions. Her chin still elevated, she added as she turned away, "I'll see you later."

Delilah could feel Lucky's gaze burning into her back as she strode away with shoulders erect and head high. She knew he was confused by her outburst. She had taken great pains to hide the darker side of herself from him and she regretted having displayed it now. But the truth was that he didn't know how hard she would fight for what was hers.

Delilah forced a smile as she strode up to the bar in the corner of the tent. She signaled the bartender and waited until he put a glass of red-eye down in front of her. She emptied it in a gulp and waited for the burning liquid to settle her nerves. Her temper had flared the moment she saw Clarice enter the tent. She had known why the woman was there. *Mademoiselle Le-Blanc* was looking for a soft place to land, and Delilah would be damned if she'd let that soft place be in the lap of *her* man.

Delilah struggled to maintain control. First a pretended innocent had managed to wriggle under her man's skin, and now a worn-out but practiced French whore, who knew all the tricks in the world, had thought she would find a spot with him.

Delilah's silent thoughts were caustic. Harley Knox had not considered her good enough to work in his house. Delilah wondered what he thought now—now that she practically had the most coveted man in San Francisco for her own.

Practically.

Delilah shuddered with that uncertainty. Nobody was going to get Lucky away from her while she had a lick of strength left in her body!

She tapped the bar for another drink. She had not handled the situation well. No one had to tell her that Lucky didn't like being told what to do. Nor did he consider himself any woman's property. Not yet, anyway. Clarice hadn't been effective with Lucky because of her condition, but the little witch with the platinum hair had stirred his sympathy, and perhaps more.

Delilah downed the glass that the bartender filled. She then straightened her shoulders and walked back toward the group of men who had gathered nearby. She'd have to keep her distance from Lucky for a while, so he could forget her outburst. And she'd have to keep her jealousy in check.

Tessa moved frantically around the cabin. Chicken stew was cooking in several pots that she had purchased at the mercantile, and several apple pies were baking at hearthside in skillets she had also purchased early that morning.

Tessa's nose twitched when she recalled the expression on Noel Richman's round, sweaty face when she'd walked though the doorway. He had thought he knew why she was there and he had leered at her greedily. She had cut short those embarrassing moments with the simple words: "I'll be cooking for Lucky Monroe's tent tonight. He sent me here to buy supplies since he has an account with you."

"Of course." Startled, he had mumbled uncertainly, "Lucky must have had a change of heart, then." He fumbled for a paper and pencil as he said, "Just let me see what you need." She saw him whisper to a boy when she reached for her list. The young fellow scampered out onto the street. She had no doubt that Mr. Richman was checking on the validity of her claim, and she was surprised at her own satisfaction a short time later when the boy returned and Mr. Richman flushed at the news whispered in his ear.

So much for the storekeeper's lechery.

Ignoring the fawning that Mr. Richman obviously felt was necessary to reinstate her good opinion of him, Tessa remained silent until her supplies were loaded onto his wagon and the driver guided it up the street toward Maggie's cabin. She turned with surprise to look at the driver when he said unexpectedly, "You sure turned the tables on that fat fella, ma'am, and I ain't afraid to say so."

Tessa was still staring at him when he continued with a frown. "My daughter is dead now for twenty-two years, but I can say that if she was in your spot—and don't get me wrong, young lady, because I've seen worse predicaments—I'd say hallelujah for making him eat his words."

A smile quivered at Tessa's mouth when she said, "And you still work for that man? Why?"

"Because he treats me well enough ever since I put him in his place. I'm no one's lackey. I used to prospect with my partner, Strike Wilson. Richman don't try none of that funny attitude on me no more, and this job suits me right now. But I'm real glad to see that you set him straight, too."

"Oh, you were partners with Strike?" Tessa was delighted at his reference to the old man. "I know Strike. I consider him a friend."

"I got to say that I heard about you, too. Strike stays with me when he comes to San Francisco. He'll always be my friend, but I figured I was getting too old to stand in a cold stream all day, sifting out sand with so little to show for it. Strike doesn't think that way. He's sure he's going to strike it rich, and I wish him luck."

Tessa asked, "What is your name?"

"It's Nugget. Nugget McDuff."

Smiling, Tessa held out her hand. "Glad to meet you, Mr. McDuff."

Accepting her hand, the old man replied, "Just call me Nugget, ma'am. And I'm glad to meet you, too."

As they continued conversing casually, Tessa recalled thinking that she had had a fruitful morning since she had taught one man a valuable lesson and had established a friendship, too.

Looking back on that moment, she sighed at the realization that those moments had been the last free minutes she had had that day. She had been peeling, slicing, and cooking anxiously ever since.

Tessa raised the lids on her pots one by one. She frowned as she checked the iron skillets containing the pies and then shoved them deeper into the fire. She was not particularly adept at fireplace cookery; her mother had taught her on the family stove. And so much was riding on what she produced for supper that evening. Looking up, she saw that Maggie looked as concerned as she did.

Tessa glanced up at the clock on the wall and shuddered. It was almost time. Pedro would be arriving soon and she needed to be done by then. If not—

Tessa raised her head, suddenly disgusted with her own negative attitude. She had come this far and she would not falter now. She would be done cooking when Pedro came, and everything would be just fine.

She hoped.

Lucky watched from his position at a nearby table when Tessa arrived at the tent. His hand paused in dealing the cards, but the protests of the other players at the table forced him to resume the game. His attention was diverted, however, his mind on the slight, platinum-haired young woman who entered carrying a heavy pot.

His mouth twitched. He was about to call out Pedro's name when the rotund Mexican entered the tent carrying an even heavier pot. They needed help, damn it! Where were Jake and Larry?

Discarding a winning hand when the two men were nowhere to be seen, he murmured, "I'm out," before striding forward to take the pot from Tessa's arms.

Surprising him, Tessa snapped, "I can carry it."

He ignored her reaction by ordering gruffly, "Get the table ready. I have the feeling we have a hungry bunch of fellas waiting."

Lucky noted that Tessa hesitated before following his instructions. Her hesitation meant that she was considering whether she should allow him to tell her what to do or not. For some reason, that annoyed him.

Lucky put the heavy pot down on the table next to the one that Pedro had carried in, aware that Tessa appeared to have cooked enough to feed a small army. He then glanced at the long line that had formed in the short time it had taken him to reach the table.

A small army it was.

Lucky withheld a frown at the sighs that echoed within the tent when Pedro brought in the first of the apple pies.

Apple pies!

Delilah's lips tightened when she saw the precious cargo Pedro was carrying toward the table. The crust was a golden brown, juice oozed from several cuts in the top, and she had actually heard several men sigh! Both Pedro and the blonde witch had been struggling under the weight of what appeared to be pots of food when Lucky threw down his cards and jumped up to help them. The fact that most of the men had actually smiled at Tessa's unexpected entrance did not sit well with Delilah.

The apple pies were the last straw.

Delilah deliberately turned her head and forced herself to smile at the men who remained nearby. She then deliberately dipped her torso to allow her admirers a better glimpse of her attributes. She smiled more broadly at their appreciative expressions and moved closer to them. If there was one thing she knew for sure, it was that she had more to offer than *apple pie*.

That thought restoring her confidence, Delilah turned away and refused to look back.

"I'm so sorry. There's no more pie left to serve you seconds." Tessa looked at Strike Walker with true remorse as the evening waned and he again stood in front of her table.

"Thirds, ma'am," Strike corrected. "Pedro cut me a second piece when you was otherwise busy."

Tessa smiled at the gray-haired prospector with true warmth. She had mentioned her meeting with Nugget McDuff to him and he had smiled. But he was her favorite. She would not forget his generosity in being the first to break the immobility that had seemed to affect the rest of the men her first night in the tent.

Besides, he reminded her of her father in a way. Not in his physical appearance, but in the honesty and true warmth that shone from his bleary eyes when he looked at her.

She worried that he was too thin and looked too weary.

Tessa realized that during the extended conversation they had had, Strike had spoken very little about himself, other than to say that his beloved wife of forty-five years had died some time ago. Without any living children, he had been alone ever since. He had told her that he'd been prospecting for more years than he could count, that he believed he had finally located the right spot to stake a claim, and that he had rushed to San Francisco to make it official. Now looking at the pallor underneath his sun-darkened skin, she asked gently, "Do you intend to take a short vacation from work on your claim?"

"No, ma'am. I'm going back tomorrow."

"Oh, is that wise?" Tessa flashed a brief smile as she continued. "I mean, wouldn't you prefer to rest a little more and let me fatten you up a bit with my cooking? That is, if Lucky keeps me on."

"He will, ma'am. I'm sure of that." Strike chuckled. "I seen the disappointment on most of the fellas' faces here when you didn't come back last night, and I heard them telling Lucky so, too."

"Well, Lucky needed to make sure. I mean, he—"

Tessa cut herself off when she realized she was about to make an excuse for Lucky's confusing attitude.

"That's all right, ma'am. I understand it wasn't your fault that you wasn't here like you planned. I know, too, that Lucky thought he was doing the right thing by offering to pay for your transportation home instead."

Tessa gasped, "You know about that?"

Strike nodded, and Tessa raised her chin. "Well, I don't take charity."

"I know."

"I prefer to earn my way."

"I know that, too."

Suddenly aware that Lucky was looking at her and indicating that it was time to leave, Tessa flushed. "I'm sorry. I have to go now."

"I'll help you take your things back out to the wagon, ma'am."

Tessa noted that the rest of her customers had returned to their tables and resumed their games. Truly touched by his offer, she smiled and replied, "That's not necessary, Strike. Pedro and I can do it."

"It'll be my pleasure, ma'am. The truth is that I ain't met a young woman like you since—" The old man's eyes watered unexpectedly. He swallowed before choosing to continue. "Like I said, it'll be my pleasure."

"Thank you, then. I appreciate your help, and I admit that I will miss seeing you again."

"Same here, ma'am."

Her progress toward the door was halted by several appreciative customers while Strike followed behind. When the empty pot she carried was snatched unexpectedly from her hands, she resisted briefly, then turned to see Lucky's frozen expression. Her response was spontaneous.

"It's empty now. I can manage it."

She did not expect Lucky to grip her arm with one hand while he held the pot in the other and dismissed her claim, saying, "Pedro can load the rest of your things back in the wagon. We have some matters to discuss before you go."

Tessa glanced briefly at Strike, who had come to a halt behind her, and Lucky said gruffly, "You can put that pot in the wagon, Strike. I've saved a spot for you at my table. I figure you need to give me a chance to get even for last night."

"Yeah, I guess I do."

Winking at her as he walked past, Strike disappeared through the doorway as Lucky guided her outside and handed the pot he carried to Pedro. But Tessa was not as confident about the discussion Lucky demanded as Strike appeared to be.

Shaking inwardly, she did her best to project a confident demeanor when she said, "Well, I sold out again with both my stew and pies. The rest is up to you."

"No, it's up to you."

Tessa asked tentatively, "What's that supposed to mean?"

"It means it's up to you to maintain the interest of the fellas if you're going to be in my tent every day. As soon as they start going somewhere else, you're gone."

"You seem to forget. Men don't have to gamble, but they do have to eat," Tessa replied defensively.

Lucky's responsive smile was caustic. "It's been my experience that men with gold fever don't always behave the way they're supposed to. You'd do well to remember that while you're here."

"Really? Well, I have more faith in people."

"I suppose that's the same faith you had when you struggled to survive while *walking* to San Francisco, and when you ended up in my room."

Tessa took a breath at Lucky's cruel rejoinder and responded, "I can't say I truly remember most of those experiences. I only know that I'm here now, and that speaks for my beliefs."

Lucky's silence at that moment triggered a vague memory that Tessa struggled unsuccessfully to recall. She was aware of his reputation as a man who did well in situations where most did not survive. Good fortune seemed to fall into the hands of the handsome, well-built gambler. Then she remembered her own vulnerability when she'd arrived in San Francisco and the sense of dependence that she still had not completely shed despite her bravado. She wondered what else she did not recall.

The thought set her heart pounding with a yearning she did not comprehend.

Remaining silent, Tessa looked up at Lucky, her uncertain thoughts clearer that she wished. She saw a silent acknowledgment of her dilemma, and an unspoken and inscrutable need registered in his gaze. She saw him lower his mouth toward hers and was somehow unable to move as his lips covered hers.

She was unsure what she felt at the moment when his mouth conquered her resistance, when his lips separated hers and the taste of him overwhelmed her thoughts. A thrill moved down her spine unlike any she had ever known, and Tessa knew only that he was suddenly the sculptor and she was the clay.

His mouth sank deeper and the thrill spread to another, more intimate part of her as she separated her lips more fully. Her arms were about to steal around his neck and draw him closer when he withdrew abruptly, his expression stiff as he mumbled, "I must have had more to drink than I thought."

Appearing unaware how deeply that comment cut, Lucky said abruptly, "Pedro will pick you up at the same time tomorrow, so be ready. We'll work out the rest."

Tessa reminded him just as stiffly, "You have to remember that I owe you and Maggie for my room and board, as well as for the supplies I'm cooking with. I expect you to take that amount into consideration so I can pay you both back."

"We'll see."

"No, I want to make sure—"

"I said we'll see."

Tessa snapped her mouth shut. Lucky then swept her up into his arms and carried her to the wagon. She turned toward him to protest, but the words died on her lips. Once again, his lips were close to hers, so close that she could taste his sweet breath and the inherently fragrant scent of pure masculinity that she remembered too well.

Lucky's dark-eyed gaze dropped to her mouth again and the pounding of her heart escalated. His mouth drew closer. Full lips, warm lips, lips that—

But the spell was broken when Lucky dumped her suddenly onto the hard wagon seat and ordered unceremoniously, "Stay there!"

Finding her voice, Tessa retorted, "I have to get the rest of my things."

"Don't move! Pedro and I will load everything onto the wagon."

"But—"

"I said, just sit there!"

Angry at his tone, Tessa turned her head resolutely forward. She did not turn back until Pedro stepped up onto the seat beside her and clucked the wagon into motion. She then said loudly enough for everyone in the general vicinity to hear, "The boss ordered me to go directly home now, Pedro."

"*Sí, senorita.*"

She turned toward the rotund driver to see that he was smiling. "Why are you smiling?" she demanded.

"For no particular reason, *senorita*."

Tessa turned stiffly forward at his response. Somehow, she did not believe him.

Lucky paused in the tent doorway as the wagon carrying Tessa and Pedro slipped from sight.

She had left just in time. Another minute would've done it. Another minute watching every prospector, cowboy, wanderer, and gambler in his tent smiling and putting his best foot forward in an attempt to impress Tessa would have been too much. It didn't matter to him that each man had paid handsomely for every portion of stew and each piece of pie that Tessa dished out. He didn't care in the least whether or not they sighed their approval of each bite of food they took. Truthfully, the last thing on his mind was whether Tessa's presence in his tent would prove to be profitable for him.

The truth was that he hadn't liked Tessa's spontaneous smiles for each and every man who appeared at her table, especially when she smiled at him so seldom. He resented the time she had taken to speak to each fellow she served, especially when she did not display such interest in him. He also despised the look in some of the men's eyes when their turn in line came up and they took the opportunity to brush Tessa's hand with theirs, or made an attempt to prolong the conversations a bit too long.

But when he had held Tessa so close, felt her slender warmth in his arms, came so close to tasting her lips—

Lucky shuddered.

What's wrong with me? He didn't like the way he felt, as if he wanted to shield Tessa from those looks.

And make her look only at him.

Lucky was astounded. He couldn't be jealous, could he?

Refusing to answer that question, he turned and walked back inside the tent.

"So, how did it go?"

Her lips in a straight line, her expression unrevealing, Tessa turned to Maggie's question as Pedro deposited the last of her supplies inside the cabin and closed the door behind him. She responded flatly.

"I don't know."

"You don't know?" Maggie appeared confused. "How could you not know? Either Lucky asked you to come back tomorrow or he didn't."

"He didn't ask me to come back. He *told* me to be there, but he doesn't know if I made him any money yet."

"Oh, but your food is gone."

"Yes."

"And Lucky set the prices."

"Of course."

"Then he must've made a profit."

Tessa replied slowly, "Oh, really?" She gritted her

teeth. "Lucky Monroe is one of the most aggravating men I have ever known! He delights in giving orders, which he expects everyone to take without question. He refuses to divulge anything that might shed light on the question. And his attitude is so fierce that . . . that everybody just ends up doing what he says!"

"Lucky learned that attitude the hard way. He wasn't always so successful, you know."

"There you go, defending him again just because you like him."

"And you *don't* like him?"

"I . . . I . . ." Suddenly aware that she didn't know how to reply to that question, Tessa swallowed, and then turned toward the fireplace. She said abruptly, "I'm hungry. In the rush, I forgot to eat."

"Then it's probably a good thing I saved you something just in case."

Turning back to Maggie and regretting with all her heart her testy attitude, Tessa managed, "Thanks, Maggie, and I'm sorry about the way I spoke to you. I don't know what's wrong with me lately."

"I do. You've had a hard time and you're just beginning to take hold of your life. Remember that things don't always go the way you plan, and things aren't always the way they seem, either, especially in San Francisco."

"I suppose."

Staring at her a moment longer, Maggie said simply, "You'll get the answers to all your questions eventually,

Tessa. Just don't be in too big a hurry." She added, "You'd better eat now. It'll be dark before you know it."

The moon was shining brightly through the window when all inside the cabin lay in darkness some hours later. The dishes, implements, pots, and pans had been washed in preparation for the next day's cooking, and Tessa had finally staggered to the cot awaiting her. Yet Maggie's unanswered question returned to haunt her.

"And you don't like him?"

Well, did she like Lucky or didn't she?

She hadn't known how to answer that question at the time. She still didn't. Admittedly, Lucky had done so much for her. He had truly saved her life by bringing her to Maggie. He had supported her until she was well again. Actually, his dictatorial attitude had fostered in her an even greater sense of purpose. Yet he continued to doubt her, to taunt her, to frustrate her, to order her about in an autocratic way that he did not seem to adopt with anyone else.

Or maybe it was that no one else ever challenged him.

She considered that thought, and then dismissed it. Maggie had told her enough about Lucky's life to know that he had been challenged by many others, and often. That wasn't the reason.

Tessa unconsciously sighed. The truth was that she *didn't* like Lucky, not entirely. She was thankful for his help and she respected the way he took control, was successful in business, and the fact that he was actually considered a friend by most of the men he dealt with. She liked the fact that he ran his tent honestly. She appreciated his genuine regard for some of the men who came there, men like Strike Walker. She admired the fact that he had found a way to make a success of a life that had seemed stalled midway, like her own.

Tessa finally admitted to herself that Lucky impressed her. She acknowledged that she felt a fluttering in her stomach each time she saw him, although he seemed to feel only annoyance. She knew it was shallow of her to consider appearances, but she was intensely aware of his masculinity. She knew every woman in his tent had difficulty tearing her eyes from his outstanding figure: his height and build, and the way he walked, as if he had a destination in mind and no one was going to stop him from getting there. The clean, earthy scent of him when he had scooped her up into his arms earlier that evening was with her still. She remembered the way her heart had leaped when his mouth was so close, and she wished—

Tessa's thoughts halted sharply at the recollection of Delilah's expression after Lucky plopped her unceremoniously onto the wagon seat. Near the doorway of the tent, the beautiful redhead had glared at them revealingly. She also remembered Delilah's spontaneous smile when another man approached her. That smile had projected a wealth of experience in dealing with men, an area where she herself was a true novice. She also knew from the scraps of information she had gathered over the past few weeks that Delilah was Lucky's mistress.

She also had to admit that she admired Lucky. He had worked hard and had created a good life for himself. She had no place in it, whatever she might feel for him. It was no wonder that Lucky wanted to send her back where she came from. It was difficult for her to acknowledge that her insistence in paying him back was actually a burden to him, but it was a burden she refused to surrender. Despite the difficulties involved, she needed to establish her independence just as he had years earlier. She needed to know that she could make it on her own, simply because she *was* on her own. It wouldn't take too long for her to accomplish her goal and return to Iowa. She only hoped that it wasn't too late for her when she did.

Tessa forced herself to answer Maggie's question squarely.

Did she like Lucky?

He annoyed her, irritated her, and chose to order her around, but despite all that, she did like him.

Tessa rescinded that thought. Maybe she didn't really *like* him. Maybe the word for what she felt was a little different.

Maybe—

Tessa rolled over in her cot and closed her eyes. Maybe it was time to go to sleep.

Chapter Five

A fair day had dawned. Maggie had watched as Tessa prepared for work in the semidarkness while the city below came to life. Tessa had since started on her way down the hillside to shop the mercantile for foodstuffs, and Maggie had remained silent as the door closed behind her. She knew that Tessa would return with another loaded wagon.

For years, Maggie had watched life from a distance. Then Lucky entered her life, and she gradually began living again because she started to care. Tessa had had almost the same effect on her. She was as proud of Lucky's success as she would have been if he were her own child. But now that he was independent of her, she had begun feeling that her work was done. With Tessa, she had rediscovered that her existence served a purpose.

She also sensed how Lucky had felt when Tessa stumbled into his tent. She knew that he had attempted to harden himself to others, yet he had recognized something special in Tessa the first moment he saw her. His intuition had been confirmed when Tessa's honesty and determination did not waver despite her circumstances. Those qualities fostered his respect, and when Tessa recovered and her beauty became apparent, he was all the more attracted to her.

Maggie shook her head. She was truly uncertain how it would all come out in the end, but she knew two things: the first was that although they didn't seem to realize it, Lucky and Tessa admired each other; and the second was that the best thing she could do was to stay out of their way until they sorted things out.

A knock on the door brought Maggie's thoughts up short. The knock sounded again, and Maggie hesitated. It was too early for most people to be about.

Maggie walked toward the door and drew it open.

"You must be Maggie. My name is Strike Wilson."

Maggie's eyes widened at the sight of the old man on her doorstep. He was apparently even older than she. His hair was gray and his face was deeply lined, but it was his pallor that concerned her. "I've heard your name," she said. "Tessa has talked about you. She considers you a friend. She's not here right now, but any friend of hers is a friend of mine. Please come in."

The old man limped into the cabin. Turning toward her as she closed the door, he said, "I know Tessa isn't here. I waited until she left. Actually, you're the person I wanted to talk to."

"Really?" Maggie was at a loss. Hesitating, she replied, "Well, I suppose you should start talking, then."

* * *

Strike gazed intently at the gray-haired woman standing opposite him, the woman who had nursed Tessa back to life. He realized he had caught her off guard.

"I wanted to talk to you before I head back to my claim. Tessa has spoken very highly of you. She told me about how she came to be in San Francisco, and how she came to live in your cabin."

Maggie was momentarily confused. She prompted, "So you're saying?"

"I'm saying thank you, ma'am, for helping Tessa like you did. It was important for me to say that to you because Tessa is special. I had a daughter of my own. Well, she didn't make it too long in this world, but Tessa's got the same kind of honesty and persistence that my wife did and that I figure my daughter would have had, too. That kind of goodness comes from the heart. I figure you helped in bringing it back to life in her. I wanted to thank you for that without embarrassing Tessa."

Maggie appeared at a loss for words, and Strike continued. "I realize you don't know me from Adam, but I loved my wife dearly, and I see a familiar soul in Tessa. I recognized it immediately and to see it again made me feel right good." He smiled sheepishly. "You can see how what I'm saying would embarrass Tessa."

Regaining her tongue, Maggie said simply, "Would you like a cup of tea, Strike?"

"I don't think so, ma'am. I don't want to run into Tessa. I'm not good at saying good-bye and I don't really want her to know that I was here." He chuckled and added, "She'd take exception to what I said about her anyways. She's that way."

"Tessa went down to the mercantile. She won't be back for an hour at least. That would give you time for tea."

"Well then, thank you, ma'am. I accept."

Talking freely between intermittent gulps, Strike listened when Maggie responded with sincere familiarity. With his cup emptied and his heart warmed a short time later, he stood up to leave the cabin.

Turning back toward Maggie when he reached the doorway, he said, "It was a true pleasure meeting you, ma'am. Whether it makes any difference to you or not, you're all that I expected you to be." He added soberly, "That's a compliment, in case you wondered."

Maggie's eyes were moist when she responded, "That means more to me than you know. Thank you, Strike."

His mission accomplished, Strike headed toward his horse. He had needed to be sure that he was leaving Tessa in good hands.

Strike was aware that the old woman watched him as he limped away and then mounted up. He waved a last good-bye before turning back onto the trail. He did not know that Maggie remained standing there with tears in her eyes long after his solitary figure faded from sight.

Agitated, Tessa busied herself among the shelves of foodstuffs. She did not want to make stew over and over again for the men who awaited her in Lucky's tent, but her circumstances were limited. Her only alternative to the salt pork in the mercantile was the game that hunters brought daily into the city to sell to Mr. Richman at top price. Today she had decided to prepare a stew made from the unidentifiable birds that now lay stretched out in the back of the wagon. She had bought extra flour to add dumplings to the stew, and for the crusts of the berry pies she intended to make from the dried berries she had discovered among the shelves.

Tessa pushed back an errant strand of platinum hair that had fallen forward on her forehead and then straightened the faded frock that she had been wearing when she reached San Francisco. She was aware that the garment had lost its original blue color, and that it was threadbare and had shrunk from repeated washings. The dress that Maggie had supplied for her was hanging on the makeshift drying line behind the cabin. The dress she had on molded itself to her slender proportions more than she would have wished. The bodice was too tight, clearly outlining the small mounds of her breasts. And the gaping hole in the back where she had sewn in a patch was in too conspicuous a spot for her peace of mind. The hemline was also too short. It clearly displayed her slender ankles.

What she did not realize was that her eyes appeared even lighter and more striking against the garment's faded color; that her skin had regained a healthful hue that emphasized the contours of her cheeks and lips;

that her flashing smile would always attract attentions; or that her appeal was especially great in a city of jaded, aggressive males and fast women.

For all those reasons, she was unique.

Reaching the counter at last, Tessa faced Mr. Richman's weak smile soberly as she said, "I suppose that will be all for today. Lucky will settle the account at the end of the week."

"Of course."

Tessa did not respond. Instead, she turned toward the doorway and the wagon awaiting her on the street outside. She was about to climb onto the seat when she heard a familiar voice.

"Good morning, Tessa."

Harley had arisen particularly early that morning so he could meet Tessa "casually" at the mercantile when her shopping was done. He had paid particular attention to his toilette and had dressed carefully in preparation for their "chance" meeting. He had known he would be scrutinized and had made sure that his appearance was faultless and that he feigned the most honest and straightforward expression. In truth, he had slipped into Lucky's tent unseen the previous evening and had taken a calculated risk in order to assess Tessa's effect on the men gathered there. Her simple beauty had been a light in the tawdry gambling tent. She had been a beacon of gentility where painted women were the norm. Those qualities had drawn men to her. The result had been that the gamblers—young and old, jaded and hopeful—had lined up for her offerings with hungery looks in their eyes. Everything she cooked was said to be delicious, and whether it was or not did not seem to matter. The opportunity to talk to Tessa, to bask in her light, to share a precious moment with someone so natural and honest, was what each man had unconsciously sought.

In short, every man there had *wanted* her. He now considered it his duty to see to it that the men willing to pay the most would have her.

Harley inwardly snickered. He was well acquainted with that duty. He had become wealthy serving it. With Tessa's help, he would become wealthier still.

Tessa turned toward him on the narrow walk and he scrutinized her petite frame. She had twisted her platinum hair into a casual bun, but the severe style did nothing to hide its glorious sheen. He noted that her worn clothing appeared to have shrunk, and that her dress hugged her slender figure more tightly than usual. The undersized bodice hinted at small breasts that were appealingly uptilted and firm. The narrow waistline of the dress hung loose, indicating an even smaller expanse underneath, and the slender ankles exposed to his eye hinted at shapely legs hidden from view. All that in a dress that was colorless and shabby.

Harley fought to conceal his excitement. After he convinced Tessa to work for him, he would see to it that she wore the best imported clothing. The styles would be modest, revealing just a teasing hint of what lay underneath. She would be the woman every man sought: perfect, unblemished, without stain of any kind, while being available to any man willing to pay her enormous price. She would be the princess that a man desired to bend to his will, but never truly expected to have. She would be the unattainable woman who was unexpectedly within his grasp. She would be all that lucky fellow had ever dreamed of, even if his dream was relatively short-lived.

Harley smiled broadly. But Tessa did not smile in return when she said, "Good morning, Mr. Knox."

"Call me Harley, please." Harley scrutinized her expression and continued. "It's the beginning of a beautiful day. I only wish your expression were as bright when you look at me."

Tessa hesitated a moment before replying, "I have always claimed to be a person who does not listen to rumors and who makes up her own mind, Mr. Knox. However, I have heard some very dark things about you."

"Harley, please, Tessa," he replied. "Tell me what you heard. I think it would be good to get these rumors cleared up as quickly as possible. My interest in you is sincere."

"But what is your interest in me, Mr. Knox?" Tessa's light eyes held his as she continued. "I have heard that you are a wealthy man, but that you achieved your success by importing women to be used at the discretion of wealthy men. Is that true?"

"If it were true, why would I be interested in you, Tessa?"

Tessa considered the honest expression that accompanied his reply and then said, "You haven't answered my question, but I suppose you dare not."

"Why do you say that, Tessa? Even if what you said were true, would my occupation be so different from the gambler you seem to have aligned yourself with?"

"If you are referring to Lucky, he plays honestly."

"I am not dishonest."

Frowning, Tessa said, "I did not accuse you of being dishonest, but I don't have time to waste, Mr. Knox. I admit to being confused by your responses and I'm afraid I must know if what I've heard is true. Did you bring women from France with the specific purpose of entertaining men in your house of pleasure?"

Harley replied vaguely, "If I did arrange for Frenchwomen's transportation to this country, I did so because they desired to come here."

"They desired to come here to work in your house and to entertain men in your house because you offered them an amount they could not turn down?"

"I offered women the opportunity to better themselves, to wear the finest clothing, to eat the finest foods, and to engage in easy work."

"On their backs."

"Tessa!" Harley appeared shocked. "You offend my sensibilities!"

"Do I? Tell me once and for all, why do you have an interest in me?"

Harley paused again. He knew he was losing this game, but he responded, "I have the interest of a man who appreciates qualities in you that are not common in any atmosphere, most especially not in this place where only pleasure and gain are sought."

"You flatter me, Mr. Knox, but I am not easily deceived. Do you run a house where Frenchwomen exchange sexual favors for money?"

"If that is the way you wish to perceive it."

Tessa raised her chin. "Do you wish to add me to your harem?"

"I do not have a harem."

"But you do keep women who are at the beck and call of any man willing to pay the price."

Harley did not reply, but the perspiration that began appearing on his forehead and upper lip told the tale. Tessa's expression was sincere as she spoke into the silence, "I do not wish to judge you, Mr. Knox. But neither do I wish to be in the company of a man who chooses to make his living demeaning women."

"Demeaning?"

"Good-bye, sir."

Tessa climbed into the waiting wagon without allowing Harley to continue the conversation.

"Tessa, wait. You don't understand."

Tessa said more softly, "I'm ready to leave now, Nugget."

"Yes, ma'am."

Harley repeated, "Tessa—"

The wagon pulled away while Harley stood immobile and unanswered.

The sound of the wheels making their way through the muddy street was all that could be heard until the wagon was a distance from Harley and the gray-haired driver turned to Tessa to say, "I'm proud of you, real proud for putting that fella in his place."

"Thank you, Nugget."

Tessa did not say more.

Rigid with anger, Harley stood motionless on the street as the wagon bearing Tessa turned onto the hilly trail. With a stiff smile plastered on his lips, he remained silently watching a few minutes longer before turning away abruptly. He nodded with a smile and a tip of his hat at a matron as she walked by, but all the while he was silently swearing that Tessa would be sorry. She had humiliated him, which was an unforgivable offense. Homeless and destitute, living on the generosity of a gambler, she was no different from the other women who worked for him, whether she knew it or not.

But he would make sure she admitted that fact to him if it were the last thing he ever did.

* * *

"All right, be patient! She has enough for all of you."

The afternoon sun was bright outside the tent. It had begun slipping toward the horizon just as the wagon bearing Tessa and her nightly offerings drew up outside. What happened then was a blur in Lucky's mind. An unusual crowd was present inside the tent for that hour of the day, and an informal line had formed at the table where Tessa was to serve. It had grown larger and more ragged as Pedro brought in each steaming pot. When Tessa took her place, the waiting crowd erupted.

Lucky frowned at the unexpected pushing and shoving all around the table. Annoyed, he glanced up at Tessa and saw that she was frowning, too. It occurred to him that when Tessa had staggered through the doorway of his tent that first time, he would never have imagined that he would end up abandoning the card table to become a policeman directing traffic for her.

He didn't like it!

Aware that the situation was getting out of hand, with several of his most easygoing patrons showing a side to their personalities that he did not expect, Lucky watched as Larry and Jake left their posts and strode toward the scene. He knew instinctively that their rough handling would only make the situation worse. He was about to shout above the mayhem when Tessa spoke up unexpectedly.

"Please line up calmly, gentlemen." Her voice was raised but controlled as she continued with obvious concern. "I have great affection for most of you and I wouldn't want to see any of you hurt." She then said directly, "Billy . . . David, I think you two were first in line. Pedro will hand you your plates while the others take their places."

When the shoving came to a halt and the men began adjusting their positions, she said more quietly, "Thank you. This is all new to me, but you may rest assured that none of you will go away hungry."

Larry and Jake halted their advance abruptly and Lucky controlled his amazement. With a few words, Tessa had checked a possible riot and had begun serving each man as if he were her old friend.

Aware that his tent was more crowded than it had ever been, Lucky continued standing beside the table until Tessa looked up. Her face flushed, she whispered, "I don't think there will be any further trouble now. You can go back to your card table."

Lucky responded gruffly, "I'll stay right where I am."

Tessa averted her gaze, but not before Lucky saw her smile even more brightly than before. The men in line did not overlook that brief exchange. His response to their accusing glances was a stiff stare. Those fellas could accuse him of anything they wanted, but he'd be damned before he'd stand by and allow Tessa to be trampled in the rush!

Lucky stood adamantly beside Tessa until he was certain the crowd was under control. Then he turned back toward his table.

As he assumed his seat, he wondered where all these

men had come from. Admittedly, he had been badgered by countless questions about Tessa since the previous night: Would she be there every night; at what time? He had responded honestly that he wasn't sure how long she'd be coming, but she'd be there at five o'clock the next day. The crowd that had filled his tent at this early hour, consisting of some men he had never seen before, was the result. His next, begrudging thought was that the crowd in the tent was good, but that didn't mean all those men would remain to play cards afterward.

Lucky then saw Harley Knox skulking nearby. It did not miss his notice that Harley was taking in the crowds of men that had shown up and Tessa's unexpected handling of them without a harsh word. Catching his eye, Harley then tipped his hat in Lucky's direction before walking back out through the tent doorway.

Lucky remembered stumbling on Harley holding Tessa's hand. He wondered if Harley had made any advances toward her, and if Tessa, as obstinate as she was, had accepted them. However, there was one thing about which he was determined. He would not allow Harley to add Tessa to his entourage.

"Are you going to deal those cards or not, Lucky?"

Realizing his thoughts had frozen him midmotion, Lucky frowned and continued dealing. He ignored the mumbles that sounded around the table. He later slapped down yet another hand and relinquished the pot he'd built to the prospector across from him. He glanced at Tessa, who was reaching down to scoop up the last of the stew. He silently groaned. Her presence interfered with his concentration; the sooner she left the tent, the better. The truth was that he didn't want to be responsible for her. He didn't want to feel that her future lay in his hands, or that her safety was his responsibility. He didn't want to feel—

He halted at that thought and looked again at Tessa as she prepared to leave. The absolute truth was that he didn't want to feel anything at all when he looked at Tessa. But that *anything* had begun turning into *something*.

Could it already be too late for him?

"I'm sorry, Lucky. I don't know what happened, but you can rest assured that I won't let it happen again."

Lucky looked down at Tessa as she stood outside his tent near the wagon that was to take her back home. She had finished serving, was preparing to leave, and Pedro was seated in the driver's seat of the wagon with his head turned resolutely forward. Lucky remained silent as Tessa continued. "All that pushing and shoving. I wish Strike had been there. He would have settled everything before it got started."

"Strike, huh? He went back to his diggings, but did it ever occur to you that my standing there should have made a difference, yet it actually had no effect at all? I doubt that Strike's presence would have helped."

"Strike would've been able to stop that behavior before it started. He's one of those men."

"So am I."

"No, you're not. You're the boss. You own this tent."

"I'm still one of them."

"Maybe you were once, but you aren't anymore."

"The only difference between me and them is that I've seen some success."

Tessa shrugged. "If you say so." She hesitated and then continued. "I just wanted to say that I didn't intend to cause you any trouble. I suppose the problem is that those men were so hungry for a touch of home that they were wild with it."

Sure.

"They wanted a good, home-cooked meal and were afraid they'd be left out."

Right.

"It had nothing to do with me. It was only what I remind them of."

Does she ever look in the mirror?

"Lucky, please say something."

Lucky looked down at Tessa's soulful expression. Damn it all, he just wanted to curl his arms around her and tell her everything was all right! He wanted to feel those trembling lips under his own and to make sure that she never felt insecure again. He wanted to protect her from everything that threatened her in this foul city.

Determined not to be trapped by the emotions suddenly running riot inside him, Lucky replied gruffly, "It's over and it won't happen again. I'll see to it."

"What do you mean?"

"I mean when you come tomorrow, I'll make sure that every man knows his place and how to behave."

"Oh."

He added sarcastically, "If that's all right with you."

Tessa shrugged. "I . . . I don't want any of them to get hurt."

Lucky tensed. "And I do?"

"No, but Jake and Larry—"

"What about them? They took care of you well enough that first night."

She remained silent.

Suddenly suspicious, he demanded, "They did, didn't they?"

"I suppose."

"You suppose?"

"I don't remember!"

"You don't remember?"

"The first night I arrived in San Francisco is a blur in my mind. All I recall is that your tent was bright and filled with music and laughter, which was in short supply those days. It drew me like a magnet."

Lucky was silent as he looked at Tessa's tormented expression. It had all been chance, then. She could have walked into any of the cluster of tents that stood in the plaza. She just happened to stagger into his.

Swallowing, Lucky scooped Tessa up into his arms

as he had done the previous night. He walked the few steps to the wagon and put her down gently on the seat. He heard himself say as he looked into her incredible gray eyes, "I guess I was just lucky, then."

Giving Pedro a signal, he said nothing more as the elderly Mexican clucked the horses into motion. He watched the wagon depart, and then walked back into his tent.

Clarice awoke in a dirty doorway on the waterfront. Her clothes were stained, she was unclean, she was hungry as well, and she had run out of medicine. She had spent the previous day wandering the city, unsuccessful in getting any type of job. Desperate, she had then approached the first man on the street that she saw. She had offered him her services, but he had turned from her in disgust. Hungry and homeless, she had approached another, only to find that his reaction was the same. Then another.

Becoming more desperate by the hour and aware that she needed the funds to purchase more laudanum, she had walked down to the waterfront, certain she would be able to find someone who would pay her for her services there. Strangely, it had been more difficult than she had imagined. She could not remember how many times she had been turned down when she finally approached a seaman who appeared to have been at sea for some time. After some persuasion, she had serviced him and obtained a pitifully small payment in return. There had been another seaman after that, and then another. She did not remember much after obtaining her medicine from a man on the waterfront who was known to sell it. But now she had awakened to another day, and her needs were again calling her.

Clarice stood up and began wandering the street aimlessly. She had no money. She could not remember the last time she had eaten. Her head was beginning to throb and her stomach to cramp. There was no work for her on the waterfront during daylight hours. Where to go? What to do?

The new day had begun and Tessa's chores awaited her. First, she needed to see what was available at the mercantile so she could plan the meal she would serve that evening. So much depended on it.

"When you lose their interest, you're gone."

Lucky had made that remark so casually, but would he follow through on his words if the men ceased to show an interest in her cooking? She did not want to put him to the test. It was a matter of pride. She *needed* to earn her way.

Those thoughts were heavy on her mind as Tessa made her way down the hill toward the mercantile. San Francisco was relatively quiet in the hours just after dawn, and she liked it that way. She saw less of the seediness of the city when the streets were clear of travelers rushing to and fro as if a few lost moments might cost them the fortune they hoped to find. The mercantile was customarily free of customers, too, enabling her to have first choice of the meager supplies available.

The sound of voices within the store stopped Tessa just outside the door. She recognized Mr. Richman's voice. No, it was the tone she recognized. He had sounded the same when he believed she was desperate enough to submit to him in exchange for a job. She would never forget that experience. Chills ran down her spine as she listened to the conversation coming from within.

"I need a position, monsieur. Anything will do."

"You don't really think I would hire someone who looks as bad as you, do you?"

The heavily accented voice responded, "Does it matter how I look if I can make you feel better than you've ever felt before?"

"That's a promise, is it?" A sneer was obvious in Mr. Richman's voice. "How much would you charge for that service?"

"I have formerly been employed by Mr. Harley Knox at a house where my services were greatly valued. The charge was—"

"You aren't employed by Harley any longer, though, are you?" Mr. Richman interrupted. "So your fee should be greatly reduced."

After a hesitation, the woman replied, "Perhaps you should set the price, then."

"How about *nothing*?"

"Nothing!"

"I wouldn't touch you with a ten-foot pole! I'm not as desperate as you seem to be."

"Monsieur."

"Get out! You're a sorry sight to see and I will not have you in my store."

"But you said—"

"But I said." Mr. Richman laughed. "I was just having some fun with you."

"But I need funds in order to purchase my medicine."

"Your medicine? You mean your laudanum."

"*Oui,* monsieur. That is my medicine."

"Get out!"

"Monsieur—"

"You heard me!"

Unable to bear more, Tessa stepped into the doorway and the conversation stopped dead. She was unable to hide her shock when she viewed the woman standing at the counter. She briefly closed her eyes. The woman's physical condition was horrendous. Patchy hair, sallow complexion, clothing that was beyond filthy covering a body that had become painfully thin. She could hardly blame Mr. Richman for his reaction to the woman's offer.

Mr. Richman looked at Tessa nervously, and then repeated more softly, "You heard what I said. Get out! I don't want any of my customers to see you here."

His insulting tone raised Tessa's hackles. She looked at the woman, noting that she was trembling visibly. Concerned, Tessa took a step toward her as the woman replied to Mr. Richman, "You are sure that I cannot do anything for you, monsieur?"

"I'm sure. Get out!"

It occurred to Tessa at that moment that she had been in no better condition than this woman when she first came to San Francisco. She had been dirty, unkempt, suffering from lack of food and water, and she had been hallucinating. She also realized that if she had walked into this mercantile instead of Lucky's tent, *she* might have faced the same harsh treatment.

"Monsieur," the woman begged.

"Go!"

The woman turned unsteadily and walked back through the doorway, roughly brushing Tessa's side as she did. Reacting with concern, Mr. Richman said, "I hope she didn't hurt you."

"No, she did not."

"And I hope you weren't offended by her presence here."

Tessa replied soberly, "I was not offended by that woman's presence, Mr. Richman, because I was a woman such as she when I first arrived in this city."

"You were never like her! She's a French whore who

was thrown out onto the street by Harley Knox because of her addiction to her 'medicine.' You have become a valuable asset to San Francisco."

"A valuable asset? I doubt that. And though I did not come to San Francisco with the same purpose in mind as that woman, she is as desperate as I once was."

"She is a whore! I don't want to discuss her."

Tessa maintained her silence for long moments. If Lucky did not have an ongoing account in this store, if this establishment were not the only place where she could buy the foodstuffs she needed, she would not set foot in the place again. It occurred to Tessa that like that woman, she was not in control of her own destiny.

"Miss White, do you have a list for me to fill today?"

Mr. Richman appeared to dismiss the Frenchwoman from his mind as he smiled and said, "I have something special today in the way of meat. It appears that the hunters that supply my store were able to bag some quail. I have enough of the birds to make excellent pot pies if you are willing to put in the time."

Tessa hesitated. Turning, she realized that the Frenchwoman had disappeared from sight.

"Miss White?"

"Yes, I will take all the quail you have. I would also like to see whatever fresh vegetables have come in on recent shipments."

"Certainly."

Mr. Richman rushed to fill her order as Tessa walked

halfheartedly around the store. She continued to be troubled by thoughts of the Frenchwoman.

Satisfied at last that she had bought supplies enough to satisfy the number of men who had been in Lucky's tent the previous evening, Tessa purchased ingredients for spice cakes according to a recipe that had been her mother's specialty.

With her supplies loaded on Mr. Richman's wagon, Tessa smiled at Nugget as he started the wagon back up the trail. She scanned the streets they passed through.

"Looking for something?"

Tessa turned back to Nugget and said self-consciously, "I guess I was looking to see where that woman went."

"The Frenchwoman?"

Tessa nodded.

"She ain't long for this world in her condition. Some-body's going to find her lying in a doorway sooner or later, and that'll be another person for an unmarked grave."

"Don't say that, Nugget!"

"Why not? It's true. Plenty of them that come here and never live to go home again are buried in a pauper's grave."

"Nugget, please." Tessa swallowed. She said more softly, "That could've been me."

"No, ma'am. Not you. Never you. You ain't the kind to give up."

"I was just fortunate."

"No, ma'am. Good fortune had nothing to do with it. A man can read in your eyes that you're not the same as that Frenchwoman."

Tessa's smile was sad as she said, "I thought not, but we'll never know for sure, will we?"

Nugget's tone did not falter. "I know."

"I wish I was as certain as you are, Nugget."

Tessa looked down when her eyes filled. She looked up again as Nugget's aged, calloused hand unexpectedly covered hers and he said, "I'm sure."

They did not speak anymore.

Chapter Six

"Don't get the wrong idea." Lucky stood in front of Noel Richman's counter. He had noted the fellow's reaction to his statement, and he didn't like it. He continued slowly. "I don't need to make explanations to you, but I want to make something very clear anyway. I'm buying a dress for Tessa because she's been successful in my tent, she needs to dress the part, and she won't buy one for herself. That's all."

"Sure, Lucky."

Lucky scrutinized the proprietor's round face and the sneer that he barely concealed. Whatever had made him think that he liked that fellow?

Lucky continued. "Just direct me to the ready-made women's clothing. I'll take it from there." He glared at the proprietor in warning. "And if I find out that you've been doing some talking that you shouldn't have, I'll make sure you're sorry."

"Okay, Lucky."

Satisfied at Noel's reaction, Lucky strode toward the section of the mercantile he indicated. He stopped in front of the rack with ready-made women's dresses and began sorting awkwardly through the limited offerings. He snorted in response to what he saw. Most of the dresses were too large for Tessa's fragile proportions. Many of them were in colors that were too outlandish for Tessa's delicate coloring. He was afraid that he would not find—

Lucky stopped short at the last dress on the rack. Obviously made for a woman of Tessa's slender proportions, it was also sewn in light blue gingham that bore a striking resemblance to the faded garment Tessa had worn when she first came to San Francisco. Lucky touched the dress gently, his mind wandering.

The past week had seen a rapid increase in attendance in his tent. He had to conclude that Tessa's arrival each night with freshly cooked food was the reason. His profits had multiplied, which should have made him very happy. The only problem was that his feelings for the determined waif had grown as well.

Feelings. The truth was that he could not look at Tessa without wanting her. He could not touch her without desiring more. His suffering grew daily, but Tessa appeared unaware of his distress.

He should be glad that she wasn't aware of his feelings, shouldn't he? He was sure they wouldn't last, and he did not want to take advantage of her innocence. He knew that although she had fought him every step of the way, Tessa had come to depend on him. He had become her hero whether she realized it or not, simply because he was there to help her when she needed it. Yet her mind still appeared to be consumed by the thought of returning home. She would be able to accomplish that goal in a month or so, at the rate she was going.

In a month or so.

Would he be able to maintain his distance that long? Would he be able to control the inexplicable longing deep inside him that made all other women pale in comparison? Would he be able to continue looking at Tessa each night while knowing that each man who approached her table wanted her in one way or another, just as he did?

Would he be able to control his unexpected *jealousy*?

Those questions went unanswered as he snatched the dress from the rack and returned to the front counter. He had not been entirely honest about his reasons for buying it. Tessa did need it. Yet *he* had needed to buy it for her just as much.

Tessa looked at the garment that she had just unwrapped. The setting sun lit the sky with brilliant streaks of red and gold, tinting the city of San Francisco with color. The night was just beginning. Lucky and she were standing outside his tent and Tessa had finished serving her loyal customers their evening meal, which was probably the only decent meal they had had that day. The hilarity in the brightly lit tent behind her had gradually risen as she gathered up her things and packed them in the wagon. The noise within the tent had grown even louder as she reached the exit and Lucky met her with a package in hand.

Tessa looked up at Lucky where he stood beside her. Tall, dark, and handsome, he was appealling from the top of his unruly dark hair to the tips of his shiny, polished, hand-tooled boots, but he had also proved to be compassionate, gentle, and considerate. He was, he was—

Tessa refused to finish that thought. Uncertain of her feelings, she only knew that each new side she saw of Lucky endeared him to her more. The sober expression he turned to her now appeared almost vulnerable as he awaited her reaction.

Emotion welled within her. She blinked back her tears and replied softly, "I can't accept this from you, Lucky."

"What do you mean?" Lucky frowned at her response. "I bought it for you. You need it, and it's your size, isn't it?"

"It's my size and it's beautiful, but I can accept it only if you allow me to pay you back for it."

"That again. You can't accept a gift from me." Annoyance creased his expression. "It would go against what you believe in."

"I've already accepted too much from you as it is." Tessa forced herself to continue. "It's not a matter of what I believe in, either. I told you that I have to learn to stand on my own two feet."

"That's what you're doing."

"With your help! You're already providing me with a place to live and food, plus the supplies I need in order to cook for the men in the tent."

"And you're making it worth my while."

"I can't allow you to clothe me as well."

"You'd rather wear those threadbare clothes, or that oversized garment Maggie lent to you, rather than something I bought."

"No, I wouldn't." She took a breath. "The dress is more beautiful than I can say, but I can't wear it if I can't pay you back for it."

"Would you accept it from Maggie?"

"Maggie wouldn't offer something like this to me."

"She can't afford it. I can."

"But Maggie wouldn't offer it to me anyway. She knows how important my independence is to me."

"And I don't?"

Tessa paused. She searched Lucky's expression. "Do you?"

In the short silence that followed, Tessa scrutinized Lucky more closely. He didn't seem to understand that she didn't want to interfere with the comfortable life he had made for himself, and she was afraid she had. Did he realize that the dark looks Delilah sent her way indicated that she had somehow gotten in the way of the satisfying relationship between Lucky and her? Did he know that to her chagrin, a part of her was glad that she had?

No, she did not think he understood, just as she did not quite understand her own feelings.

"I don't want the men in my tent to wonder why all your hard work hasn't netted you decent clothing."

"My clothing is decent!"

"It is decent, but only barely. You should be able to afford better when working for me."

"Oh."

"Besides, I want you to have that dress."

At a loss for words, Tessa looked at Lucky. She asked straight out, "Why is what I wear so important to you?"

The answer to that question would reveal too much. He knew he didn't actually care what she wore. But he felt a strong need to buy something for her so that she would wear a visible link to him.

Realizing he dared not tell the full truth, he replied, "I don't think you'd buy it for yourself, but you deserve it. You've worked hard."

"I owe you too much already."

"Do you?"

"I told you how I feel."

Lucky responded, "I suppose, then, that I haven't made the way *I* feel very clear. I've been lucky to have made a comfortable life for myself in this transient city. I know that now. So many others with a history like mine tried and failed."

"You did that because of your determination and your will to succeed."

"The same determination that you have."

"No, you can't put me in the same class as yourself. You made it on your own, but I've been helped every step of the way. As much as I hate to admit it, I might not have seen as much success as I have if I hadn't stumbled into your tent that first night."

"You would've made it somehow."

"Maybe, but I'm not sure how."

"Don't talk like that."

"It's a truth I wouldn't admit before."

"The truth is that you stumbled into my tent, but you never made me sorry that you did."

"Never?"

"Well, almost never."

Tessa held Lucky's serious gaze with hers and said softly, "This is one of those 'almost' times, Lucky. I love the dress, but I can't accept it from you unless you let me pay you back for it."

Lucky did not respond. Tessa saw his chest heave as he took a deep breath. Something she could not quite identify flashed in his dark eyes before he scooped her up into his arms without another word and walked to the waiting wagon. Putting her down firmly on the seat, he said in a tone that suffered no refusal, "Just take it. And go home."

Pedro flicked the reins before Tessa could reply. The wagon leaped forward onto the trail, and the issue was temporarily settled.

* * *

Delilah allowed the calloused hand to remain on her shoulder as she watched Lucky enter the tent. She pushed it off with a smile when it sank a few inches closer to her breast. Reaching for her glass, she emptied it in a gulp, and tapped the bar for another as the nameless prospector beside her laughed. She laughed also, knowing that in another few minutes, she'd move that fella toward the gaming tables where he'd do the most good. Her thoughts were on another man anyway.

Delilah followed Lucky to his customary seat with her gaze. She watched as he was greeted by the mumbled comments of the men there. Whether they wanted to admit it or not, they missed the challenge of having him at their table. She missed Lucky, too. Lucky hadn't visited her tent since *sweet Tessa* had stumbled into their lives. She knew she couldn't compete with the girl's sweetness and innocence. She was losing him. She had to do something before it was too late.

But what?

Tessa rose from her cot to another new day. Dawn was just beginning to lighten the night sky when she began moving around the cabin in the semidarkness. She had had difficulty falling asleep the previous night even though she had been exhausted. She could not seem to forget the vulnerability she'd glimpsed in Lucky's eyes. The unspoken need there had summoned a deep response within her. When Lucky's strong arms had closed around her, she'd wanted to turn toward him so that their lips—

Maggie spoke up unexpectedly from the shadows and Tessa jumped.

"What's wrong, Tessa? Don't you feel well?"

"I'm fine." Tessa managed to smile in the direction of Maggie's cot. "It's only a little earlier than usual. I'm sorry if I woke you up but I wanted to get a head start today. Some of the fellas asked if I could make them a pudding for dessert. I said I would if Mr. Richman could provide the ingredients. I figure the earlier I get there, the better."

"Oh, I see." Maggie continued uncertainly. "I was just wondering if your restlessness had something to do with the dress Lucky bought for you."

Tessa replied flatly, "I'm not going to wear it, Maggie. Not unless Lucky says I can pay him back for it."

"He said he wanted to buy it for you, Tessa, didn't he? It would be kinder to let him do that than to turn him down."

"I can't, Maggie. That's all there is to it. If I give up on this, I may as well—"

"You may as well what?"

Tessa hesitated, and then responded, "I may as well give up on everything else that I swore to do, too."

"It's only a small point, Tessa."

"No, Maggie." Tessa stared in Maggie's direction as the daylight brightened the room. "It's more important than it seems."

When Maggie did not reply, Tessa slipped on the oversized dress that Maggie had provided, twisted her hair into a casual bun, and said, "I'm going down to the mercantile now."

"Whatever you say."

Tessa was still distracted when she reached the board sidewalk outside Mr. Richman's mercantile. She was about to enter when she heard moaning from a dark corner nearby. Startled, she froze for a moment, then moved hesitantly toward the sound.

Tessa gasped when she drew near. It was the woman with the accent whom she had seen talking to Mr. Richman earlier. Her condition was even more deplorable now than before. She obviously had not washed and had eaten very little in the days since she had staggered out the doorway past her, but it was more than that. The woman twitched and moaned again in a kind of semiconsciousness. No wound was visible, but Tessa could not help remembering the word that Mr. Richman had spoken.

Laudanum.

The woman groaned again, and Tessa said softly, "What can I do for you, mademoiselle?"

The woman looked up at the familiar sound of her native tongue. Her darkly ringed eyes were sunk deep within a skull that appeared to have shrunk in size. Her hair stuck out from it in unhealthy, untended spikes, and her skin was dirty and covered with weeping sores. She whispered, "I am sick."

Tessa repeated, "What can I do for you?"

"My medicine."

Tessa's heart sank. "I have no medicine to give you."

A single tear slipped down the hollow of her cheek as the woman rasped, "Then I will die."

Heartsick, Tessa said abruptly, "No, you will not die. You'll come with me and you'll grow strong again."

"Non . . . non . . ."

Suddenly determined to help despite the Frenchwoman's negative response, Tessa hastened inside. Speaking firmly to Mr. Richman, she said, "I will need your wagon before I make my purchases this morning as well as afterward. I would appreciate it if you would send Nugget around with it now. I will wait for him on the walk."

"Of course, ma'am, but why do you need the wagon?"

Not allowing the lecherous proprietor another word, Tessa insisted, "I will wait for Nugget outside."

Her heart pounding, she heard the wagon's rattle a few minutes later. She saw the expression on Nugget's face when she whispered, "Help me put this woman in the wagon so I can take her up to the cabin on the hill."

"You're making a mistake, Tessa."

"I hope not."

"She won't live long in this condition."

"Just help me put her in the wagon, Nugget. I'll take care of the rest."

The old man stared at Tessa for long moments before stepping down from the wagon and raising the Frenchwoman to her feet. Together, they helped her into the back of the wagon, where the woman slipped into unconsciousness.

Tessa took the passenger seat beside Nugget as he silently flicked the wagon into motion. Noting that Tessa glanced back at the unmoving woman in concern, he repeated, "You're making a mistake."

Tessa remained silent.

Morning light shed its glow on the hillside when they reached the cabin. Maggie rushed outside with obvious concern, but she halted at the sight of the unconscious woman in the rear of the wagon.

Tessa said simply, "I'm sorry, but I need to help her, Maggie, and I had nowhere else to bring her."

Maggie hesitated and Tessa held her breath. Maggie was generous, but was she asking too much?

Maggie walked to the wagon and instructed, "Help us get her down so we can bring her inside, Nugget."

Tessa knew at that moment that she would never love the dear woman more.

The sun was approaching the midpoint in the sky when Tessa returned to the mercantile. Mr. Richman's expression was haughty when he said, "So you finally returned."

Refusing to comment, Tessa put a piece of paper down on the counter in front of him and said with equal hauteur, "Here is the list of what I will need for today. Do you wish to fill it?"

"I'll fill it. I'll call Nugget so you can use the wagon again, too."

"Good."

"But remember this. I contributed to your rescue this time. I will not do it again."

Tessa nodded. She knew she would remember what he said. She would remember every word.

The sun outside his tent entrance had begun setting as Lucky sat at his card table within. He heard the mumbles of the impatient crowd surrounding him and withdrew his watch from his pocket to stare at the hands.

"She's late."

Lucky looked at the bearded prospector who had spoken. He did not reply.

"It ain't like Tessa to be late. She should've gotten here about an hour ago if my calculations are right."

Lucky responded sarcastically, "You mean if the rumblings in your stomach aren't wrong."

"Yeah, that, too."

But Lucky did not smile at the reply. Instead, he put his cards down on the table, mumbled a few words, and stood up. Aware that he was being watched, he stretched his muscular frame in a deliberately casual fashion before walking outside. As soon as he could not be seen from inside, he stared up apprehensively at the trail nearby. There was no wagon in sight. He had sent Pedro up to gather Tessa and her things more than an hour ago. Where were they?

"Where are they?"

Lucky turned toward Delilah. Her words echoed his own thoughts, but her reaction to Tessa's tardiness was obviously far different from his. Lucky stared at Delilah as she approached. Was it his imagination, or was her hair a gaudier red than before? He wondered why he had never noticed before that the neckline of her bodice was drawn down especially low, or that her manner was as deliberately provocative as her dress.

Delilah smiled at his perusal as she moved closer. Butting herself up against him in the shadows, she whispered, "Maybe she isn't coming tonight, Lucky. Maybe you'll have the night off and you'll be able to think about other things."

"Other things?" Lucky took an involuntary step backward. Something about Delilah annoyed him. She was too happy that Tessa hadn't shown up.

Lucky's eyes narrowed as he stared over Delilah's head at sudden movement on the shadowed trail. He took another step backward and muttered with relief, "Here she comes. She's late, but she's coming."

"Isn't that *gratifying*?"

Lucky heard the sarcasm in Delilah's voice, but her tone was the furthest thing from his mind. He did not notice that she walked back inside the tent when the wagon drew closer. Tessa's tense expression was clear. He waited only until the wagon drew to a halt before swinging her down from the seat.

"I'm sorry I'm late, Lucky." Tessa's apology sounded

sincere. "I hope it didn't cause a problem. I'll get inside as quickly as possible."

She started to walk past him, but Lucky said, "I thought something might be wrong."

"No, nothing's wrong."

Tessa picked up a basket of freshly baked bread and then disappeared through the tent doorway. The spontaneous cheer she received turned Lucky's frown even darker. Something *was* wrong. Tessa was wearing the dress he had bought her. She looked beautiful, but he had the feeling that her appearance was the furthest thing from her mind. He turned to Pedro as the rotund fellow lifted the first of the large pots down from the wagon.

"What happened, Pedro?"

The burly Mexican smiled. "I do not know, *senor*."

He pressed, "Why is Tessa late?"

The Mexican rushed through the doorway, calling over his shoulder, "I do not know, *senor*."

Lucky snorted. He had expected as much. Yet he knew tension when he saw it. He would wait until Tessa was done serving and then he'd find out.

Lucky grumbled to himself, "Damned if I won't!"

Maggie walked slowly down the trail toward town. Tessa and Pedro had left a while earlier with the wagon and the setting sun had slipped below the horizon. All was temporarily quiet within the cabin, allowing her the opportunity she sought. She knew it would soon be dark and unsafe on the trail for anyone walking, yet she needed to talk to Lucky. For many reasons, Tessa and Pedro would say nothing about the Frenchwoman's presence in the cabin, but the situation affected Lucky and he ought to be aware of it.

Maggie reached the tents in the plaza and walked toward the brightly lit structure that belonged to Lucky. Pausing for a breath, she pushed back a wisp of gray hair and straightened her stained clothing. Clarice had been difficult. She had called for her medicine throughout the day, even when they told her they had none to give her. Her crying had not ceased. Basin after basin of water was filled and then knocked irritably to the floor before Clarice allowed anyone to wash off the dirt that had accumulated on her painfully thin body. Maggie remembered the woman's stench and the retching that had caused Tessa to make a last-minute change into the dress that Lucky had bought for her.

Maggie smiled. Perhaps that was the only good thing that had come of the situation. But she knew Lucky. He would sense that there was a problem, and she needed to set his mind at rest.

She had been hesitant about allowing Clarice into her cabin at first, but that was before she saw Tessa's expression and realized how much helping the woman meant to her. A local doctor had concluded in his brief visit that they could do no more than wash, feed, and clothe the Frenchwoman, give her the powders he left, even though he knew they would not be of much help, and hope that she would live to recuperate. If she did not survive, he had said he would take care of the rest.

"What's wrong up the hill, Maggie?"

Maggie started when Lucky appeared unexpectedly beside her at the tent's entrance. She did not immediately respond.

"Tessa is inside." Lucky went on. "She's smiling and trying to pretend that nothing is wrong, but it's easy enough for me to see through her pretense. Pedro isn't saying anything, either, but I know something's happened."

"It's not Tessa's fault, Lucky," Maggie began defensively. "It's just that she has a big heart."

"A big heart?"

"She . . . she took in that Frenchwoman that Harley Knox threw out."

"What?"

"The woman was lying on the sidewalk in front of Noel Richman's store when she went there this morning. Hell, the poor creature's in terrible shape! She's just a step away from the Almighty. She kept calling for her medicine, wouldn't take food or drink. She caused a general havoc in the cabin all day, pushing aside the water when we attempted to wash her and upchucking all over us even though her stomach was empty."

"That's why Tessa is wearing the dress I bought her."

Maggie nodded and offered a half smile. "It's not that she doesn't like it. It's just that—"

"It's just that she's damned stubborn. And now she has another cause to defend."

Maggie did not immediately respond. Then she explained softly, "Tessa thinks that woman could have been her if she hadn't been fortunate enough to stumble into your tent."

"That's nonsense! Clarice is nothing like Tessa. Clarice came here promising anything I could think of if I gave her a job. I told her this wasn't that kind of place, but it didn't do any good, and she walked out just as arrogantly as you please."

"That was before, when she still had a spark of spirit left. She doesn't anymore."

"I told you, she's nothing like Tessa. Tessa was out on her feet and she still wanted to earn her own way."

"You'll never convince Tessa of that."

Lucky mumbled, "She'll get tired of that woman's demands."

"I don't think *that woman* is going to last too long."

That pronouncement silenced Lucky momentarily. He asked, "Where is Clarice now?"

"She's back in the cabin, temporarily asleep."

"I'll tell Jake to take you back to the cabin with the wagon."

"No, I can walk."

Lucky's brows drew together. "Jake will drive you back."

Maggie smiled as Lucky strode back into the tent.

* * *

"I'm sorry, Lucky." Appearing exhausted despite her formerly bright smile, Tessa approached him quietly when she emerged from the tent at last. She appeared to expect Lucky to respond to her apology. When he did not, she continued. "Something came up, but I won't let it interfere with my work in the tent again."

"Can you guarantee that? What if Clarice continues to act up?"

Tessa's expression fell. "Who told you?" When Lucky did not answer her, she whispered, "I intended to explain what happened, but I wanted to see if Clarice would last through the night first. She's in terrible shape, Lucky. I don't know if she will."

"Addiction to laudanum is one of the hazards in her line of work."

Suddenly angry, Tessa said, "I don't care what's wrong with her! Clarice is a victim of circumstance. If things had worked out differently, that could've been me lying outside that mercantile."

"You're wrong."

"I'm not wrong."

With no anger in his tone, Lucky replied, "I won't argue the point with you, Tessa. If you feel you want to help someone like Clarice, that's all right with me. Just don't compare yourself to her."

"Lucky, I—"

"You're not the same, Tessa. Clarice may be a victim of circumstances, but she gave in to her misfortunes.

You rose above them. And you'd die rather than betray what you believe in."

Ignoring his statement, Tessa pressed, "The cost of living in Maggie's cabin will double while Clarice is there."

"The cost doesn't matter."

"It does! I don't expect you to pay my way. I'll pay you back for any expenses that Clarice adds. I'll make sure I keep cooking in your tent until we're squared away. Providing that's all right with you."

"I guess."

"It's a deal, then?"

"Yes, it's a deal."

Tessa's sudden smile was filled with relief, but it hit Lucky like a blow to the stomach. He offered softly, "That dress looks real fine on you."

Surprising him, Tessa flushed and pressed a quick kiss on his cheek. "Thank you." She paused, and then added, "And in case I've never said it before, thank you for everything, Lucky."

She turned without giving him a chance to respond and strode back to the wagon where Pedro waited. Lucky watched as she climbed up onto the seat and the wagon started forward.

Lucky had only one thought as the wagon disappeared on the trail. He couldn't deny the truth any longer.

Damn it all, he loved her.

* * *

The men would love her!

They'd pay any price to have her.

Harley watched from a distance, the shadows hiding his glee as Tessa rode away in the wagon. She was beautiful, and she became more delicious every day. Instead of becoming accustomed to her, men were becoming more and more obsessed with her. She was a golden girl, a vision from home, every man's dream.

Tessa's wagon disappeared on the trail as Harley's lascivious thoughts expanded. He would bide his time. The right opportunity would present itself. He hadn't been able to hear what Tessa and Lucky had been discussing, but he had seen Lucky's face before he turned his back, and he knew Lucky was upset. Yes, the right opportunity would present itself.

Harley smiled. He would use the power of his personality to finally convince Tessa that he was her friend. He'd sympathize with her. He'd coax her slowly into leaving Lucky by insinuating that the gambler had taken advantage of her situation and that he was using her.

It appeared Lucky's attitude would be his rival's greatest asset. He continued giving her orders, and she resented it. He could not seem to understand that Tessa wanted to take her own path.

Harley would tell Tessa that Lucky thought she should do everything he said, but that it would be different with him. He would tell her that he would treat her right, and he would, too. He would shower her with luxuries that she had never dreamed of. He would introduce her slowly into the demimonde, never pushing her new lifestyle on her until she was ready to embrace it wholeheartedly. Then he would teach her how to use her natural assets to seduce a man.

Tessa was stubborn, but he had handled stubborn women before. With the drugs at his command, none of them stood a chance against him.

How he would enjoy the lessons he'd teach her. He would make sure that he was her only instructor until he handed her over to the highest bidder.

Lucky turned away from the trail abruptly and walked back into his tent. The shadows darkened as Harley watched him, aware that Lucky would be his biggest problem. The gambler would not take losing Tessa's services well. He was more accustomed to winning than losing.

Harley silently scoffed at that thought.

Well, so was he.

Chapter Seven

Another week had passed, and at first glance, nothing seemed to have changed. Lucky knew better. He looked at Tessa as she stood with a frozen smile on her face serving the food she had prepared for the men in his tent. His profits continued to soar. Word seemed to have spread and the line at her table increased every evening. There seemed to be nothing she could cook that could displease the prospectors. They came in droves.

Contrary to his first concern, many of the men remained after eating to gamble at the tables or to drink. He'd actually needed to increase his orders for liquor and to provide more seating for the crowd.

Yet Tessa was exhausted. The extra work she had undertaken in caring for Clarice was taking its toll. Her formerly delicate appearance had grown more fragile. Rings under her eyes attested to her sleepless nights.

Lucky wasn't sleeping, either, because he knew that *she* was not sleeping. That morning he had risen from a solitary bed that he refused to share lightly anymore. He had walked to the washstand to splash water onto his face and had gazed in the mirror as the liquid dripped from his chin. He had needed a shave, and the edges of his unruly black hair were wet, his eyes as deeply ringed as Tessa's. He looked like hell and didn't feel much better.

He had tried for the past week to maintain his distance and allow Tessa to come to terms with the extended care that Clarice would need. It hadn't been easy. Observing her obviously fatigued condition this evening, he knew it was time to take a stand.

Lucky watched as Tessa emptied her last pot of food and turned the next fellow in line away with a weary smile. He had abandoned any attempt to play cards while she was there, preferring instead to stand in the doorway until she left. He strode to her side the moment the line dispersed.

When he approached, she protested, "You don't have to help me, Lucky. I can manage."

He did not bother to reply, scooping up two empty pots and walking toward the exit. Tessa walked behind him as he carried them to the wagon. She placed the bread basket that she carried inside, then said apologetically, "I'm sorry, Lucky. I know you've been watching me. I hope I haven't been a burden to you."

"You're not a burden."

Tessa shook her head and mumbled again, "I'm sorry for all the trouble I've caused you."

Trouble? That did it!

Suddenly angry at her exhaustion and the changes in her that it had wrought, Lucky dismissed Pedro by saying, "I'll drive Tessa home tonight."

"No, that isn't necessary! I mean—"

Tessa sighed, too tired to continue, and Lucky's heart squeezed tight in his chest. He swung her up onto the wagon seat without comment and took his place beside her. He clucked the horses into motion, his mind racing. Didn't she see what she did to him? Didn't she realize that he had watched her every night, seeing her grow more exhausted with each appearance, wanting to help her but knowing that she would resist him at every step? Didn't she realize that he was at his wits' end, that he wanted nothing more than to console her, to make everything right for her?

Lucky knew that the answer was simple. No, she didn't.

Lucky stared at Tessa's profile a moment longer. Her head was averted but the glow of twilight turned her platinum hair to pure silver before his eyes. Her dark eyelashes swept out in dark relief against the backdrop of the trail, her profile so perfect as to seem unreal. The lips that he dreamed of touching with his own quivered slightly. He could not see her expression, but he knew that despite the brief bout of weakness he had witnessed, the sudden lift of her chin meant renewed determination.

He realized it was not simply Tessa's natural beauty that made him cherish her more each day. He loved her inner beauty, and her insistence on conducting life according to her own standards awed him. She had an instinctive pride in herself that would not allow her to surrender despite the harshest of circumstances.

He also understood that her determination to accomplish everything she had set out to do was another way of remaining faithful to the past. She was bent on erasing from her mind all the days of hopelessness she had suffered on the trail.

He sensed that because he had suffered the same kind of hopelessness and had become equally determined to escape his circumstances. He wanted to tell her that he understood. Like her, he was his own harshest critic. Now every day was more difficult for him, because he wanted desperately to ease her way.

Halting the wagon on the spot, aware that the trail was lit only by the fading twilight, he turned toward her and said simply, "Please, let me help you, Tessa."

Tessa looked up as Lucky spoke. Aware that Maggie was tending to Clarice in her absence, she murmured, "I need to get back to the cabin, Lucky."

"And I need to help you."

Tessa's throat tightened at the sincerity of Lucky's deeply voiced response. The previous night had been difficult and long. Clarice's withdrawal from the "medicine" that Harley had supplied had ravaged the poor Frenchwoman. Aside from her obviously deteriorated physical condition, there were other problems that were even more debilitating. The strange restlessness that allowed her no peace no matter which way she turned was her greatest problem.

Clarice moaned and cried out during the night, allowing neither Maggie nor Tessa any rest. It was during one of those restless nights that Clarice related how Harley Knox had convinced her to take the "medicine," how he had supplied it to her in ever-increasing dosages, and how he had then thrown her out onto the street when her addiction took over. Harley Knox was the demon who had fostered Clarice's sickness. Tessa would never understand the complete selfishness of that act.

"I don't want you to get involved in all this, Lucky," she tried to explain. "I have to do what I intended. You do understand, don't you?"

"I understand more than you know, Tessa," Lucky whispered hoarsely. "I know that you're attempting to make sense of your own life, but you don't need to justify your existence. You escaped your parents' fate because you were meant to escape it."

"Yes, so I could save others from a similar fate. People like Clarice."

"No, Clarice is too far gone to matter now. She had her chance and she chose the wrong path."

"You're wrong, Lucky! Clarice is—"

Drawing her into his arms with sudden urgency, Lucky held her close. His large hands smoothed her back. They tangled in her hair as he pulled her closer still and said, "Don't say anything else about Clarice, please. It's you I'm thinking about now. You've done everything right, but you've taken on a fight you're not prepared to handle. You need help, and I want to help you."

Tessa closed her eyes as the warmth of Lucky's arms enclosed her. She had wanted this. She had *needed* to be close to him. His action meant that he cared, just as *she* had come to care about him.

Suddenly worried that the embrace might be motivated by sympathy, Tessa attempted to draw back. He allowed her to withdraw only far enough so he could look directly into her eyes. His lips brushed hers as he whispered, "Did you hear what I said, Tessa?"

His breath was sweet on her lips. His gaze drilled into hers. Breathless, suddenly beyond control, Tessa could no longer hold back her tears as she whispered, "I heard everything you said, Lucky. I wanted to hear you say those things because I—"

Tessa turned abruptly toward a sound on the trail ahead. She gasped when Maggie appeared unexpectedly out of the shadows and ran toward the wagon. The old woman's oversized clothing was sweat stained and her hair flew out wildly from her careless bun.

"Tessa, it's Clarice!" she exclaimed breathlessly. "She's getting dressed. She's determined to go down into town for her medicine. I tried to stop her but she won't listen to me."

Lucky did not allow Tessa to reply. He swung Maggie up into the rear of the wagon and started the horses forward at a gallop. They reached the cabin just as the door swung open and Clarice stepped into sight. The

Frenchwoman froze, a ghastly vision framed in the doorway, her skin drained of color, her hair askew, and her clothing wrinkled and stained. "I am going into town to obtain some of my medicine," she announced in a croaking voice.

His expression dark, Lucky stepped down from the wagon. He walked toward her, saying firmly, "No, you aren't, Clarice."

"But I need my medicine, *monsieur*!" Clarice whined. "I am hardly able to stand without it!"

Tessa did not interfere when Lucky took Clarice's arm, turned her back inside the cabin with a firm touch, and replied, "You're not well enough yet. If you still want laudanum when you are, we won't stop you. Do you understand what I'm saying?"

Clarice looked up at Lucky, and then at Tessa for long moments. Turning back to him with a strangely solemn acceptance, she allowed him to lead her through the doorway without protest. "I understand, *monsieur*," she muttered sadly. "I understand far better than you know."

Tessa released a shaky breath when they disappeared from sight. She followed them inside with Maggie at her heels and the bewildered hounds slinking in at their side.

When everyone quickly settled in for the night, she breathed a sigh of relief. Clarice and Maggie soon fell asleep, and Lucky sat on a chair beside the fire and drew her comfortingly into his arms. Tessa remained in the tempting warmth of Lucky's embrace until she was sleeping as well. It was where she wanted to be.

Harley stepped out onto the early morning silence of the street in front of his exclusive bordello. He started toward the mercantile, carefully avoiding the mud and debris that sucked at his imported boots. He had spent a considerable amount of money seeing to it that the thoroughfare in front of his bordello was free of the debris that seemed to overwhelm the city. Also, there were no penniless, drunken prospectors sleeping in doorways near his place of business. It would not do to offend his customers when they entered his establishment. Men who had large sums to spend expected the show of opulence.

He had spent the previous evening with one of his favorite harlots in the quarters he maintained in the brothel. Harley recalled that the brunette French beauty had been particularly inventive the previous evening. She had proven her worth many times before, but he never grew tired of testing her. He enjoyed the thought that the women of his house strove to satisfy him in any way he asked, with every deviation that he demanded, and that they usually provided him with many surprises, too. Such was the case with Simone. It was a mystery to him why her popularity with his customers had slipped during the past few months. He could only think that some of his wealthy men had become bored with the French whores, no matter how inventive his women sought to be, and were now looking for something a little different.

That thought brought Tessa to mind. Yes, she was something different. He continued to watch her carefully when she arrived at Lucky's tent. He had noted her exhaustion over the past week and had decided that he would give her a little more time to become tired of the hard work there before approaching her. He could only hope that she was a virgin and that rape was not included in her experiences on the trail to San Francisco. He would have her examined by a doctor to see if she was still a virgin. He knew that if she were, he would have to alter his plans about indoctrinating Tessa into the methods of pleasing a man. It would be another man, someone willing to pay the enormous price that he would ask for her virginity, who would have the privilege of deflowering her.

That thought brought a temporary frown to Harley's face. He erased it by telling himself that although he would not be Tessa's first, he would be the only one to enjoy the wealth she brought him. And in due time, he would sample everything she had to offer. His demands on her would be slight at first, but would grow in scope until she was addicted to the sexual satisfaction that being with a man could bring. He would make sure that she became well versed in the many sexual acts possible between a man and a woman. He would accomplish all that easily since he had the deflowering of many willing, as well as unwilling, virgins to his credit.

Experience is the best teacher, and he would teach Tessa everything he knew, while showing her how to maintain the guise of innocence. She would be well worth the price he'd demand.

Perhaps he would even allow Tessa the privilege of spending the whole night with him while he instructed her, something he rarely did. The previous evening, he had turned Simone out of his bed to resume her work despite her efficient servicing. He had then cleaned himself up and had slept alone, enjoying the feel of his naked body between the spotless sheets.

Harley drew closer to the mercantile and sidestepped some particularly foul-smelling garbage before taking the few stairs onto the boardwalk in front of the store. It annoyed him that he was forced to deal with the insufferable Noel Richman, yet he had run out of cigars and Noel was the only person who stocked his particularly expensive brand.

Harley entered the emporium with a smile reserved specifically for the overweight proprietor. His unspoken greeting was met with Noel's enthusiastic "Good morning, Harley. It's nice to see you again, although I admit that I didn't expect to find you smiling so broadly."

"You didn't?" Harley maintained his smile despite Noel's attempt to disturb him and asked casually, "Why is that?"

Noel shrugged.

More annoyed than he cared to reveal, Harley said

flatly, "All right, out with it, Noel. You have something you want to tell me. What is it?"

"I don't want to be the harbinger of bad news."

"Really? Since when?" With a sarcastic smile, Harley
demanded, "Just say what you wanted to say."

"Well . . ."

Noel drew out the suspense, Harley's smile disappeared. He would not ask again.

"Your old friend, Clarice LeBlanc, was lying in a
doorway on the walk outside a week ago. She wasn't in
good shape. About ready to kick the bucket. I figured
she deliberately chose a doorway close to mine just so
as to inconvenience me, so I ignored her."

"Clarice isn't my responsibility any longer."

"I know that." Noel's round face creased into an
unexpected smile. "Everybody knows that."

"So what does all this have to do with me?"

"Nothing. It's just that I've noticed your interest in
Tessa White."

Harley's casual attitude became suddenly alert.
"What about Tessa?"

"Well, Tessa used my wagon last week to transport
Clarice to Maggie's cabin. Of course, I never would have
lent it to her if I had known what she wanted to use it
for, but she—"

"What do you mean?" Harley interrupted boldly.
"Are you saying that Tessa took Clarice in?"

"For as long as Clarice lasts, I guess. She's still hanging on as far as I know."

A slow fury swept through Harley. Why hadn't he been informed about Tessa's involvement with Clarice?

The question reverberated in his mind, but Harley did not speak.

Noel brushed his hands on the stained apron tied around his wide girth and said, "I figure that's a complication in whatever plans you had for Tessa. I mean, Clarice doesn't have much that's good to say about you, if she can still talk, that is."

Harley's jaw stiffened. He managed, "You're sure of this?"

"I'm sure." Looking past him, Noel added more softly, "But you can find out for yourself. Here comes Tessa now."

Harley turned abruptly as Tessa entered the mercantile. She stopped short on seeing him but then resumed her approach. Nodding in his direction, she placed a list on Noel's counter and said, "I'd like these groceries when you're done with this customer if you please."

Harley turned toward Tessa and smiled. Using the full power of his practiced charm, he said, "Tessa, what a delight! I suppose you're here to buy supplies for this evening's meal."

"Yes, I am."

"I can only hope it's as good as the last. The men in Lucky's tent rave about your cooking. They say—"

Tessa interrupted, "Please, spare me your conversation, Mr. Knox."

"Tessa, don't act that way."

Tessa turned fully toward him. Her gaze direct, she continued. "I'm sure Mr. Richman told you that Clarice has been staying with Maggie and me for the past week."

"He did, but what does that have to do with me?"

"Feigning innocence does not become you, Mr. Knox." Tessa's expression was cold. "Maggie and I have heard enough of Clarice's ravings to learn how she came to be out on the street."

"But that has nothing to do with me, Tessa."

"Please, don't attempt to deny what you did."

"Tessa, I ask that you give me the opportunity to defend myself!"

Silent for a few moments, Tessa then turned to Noel and said, "I'll leave my list with you. If you will have Nugget deliver it to me as soon as possible, I would appreciate it."

Noel nodded.

"Tessa?"

"Good-bye, Mr. Richman."

Harley watched as Tessa left, her head high.

"I guess she ain't the forgiving type," Noel commented with a grin.

Unable to bear Noel's obvious glee, Harley said abruptly, "You can fill her order now and have it delivered. Have Nugget deliver my supply of cigars later."

Harley did not wait for Noel's response and walked out of the store without another word. Out on the street, he felt the heat of fury consume him. Damn Clarice, and damn the haughty Tessa! Clarice was done for, but he'd cut Tessa down to size. His charm never failed in the end, and it wouldn't fail him once he got the chance to use it on her.

Harley turned toward his primary residence, which was a few streets away. His step was harried and his formerly good mood was shattered. He had no desire to return to his rooms at the bordello, where he had spent the night. He needed the comfort that solitude provided so he could devise a way to achieve his ends.

As the situation now stood, Tessa was beyond convincing of his innocence. He needed the help of the drugs that had never failed him, and he needed privacy in order to use them.

Tessa would belong to him one way or another.

Delilah peeked at the early morning outside her tent and saw that the sun was beginning to make bright inroads in the sky. She dressed and stepped out to start down the hillside where her tent was perched. She was not usually up at that hour, but finally admitting to herself that she was losing Lucky had kept her sleepless. He was totally enamored of Tessa White's innocence, which, in the light of the deft way Tessa handled the men in the tent, Delilah knew she needed to do something quickly, before it was too late.

The solution had come to her in a flash. She had noticed that Harley Knox had been watching Tessa and the lines of men awaiting her appearance in Lucky's tent each night. Yet she had not seen him attempt to talk to Tessa since that first night. She suspected that there was some history between Tessa and him that kept him from making his move.

She guessed that if Harley had already made an effort to entice Tessa into his elaborate "house," he had not been successful. She knew Harley's type very well, however. His arrogance would not allow him to give up, especially since he had recently lost Clarice LeBlanc.

Delilah sneered as she walked around another pothole and continued on through the quiet streets of early morning. She recalled the day that Harley had turned her away from his house when she first came to San Francisco. He had considered her manner too brash and her appearance too common to appeal to the gentlemen who patronized his establishment. He had said that she was more suited to the tents recently erected in the town square. When she realized he was not going to relent, she left for the tents he had mentioned. That was where she met Lucky.

Delilah slowed her step when Harley's primary residence stood before her. She had to approach him the right way. She had to make sure not to insult his intelligence. She had to be certain—

"What are you doing here?"

Delilah turned with a start to find Harley Knox behind her. Taken off guard, she replied, "I . . . I came to talk to you."

"I told you I'm not going to hire you. That is the end of any conversation between us."

Ignoring his insulting manner, Delilah replied sharply, "But you don't feel the same about Tessa White, do you?"

Harley's stance grew rigid. "Why do you bring up Tessa?"

Delilah replied boldly, "I need to know if you're as *interested* in her as it appears to me that you are."

Harley paused. His small eyes narrowed as he replied hesitantly, "I may be interested."

"Then perhaps I can help you."

"Help me?"

"Mr. Knox, I do not wish to be seen conversing with you on the street. If you want to continue this conversation, I—"

"Come inside," Harley interrupted boldly. "But I warn you, you'd better not waste my time or you'll be sorry."

Delilah felt momentary fear. Harley Knox was a dangerous man. Then, remembering that desperation made strange bedfellows, she smiled and turned to precede him up the stairs to his residence.

"All right, you have the seclusion that you requested. What do you have in mind?"

Delilah paused as Harley closed the door of the most spectacular home that she had ever seen. From the outside, the house had appeared to a typical San Francisco residence. But the intricate carving that adorned the marble staircase leading to the second floor and the glittering crystal chandelier in the sophisticated foyer made it clear that the residence was anything but common.

Harley did not offer her the courtesy of a chair as she entered his office and scrutinized the piles of paperwork and other articles on the enormous desk near the window. Elaborately furnished, the space was large and bright. The leaded-glass windows were surrounded by woven drapes that enabled Harley to shut out the scene of great ships approaching in the distance. Mahogany bookshelves boasted leather-bound volumes with titles she could not even pronounce. The matching desk and chair were as impressive as the overstuffed, leather furniture. An imported rug partially covered what appeared to be mahogany floors that were polished to a high sheen.

While she lived in a tent.

But that condition was only temporary.

"I'll say it just one more time. Speak up or leave."

Delilah turned toward Harley. "The magic word here appears to be *Tessa*."

"What about her?"

"You've been watching Tessa White. You want to use her in your 'house.'"

"That is all you have to say?"

"Tell me at the outset if I'm right, Mr. Knox. I do not intend to proceed unless I am."

Delilah watched as Harley's face twitched. He hesitated to respond. Speaking to him as rudely as he had spoken to her, she said, "Speak up, Mr. Knox. I don't have time to waste."

Harley's glance was deadly as he replied, "You appear to learn quickly. Yes, I have considered hiring Tessa White."

Delilah nodded. "But she won't let you near her."

"I've had some difficulty in that regard."

"You know she has taken in one of your cast-off women. The possibility that she will agree to any of your propositions is now nil."

"I don't actually see it that way."

"Well, you should! Tessa White is establishing herself in San Francisco in a way that will not aid your cause. If she succeeds, you can give up the hope of ever getting her to accept your offer."

"And she is getting in *your* way, is that it?"

Delilah smiled. "She can't compete with me in the ways that count most with a man, but she may end up with the prize she seeks if she succeeds in springing the trap she is planning."

"You're talking about Lucky Monroe. He's not yours exclusively anymore."

Delilah raised a hand to her upswept hair in a characteristic gesture. She smoothed the surface with her palm as she said, "Temporarily, no. But I have a plan of my own that may change everything."

"And you expect me to play a part in your plan."

"That would be to both our advantage."

Harley pressed, "I also need to know something from the outset. How much do you expect to gain from this endeavor?"

"Monetarily?" Delilah's laughter was caustic. "Nothing. I expect only to return to my former status of being inches away from becoming Lucky's woman."

"That alone would satisfy you?"

"That, and the easy life that comes with it. I will make sure Lucky turns to me in his distress. He will then be all mine again; and yes, that would satisfy me."

"What am *I* supposed to gain from your plan?"

"You will have Tessa White to do with as you please, of course."

"You're sure?"

"I'm sure, if you follow through with my plan."

Harley stared at Delilah coldly for a few moments and then withdrew a gold watch from his vest pocket. Glancing at its face, he said, "I'll give you five minutes to explain what you propose. I warn you to make good use of the time, because I will never afford it to you again."

Delilah's face flushed. If she had any other choice, she would not help this man. He was insufferably rude, and she knew he had no scruples at all.

But neither did she.

Delilah started to speak.

She emerged later through Harley's front door with a smile on her face. She scrutinized the street carefully before walking swiftly back in the direction she had come.

Clarice stood up warily and glanced around the small cabin. Maggie had gone outside to hang laundry on the clothesline she had strung there. It would take her a while to accomplish that task with hands that had become clumsy from arthritis, but Clarice knew it was important to Maggie to be able to accomplish her work. She had pretended to be asleep when Maggie left, since Tessa had gone into town to buy supplies. At last, she had been left totally alone.

Clarice thought back briefly on Lucky's unexpected appearance at the cabin the night before. She was sick and she was in desperate need, but she was not *unobservant*. She had seen the way Lucky looked at Tessa. It was written in his eyes. He loved Tessa in a way Clarice never expected a man to love her: for the woman she was, and not for the woman she pretended to be. She had known she was no match for him when he ordered her back inside and promised that he would allow her to leave when she was well. She had pretended to agree and had also pretended to sleep when Maggie's breathing became regular.

She had watched through slitted eyes, however, as Lucky drew Tessa into his arms and sat holding her in a comforting embrace, his strong body surrounding her in sweet consolation. She had listened as he mumbled lovingly into Tessa's unhearing ears long after she had fallen asleep. She had sensed the self-control he practiced as he held her so intimately close.

Tessa was still asleep when Lucky carried her to her cot as morning neared. He then left, probably so the wagon would not be seen returning from the cabin in the morning. She knew he did that with Tessa's reputation in mind because Maggie was too old to be considered, and she had no reputation left to protect.

The truth was that she could not even pretend she was going to get well. The "medicine" still called out to her despite two agonizing weeks of withdrawal. It had changed her permanently in body and soul. She sensed that her time was limited, though both Tessa and Maggie had tried to convince her otherwise. She felt that the only consolation left to her was the medicine that had destroyed her.

Desperate to procure some, Clarice arose from the sleeping pallet that Maggie and Tessa had prepared for her. She was already dressed, having slept in the clothes that she had worn the previous evening. It was just a matter of stealing down the mountainside while Maggie was otherwise occupied, and avoiding Tessa if she were returning from the mercantile. She would work the streets of the city until she had enough to purchase what she needed.

Her medicine was all she had left.

Clarice patted the three faithful dogs that arose from their corner, calming them before slipping out the doorway and starting unsteadily down the trail toward town.

"She's gone, Lucky! Clarice stole away while Maggie was occupied and I was in town. I don't know how she got past me, but she did."

Lucky looked at Tessa as she stood in his hotel room. He had answered the frantic knocking on the door only moments earlier and had been stunned to see her there. Her hair askew, her cheeks wet from tears, she had thrown herself into his arms, whispering against his chest, "Please, please help me find her."

Please help me.

Lucky curled his arms around her, recalling the last time she had been in his room. She had been thin, starving, and weary to the bone, but she had not asked for his help. Instead, she had insisted that she could make it on her own.

So much had changed since then, but one thing had not. Tessa would not ask him for help for herself. She asked only for Clarice. When Tessa looked up at him pleadingly, he released her and instructed, "Go home. I'll find her. You can finish cooking for tonight's meal."

"No, I . . . I couldn't."

"The men are depending on you."

"So is Clarice!"

No, Clarice was not depending on her, but Lucky could not tell Tessa that. Clarice was *escaping* from her and returning to the only comfort she knew. Instead, he repeated, "Go back to Maggie's cabin and finish your work so you can show up at the tent on time. I'll find Clarice for you, and Maggie can take care of her until you return."

"Lucky?"

"Go. I'll find her. I promise."

But Tessa did not move. Her gray eyes damp as they stared up into his, she said, "Before I do, I need to apologize to you for the way I've behaved, Lucky."

"No, you don't."

"Yes, I do."

"You were finding your way. You did what you needed to do at the time in order to retain your self-respect. You worked hard and everyone respects you for it. I want—"

Lucky paused as his mind worked to complete his statement.

I want what? For her to feel confident enough to return to Iowa?

No! I don't want that.

For her to regain the self-respect that she feels she's lost?

Yes . . . no . . . that isn't it.

Or do I just want her to love me?

"Lucky?"

Tessa was still staring into his eyes as if mesmerized by his expression. Her lips separating, she stood on tiptoe and pressed a brief kiss against his mouth. She said in a choked voice, "Thank you so much, Lucky."

His heart pounding, Lucky watched as Tessa turned

and walked out the doorway of his room. Astounded, he stared at the closed door. Why had he allowed her to leave before he could tell her how he felt?

"Clarice!"

Clarice turned unsteadily at the sound of her name. Her heart thumped wildly. She had not been expecting to see anyone she knew in this area of San Francisco, which respectable people avoided if possible. The streets were particularly busy and dirty near the wharves, although the usual traffic had temporarily subsided because of the early hour. This was the place where she could buy laudanum, but what was that well-dressed woman doing here?

"Clarice, *ma amie!* Don't you recognize me?"

Clarice strained to see the overweight woman more clearly as she drew closer. She swallowed at sudden recognition.

"Clarice, *ma cherie*, what has happened to you?"

Clarice stepped back as Madame LeFleur rushed to her side and embraced her. The older woman brushed tears from her cheeks as she said, "You look . . . you look . . ."

"I look *atroce*." Clarice muttered the words that Madame LeFleur could not seem to make herself say. She was only too aware that her formerly stylish attire was no longer elegant, and neither was she.

Clarice continued evasively. "I have been ill. A young woman took me in and has been trying to nurse me back to health." She took another breath and said truthfully, "I say 'trying' because I do not believe I will ever be truly well again."

"I am so sorry, *ma amie!*" Tears ran down the madam's face as she confessed softly, "This is all my fault, and I have regretted the day I spoke to Monsieur Knox about you from the moment I left his office."

Hardly able to keep herself upright, Clarice said, "You spoke to Monsieur Knox about me?"

"*Oui,* I confess that I did!" Her tears falling more rapidly, Madame continued. "But I did not expect or ever believe he would take the steps he did. You were out of control, you see! I had no choice but to go to Monsieur Knox with the problems you were causing. But I explained to him that you were unhappy in this new land, and that all might be well if he would only send you back to France so you could recover from your illness."

"An illness he induced with the 'medicine' he provided."

Madame LeFleur whitened. "You are speaking of laudanum?"

"*Oui,* I am."

"*Mon Dieu!*" The madam's aging eyes widened. "He sent me to this portion of the city so I might buy him a supply of laudanum for another of the women he expects to bring to the house."

"Another woman? Who?"

"I do not wish to say."

"Who is this woman?" Clarice's voice quaked. "You

must tell me her name so I may talk to her. I do not want another to suffer as I have."

"This woman has not arrived yet."

"Monsieur Knox is bringing her from France?"

"*Non*, he . . . he . . ." Suddenly breaking down into sobs, Madame LeFleur drew Clarice deep into the shadows. She brushed the tears from her painted cheeks when she regained control. "I am not supposed to know, but when Monsieur Knox returned to the house in a rush and ordered me to procure such a large supply of laudanum, I became curious. My curiosity grew when two suspicious-looking men almost immediately entered the house and were called to his office."

"Two men?"

"Two men unlike those the women of the house service. They were hoodlums, Clarice, bad men, so I listened at the door of the office when they went inside."

Madame started to cry again, and Clarice's waning patience snapped. She demanded, "What did Monsieur Knox tell them?"

"He . . . he told them to kidnap a local woman so he could force her to work in his house. He said it would be perfectly safe because another woman had arranged it all and this other woman would see to it that the victim came to a place where they would not be seen and could easily accomplish the task."

"A young local woman? What would they want with her in a house where only Frenchwomen work?"

"He told them the young woman is well-known and

that they must not mar her beauty or compromise her in any way because he believes she is a virgin and he intends to offer her at a phenomenal price that will make all his expenses worthwhile."

Non, it cannot be!

"Clarice!" Grasping her arm when she swayed visibly, Madame LeFleur said, "You must be strong, Clarice. I will help you get away. I have some money saved that Monsieur Knox does not know about, and I will purchase a ticket for you so that you may return to France—"

Regaining her composure, Clarice interrupted, "What is this young woman's name?"

"I do not know. Monsieur Knox was whispering. It was Melissa or a name such as that."

"Was it Tessa? Tessa White?"

"*Oui,* I believe that is the name!"

"When, Madame? When do these men intend to do this thing?"

"Sometime today, which is the reason for Monsieur's rush to obtain extra medicine. I am not sure of the time, but those men are to wait for Mademoiselle White at an appointed place near here. He told the two hoodlums that she would probably protest after she arrived, that they might have to restrain her in some way, but to be certain not to mark her."

"What is the plan?"

"The other woman is supposed to send a note to Mademoiselle White, asking her to come to a warehouse in this area with a reason that she will not dare disregard."

"Which warehouse?"

"I could not hear that detail."

"She is supposed to go there to find someone she cares about, perhaps?"

Madame replied, "*Oui,* perhaps. I am not sure."

Clarice briefly closed her sunken eyes. In leaving the cabin, she had inadvertently fallen in with that plan. Filled with dread, Clarice pressed, "And then?"

"The two men will overwhelm the young woman and hold her captive until Monsieur Knox comes. He will drug her with laudanum until she finally succumbs to his persuasion."

"And if she does not fall in with his plans?"

"That possibility was not discussed, but we both know what Monsieur Knox's alternatives are."

Clarice paled further as she whispered, "Monsieur Knox does not expect any interference?"

"When one of the hoodlums asked that question, Monsieur Knox told them that this other woman guaranteed to divert the only person who could possibly cause them a real problem."

"*Mon Dieu . . . mon Dieu . . .*"

Clarice's exclamations were weak and Madame panicked.

"Clarice, please, what is wrong?"

Hardly able to stand, Clarice trembled as she instructed with visible effort, "You must make your purchase as you were told and then go back to the house, Madame."

"But I cannot allow you to remain as you are. I must help you!"

"You have already helped me, Madame. Please do as I say."

Breathing laboriously, Madame whispered, "You will agree to meet me again, then, so I may provide you with a ticket to return home?"

"Home?"

"To France."

Clarice replied as gently as she could manage, "Look at me, Madame. I have no home."

"Clarice, please."

"Finish the chore that Monsieur has set for you, Madame. I will take care of the rest. But you must promise me that you will not tell Monsieur Knox what we have discussed."

"*Non!* I would not dare!"

"*Bon*. I must go."

At those words, Clarice turned unsteadily and left the flustered woman behind her. She could not afford to waste time.

"Maggie, where are you?" Ignoring the effusive welcome of the dogs as they bounded toward her, Tessa closed the door behind her as she entered Maggie's cabin. She glanced at the table nervously when she spotted a scribbled note. It read:

Tessa,

I have gone down to the city to search for Clarice.
Maggie

Torn by indecision, Tessa fingered the note. Lucky had told her to go back to the cabin and that he would find Clarice for her. She trusted him, but she was concerned about Maggie. Did he know that Maggie was also searching for the Frenchwoman? Had they joined forces? Should she join the search as well?

Tessa shook her head. Lucky had insisted that he would locate Clarice and had asked that she leave the problem in his hands. Tessa looked at the fireplace, where a small fire flickered, and then made a decision. She would do as Lucky instructed, but she would wait only until the noon hour. If Maggie and he had not returned by then, she would attempt to find them.

Still uncertain, Tessa took the vegetables that had been delivered earlier and began preparing them for that evening's soup. The meal would be smaller than usual and the men would complain, but it was the best she could do under the circumstances.

Tessa looked at the window where the morning sun rose gradually toward the midpoint in the sky. Yes, she would wait only until noon.

Tessa's gaze was still fixed on the cloudless sky outside the window when she heard an unexpected knock on the door. Startled when the dogs began barking, she shushed them and walked cautiously toward it. She was unprepared when the animals pushed past her and rushed the young fellow standing there with a note in his hand. Appearing terrified by the animals, the boy dropped the note and ran. Tessa called the dogs back when they attempted to chase the boy. She shouted out to him that they were just overly friendly, but he paid no attention.

The young fellow slipped from sight, and Tessa sighed at the unexpected fiasco. She then picked up the note the boy had dropped and opened it. She started to shake when she read:

> *Tessa,*
> *Come to the warehouse on the dock opposite the ship named* The Painted Lady. *I need your help.*
> *Lucky*

Lucky had found Clarice! The confused French-woman must have returned to the docks, where she would only sink further into despair. Although Lucky had found Clarice quickly, the poor Frenchwoman obviously resisted returning with him. She needed to go there. She needed to convince Clarice that coming back to the cabin was her only path to recovery.

Making certain to leave the dogs confined, Tessa hurried off with them barking wildly behind her as she started down the hill.

*   *   *

"What do you mean I cannot enter?" Clarice demanded of the burly fellow who barred her entrance into the hotel. "I have a message for Lucky Monroe. I must see him quickly."

"Go back where you came from, lady. Lucky don't have nothing to do with women like you."

"Like me?"

Clarice stared at the short, stocky man whose muscular arms shouted a strength she could not ignore. She still had trouble remembering that her appearance had slipped to the degree that she would no longer be allowed entrance into places where the successful few resided.

Tears filled Clarice's eyes. *Oui,* the successful few whose company she was no longer fit to keep.

With no recourse, Clarice said softly, "What is your name, monsieur?"

The fellow responded warily, "My name is Wally. Why?"

Clarice begged, "Please, Wally, I must see him. I have an urgent message to give to him."

"You're wasting your time." Appearing amused by her approach, the man commented, "He ain't here anyway. He left a while ago."

"Where did he go?"

The burly fellow raised his brow. "That ain't none of your business."

"I must know if I am to deliver this important message."

Wally shrugged. "I guess there ain't no harm in telling you right off that Lucky has as many women as he wants. As a matter of fact, he left right after he got a note from one of them who works in his tent." He shrugged his beefy shoulders again. "I got to admit that he looked annoyed by it, but he said to tell anybody who came looking for him that he would be back down as soon as he could."

"He would come back down? Who did he go to see?"

"Why do you want to know? You'd never make it up to her tent on the hill in your shape."

On the hill.

Clarice briefly closed her eyes. The man was right. She could not manage the climb. She was weakening even now.

Infused with a new determination, Clarice forced her chin upward. She would not give up! She had to stop Harley's plan from succeeding.

But Madame had not been specific about which warehouse those two men would be waiting in. Would she have the strength to find Tessa before it was too late?

Clarice turned unsteadily back toward the docks.

"Delilah! Are you in there?"

Standing outside Delilah's tent on the hill, Lucky called out her name. He was irritated by her urgent summons. He could think of no reason why he must go to her immediately, or why it was "a life or death situation" as she had insisted.

He called out again, only to hear Delilah respond weakly, "Lucky, is that you?"

His brow knitting, Lucky pushed aside the flap to see Delilah lying on her cot in a state of dishabille. "I'm so glad you came," she murmured. "I'm ill, Lucky. I needed someone, and the only person I could think of was you."

Unable to feel the sympathy she obviously expected, Lucky asked, "What's wrong?"

"I don't know. I'm just unwell. I think I have a fever because I was haunted with hallucinations throughout the night, and now I'm too weak to pull myself upright."

"Did you send someone for Dr. Riker?"

"No."

"You found someone to send for me, but you didn't send for Dr. Riker?"

Aware that her face had flushed at his questioning, Lucky turned toward the exit. "I'll summon Dr. Riker for you. He'll come up here and give you something."

"No! Don't!"

Delilah attempted to stand as he moved away from her cot, but she stumbled and fell weakly to the ground. Silently cursing, Lucky gathered her up and placed her back on the cot, but his irritation did not abate. He had no time for this! He could be no help with whatever ailed Delilah. She needed someone with Dr. Riker's knowledge.

Lucky said softly, "Who delivered your note to my hotel, Delilah?"

Delilah's eyelids fluttered weakly. "I called a boy who lives with his mother a few tents away."

"I'll send him to Dr. Riker for you."

"But you'll stay with me until the doctor gets here, won't you, Lucky?" Delilah's voice was a weak plea. "I don't want to be alone."

Lucky was fast losing patience. He needed to find Clarice. Tessa and Maggie had struggled so hard to restore her health, and with every minute that passed, the possibility increased that she might do something to weaken the meager strength they had restored.

"Lucky, please."

Lucky looked at the woman who had formerly filled all his needs. Despite her illness, she was dressed provocatively in a sheer garment that displayed her bountiful female flesh. Her hair was strewn against the pillow, a deep red that now appeared garish to him. Her tearstained but otherwise carefully painted face was composed in a plea that somehow appeared contrived. Incredulous that Delilah could have appealed to him at all, he instructed tightly, "Cover yourself against the chill. I'll find the boy."

Satisfied that Delilah had pulled the coverlet back

over her seminakedness, Lucky stepped outside and walked briskly toward the nearby tents. He found the boy that Delilah had mentioned, sent him to summon the doctor, and then strode back to Delilah's tent. He said tightly as he looked down at her, "The doctor will be here shortly, but I can't stay. Something has come up that I have to tend to."

He turned to leave as Delilah whispered, "So you no longer care."

Lucky responded, "Someone is in dire straits, Delilah. I promised to help."

"Is her situation more dire than mine?"

"Truthfully, I'm not sure."

"Is this person more important to you than me?"

Lucky did not reply.

"Please stay with me, at least until the doctor arrives. Please, Lucky."

Lucky frowned. There was something wrong here, although Delilah's skin was hot to the touch and she doubtless did have a fever.

"Lucky?"

"All right, I'll stay until the doctor comes."

"Thank you."

Was he mistaken, or did Delilah's eyes flash a gleam of triumph before she urged, "Come and sit beside me until then?"

"No, I think not."

Uncertain exactly why he refused, Lucky remained

near the exit. He had the uncomfortable feeling that however long the doctor took to respond to his summons, it would be too long.

Tessa was still breathless when she arrived at the warehouse. The only thought in her mind was that Lucky needed her help with Clarice, so she ignored the conditions in the area where she had been directed. She found *The Painted Lady* tied to the dock among the other ships there, and then glanced at the deserted warehouse across from it. That abandoned building was exactly the kind of place Clarice would seek out, somewhere where she could indulge her weakness without anyone as a witness.

Tessa approached the building but hesitated at the darkness within as she entered. She wondered how Lucky had found Clarice so quickly, but then reasoned that he had countless contacts in the city. She called out as she walked cautiously forward.

"Lucky, Clarice. Where are you?"

A chill ran up her spine when there was no response. She called out more loudly, "Lucky, please answer me."

She heard the sound of a step in the darkness and turned toward it with a smile, and then everything went suddenly dark.

Lucky made his way back down the hill with a frown. Dr. Riker had taken too long to respond to his summons.

By the time the old man arrived, Delilah appeared to be recovering with amazing speed, but somehow that had not surprised him. She had attempted to talk to him while he waited, but he had asked her to save her strength. She had again attempted to breach the silence between them, but he had insisted that she try to sleep. She had even uncovered herself as if she were warm, revealing her state of undress, but all her actions became utterly transparent when she tried to seduce him.

Lucky looked at the position of the sun in the cloudless sky. Realizing that it was past noon, he made a snap decision and turned abruptly toward the cabin on the hill. He needed to make sure that Tessa has not reconsidered her promise to remain behind. With his mind free of that concern, he could then search out the places where Clarice might have gone.

The wild barking of the dogs as he approached the cabin caused Lucky to frown with concern. Neither Maggie nor Tessa would allow that noise to continue. He pushed open the cabin door moments later and entered to find the animals in a strange state of excitement. "Tessa, Maggie, where are you?" he called out.

No response.

Lucky was about to search the premises behind the cabin when a slip of paper on the floor caught his eye. He picked up the note signed with his name and read it with burgeoning fear.

He then turned abruptly and headed for the warehouse across the dock from *The Painted Lady*.

* * *

It took tremendous effort for Clarice to move, but she knew she must go on. She had already entered the first two warehouses in the area, and had been thrown out of both with insulting comments that she did not choose to recall. There was only one left and Clarice approached it cautiously. The warehouse was deserted and dark, and it was on a street less traveled. She had avoided it for that reason, hoping that she would find Tessa under better circumstances, but it appeared that was not to be.

Taking a breath, Clarice entered. Her steps shaky, she summoned her courage and called out, "Tessa, are you here? I have come to speak to you."

No response. The interior of the building was dark despite the light outside, but the darkness was not silent. She heard the sound of small, scampering feet in the corners, and her flesh crawled.

"Who are you, and what are you doing here?"

Clarice turned so swiftly toward the voice behind her that she swayed. The shadowy male figure accused, "You're drunk, aren't you?"

"*Non,* I am not." Suddenly aware that she had no plan to help Tessa escape even if she found her, Clarice replied with as much hauteur as she could manage, "I have come to find a friend of mine who . . . who told me that she was coming here for an assignation."

"You did, huh?" the fellow said. "You called a name. Tessa."

"Tessa is the name she prefers while in this country.

She is otherwise known as Mademoiselle Montessa Victor."

"So, you aren't looking for Tessa White?"

"Tessa White? Who is she?" Her eyes rapidly acclimating to the darkness, Clarice saw that although the man addressing her was only a few inches taller than she, he was bulky and muscular. Clarice managed, "If my friend is not here, perhaps you will be interested in some intimate play. I might surprise you with my ability."

Incredibly, the fellow's expression became lascivious as Clarice added more boldly, "My fee is small, and the pleasure I give is well worth the price."

The man's smile broadened, and he called out, "Lester, it looks like we can have some fun while we wait."

"Lester . . . while you wait?"

"That doesn't concern you. From the looks of you, all you want is enough to buy whatever brings you relief, and my friend and I can provide that sum if you satisfy us."

Taking her by the arm, the man drew her toward the rear of the warehouse.

Clarice saw the other man approach with a leering smile before she noticed the bound, squirming figure lying in the corner.

Noting her glance, the first man ordered, "That's none of your business. You have other things to take care of. I'm first. My friend will come later."

Clarice heard the mumbled protests from the prone,

gagged woman on the floor as she responded, "Whatever you want, monsieur. I hope to please both of you."

Clarice raised her skirts.

"No, that's not enough. I want more. It's been a long time."

"Whatever you say, monsieur."

Clarice fell back into the shadows with a show of modesty that she did not feel. She reached behind her in the darkness, hoping for something she might find on the boxes stored there that would serve as a weapon. She nearly gasped when she found what seemed to be a metal bar of some sort that had been discarded there. Clutching it behind her, she cooed, "Perhaps you would enjoy helping me remove my clothing, monsieur. Perhaps the fantasy that I do not comply with your desires will help excite you."

"I'm ready for you right now, lady, but what you're saying don't sound like a bad idea at all."

The man stepped into the shadows as Clarice smiled. He did not see her first blow coming, nor the second or the third as he slumped over with blood gushing from his head. Breathless, aware even as the first man hit the floor that the second fellow was rushing toward her, Clarice raised the bar to strike again. Too late, she saw the gun in his hand. The bullet struck her breast with hot, breathtaking pain, and she fell to the floor.

Helpless, she heard the gunman's footsteps approaching. She heard him start at the sound of voices and new footsteps growing near.

And then she heard no more.

"Clarice, can you hear me?"

Clarice came back to reality slowly. She became aware of the arms that held her gently and recognized the woman's voice calling her name even as the pain in her chest stole her breath.

"You must hold on, Clarice. One of these men who came to investigate the sound of the shots has sent for a doctor. He will take care of you."

"You . . . you are free?" Clarice asked.

"Yes, these men untied me." Indicating the men who hovered nearby, Tessa whispered, "Whatever those two were planning, you stopped them." She continued more slowly. "The fellow you hit is dead. The other one got away."

"Bon . . . bon . . ." Her mind beginning to wander and her breathing short, Clarice whispered, "You must take care. These men . . . these men . . ." Losing her train of thought, Clarice said suddenly, "I am cold."

"The doctor will be here soon. He will see to it that you aren't cold anymore."

"Oui, he will see to it that I drift away. That is want I wanted, to drift away."

A teardrop touched Clarice's face as Tessa replied, "And when you awaken, you will feel better than before."

"I will not awaken."

"Clarice!"

Clarice forced a smile past her quivering lips. "Do not be sad, for I do not wish to awaken. The world has become a bitter place for me."

"No. I will help you."

"Do not despair. These last moments are my best. I do not . . . I . . ."

Clarice suddenly smiled. The coldness disappeared and she felt well. She then closed her eyes, never to open them again.

Lucky's heart lurched at the crowed gathering in front of the warehouse. He had run every step of the way from Maggie's cabin. His suit soaked with perspiration, his face gray, he came to an abrupt halt, and then ran even faster as he entered the warehouse breathlessly. He heard one man whisper to another, "She's dead. She didn't stand a chance."

No! Lucky staggered.

"She wasn't in good shape anyway. Hell, I ain't never seen nobody look so bad."

"Yeah, but—"

As his eyes grew accustomed to the darkness, he saw her. Tessa held Clarice in her arms.

Lucky crouched beside Tessa as she turned toward him.

"She saved my life, Lucky. She allowed those men to think . . . to believe . . ."

Tessa was suddenly sobbing. Her slender body shook with the emotions rocking her as she clutched Clarice gently. Aware that men stood behind her ready to remove Clarice's body, Lucky took Tessa into his arms. It occurred to him as he held her, as he felt sorrow shuddering through her, that she didn't care how close she had come to meeting Clarice's fate. Nor did she realize how much love he felt for her as he raised her to her feet and walked her toward the door. Or how much gratitude he felt toward the Frenchwoman he had never believed in, but who had proved herself in her final hour.

Harley's steps stopped short as he rounded the corner near the warehouse and spotted the waning crowd congregating there. Something was wrong!

Hurrying back behind a few abandoned bales, Harley saw Lucky emerge through the doors with his arm around Tessa. Tessa walked slowly, as if disoriented, and Lucky's arm tightened. Harley held back a curse with pure strength of will when Tessa moved closer to him and rested her head against his shoulder.

The "foolproof" plan that the bold Delilah had offered him had been foiled! It had failed! It had fallen apart, and he had yet to discover what repercussions that failure would carry with it. If he went down, however, he promised himself one thing. He would take her with him.

He waited a moment longer and saw two bodies being carried out. The first was a man, and the second was a woman. The woman was unmistakable. It was Clarice, but however she'd become involved in the fiasco, he did not care any more than he cared about her. The other body was one of his hirelings, but there did not appear to be a third.

Harley listened to the conversations as observers passed. Apparently the crime was adjudged a kidnapping. The first kidnapper had been killed and the second one had gotten away without being identified.

Far away, he hoped.

He listened intently to the conversations and learned that the events remained mysterious, most especially how Clarice became involved. The supposition was that the Frenchwoman had saved Tessa's life.

He doubted it.

A new agitation rose inside Harley. He was finished with Delilah. He had learned the hard way that he could not depend on Delilah's "plans." But he was not finished with Tessa yet. He would not suffer his plans for her to come to so ignominious an end. He would bide his time. She would pay for insulting him, for escaping him, for turning his plans upside down. So would Lucky, who seemed to have earned a spot in Tessa's regard that infuriated Harley.

When he was finished with them, Lucky would not be so lucky anymore, and Tessa's life would be in his hands. He would see to it, one way or another.

Chapter Eight

Clarice was buried in a pauper's grave just as Nugget had said she would be, but at least she had a marker.

Tessa kept the thought of that marker in mind while Pedro carried in the food she had cooked. She was standing outside Lucky's tent, preparing to follow with a basket of bread. It had become Lucky's policy since her abduction to meet her at the entrance to his tent and escort her inside. It was his way of showing everyone concerned that he intended to protect her from all harm. Involved in a card game just now, he had signaled that he would be with her as soon as the hand was finished.

Tessa had been surprised when so many of the prospectors she had come to know voiced their angry reactions to her abduction. Their visible fervor was the first sign of community that she had seen in that transient society. She had not expected it, and their concern brought her to the edge of tears.

But she'd had no time for tears in the confusing aftermath of that day. The second kidnapper had not been found and many mysteries remained. How

Clarice happened to learn where Tessa had been taken was one of those mysteries. The only certainty in the situation was that Clarice had sacrificed her life to save Tessa's, and she had done it with a selflessness that Tessa would never forget.

Lucky's lips had tightened when Tessa said she did not understand why those men had kidnapped her when there were so many other women ready to accommodate them—if that was what they had in mind. He had chosen not to respond, yet he no longer entrusted her safety to Pedro once twilight fell. He had begun taking her back to the cabin in the wagon each night. Strangely, as much as she liked and respected Pedro, she hoped Lucky would continue to do so. She felt safe with him. She supposed that was the reason for the fluttering in her stomach when he sat beside her, when he spoke to her in that husky tone he used with no one else, or when he smiled in the way that shook her down to her toes.

But the dark looks Delilah continued to send her way did not escape her. She could not blame the woman. Tessa had gradually begun taking up so much of Lucky's time that he appeared to have none left for . . . well, for other things that were important to a man.

She was torn in two directions. One part of her did not want to interfere with the life that Lucky had made for himself, yet another part of her was selfishly glad about the distance he was putting between himself and Delilah.

She was floundering. It had been a blow for her to admit to herself that she was not as strong, as independent as she had once believed. Or that she wanted—

But what did she want?

Two weeks had passed since that fateful day, and although Lucky and she had drawn closer, she sensed something was missing in the relationship between them. She was uncertain about the jolt she felt each time Lucky looked at her, about her avid anticipation of the moment when Lucky would meet her outside his tent, or lift her casually onto the seat they shared on the way back to the cabin after her work was done. For those brief moments, she would feel his strength enclosing her, his breath on her cheek, and the soul-shaking effect of his nearness.

They had begun to talk confidentially during the ride home. She had told him things she had told no one else about the dreams of prosperity that had convinced her to join her parents in their quest, dreams that had been sadly shattered. Lucky had quietly confessed that he still searched the faces of new arrivals on wagon trains, hoping that he'd find his parents one day, although he knew in his heart that he would not. He had laughed at that confession, but she hadn't. She had learned the hard way that hope was not easily dismissed, even when reality raised its sensible head. The truth that she hoped those rides home would never come to an end was proof of that point.

"When are you going to get over what happened to

you?" Delilah demanded, suddenly appearing beside her. "Everybody has bad experiences, but you're taking advantage of Lucky because of yours. You're disrupting the life he worked hard to make for himself. He was happy until you came, and now everyone notices that he's more quiet and withdrawn."

Tessa remained silent under Delilah's unexpected vocal attack. Standing opposite the beautiful red-haired woman and noting the voluptuous assets she displayed so casually in her gold satin gown, Tessa felt the rise of familiar guilt. She could not hope to compete with all that Delilah was, or with all that Delilah had provided for Lucky, without asking anything in return.

Delilah continued venomously. "You're a weight on Lucky's shoulders. It's about time you thought about someone other than yourself. Take the money Lucky offered you and go home! It should be obvious to you by now that's what Lucky wants you to do. The sooner you leave San Francisco, the better it will be for him."

"I didn't mean to . . . I only wanted—"

"Whatever you wanted didn't work out, though, did it? All you've done is pile more debt on your shoulders and create a heavier load for Lucky to carry."

"I know, but—"

"You know." Delilah's heavily rouged lips tightened. "So *do* something about it! Go home! Let Lucky enjoy the life he worked so hard to achieve."

Halting abruptly when she saw Lucky rising from

his card table to start toward them, Delilah mumbled, "That's all I have to say. You can tell Lucky what I said if you want to aggravate him even more, but that's up to you. It won't change the truth."

Delilah sauntered back through the tent entrance. Her broad smile flashed at a prospector who made his way directly toward her when she called out, "Hector, are you ready for another night's fun?"

Hector responded with a leering smile that caused Delilah to laugh as she swayed confidently across the crowded floor.

"What's wrong, Tessa?"

Tessa managed a smile when Lucky walked up beside her. "Nothing. I was just thinking."

Lucky picked up the bread basket and took Tessa's arm possessively as he urged her through the entrance. "You don't have time to think right now. The fellas inside have been waiting for you."

But Lucky's glance at the line that had already formed in front of her table was not accompanied by a smile.

Halting abruptly midway toward it, Tessa waited until Lucky frowned down at her to whisper, "I suppose I've been selfish."

"What are you talking about?"

"Selfish because I didn't really care what it would cost you in order for me to reach my goals."

"Your goals?"

"Paying you back and going home without debt."

"I came to terms with that a long time ago. I had my chance, and now it's time for you to have yours, that's all."

"Really? You're not just saying that?"

Lucky searched Tessa's expression with a deepening of his frown and then said abruptly, "This isn't the time or place for this discussion, but no, I'm not just saying that."

"You know," Tessa said, "I think I'm the one who turned out to be lucky, not you."

Lucky stared down at Tessa as she looked up at him with sincerity bright in her eyes. He wanted to tell her that *he* had indeed been the lucky one that night she had walked into his tent. He knew that now.

Glancing at some of the prospectors in line who called out Tessa's name, Lucky gripped her arm more tightly. He drew her along with him to the table where they waited. They were hungry.

Lucky momentarily considered that thought and then looked down at Tessa. He was hungry, too, but it wasn't the same kind of hunger, and no one but Tessa could sate it.

Maggie was tired. She wasn't herself of late. Too many things were on her mind. Like Clarice's tragic end. Though initially she'd been repelled by the young Frenchwoman, she had quickly come to realize that Clarice could not escape the physical pain controlled by her addiction. Her excruciating need for laudanum allowed Clarice to think of nothing else. Pity had then overtaken Maggie.

She had just begun feeling that Tessa and she were making inroads into Clarice's misery when Clarice left the cabin and stole back down into town.

As soon as Maggie had realized Clarice was gone, she'd set out to search for her, only to discover when she returned many fruitless hours later that Clarice had sacrificed her life to save Tessa.

Tessa had outwardly recovered from her ordeal, and now she was being watched over by Lucky far better than Maggie ever could have. Except for providing a place where Tessa could stay, her work with the girl was done.

Yet, somehow, she had the feeling the story was not over.

The sound of a horse's hooves on the trail raised Maggie's head. She opened the door to see Nugget McDuff dismounting from his gelding. She waited until he approached her, frowning as he said solemnly, "Hello, Maggie. I'm not delivering groceries this time. I wish I was. Instead, I'm the bearer of bad news."

A knot of apprehension clenching tight in her stomach, Maggie stepped back and allowed Nugget to enter.

Delilah watched from a distance, her disgust barely concealed as Tessa looked down at the empty stew pot in her hands and then at the emptied pie plates on the table. When the next prospector in line growled his disappointment that he would not get "seconds" that evening, Delilah mumbled an unladylike curse.

The fools! They salivated over platinum hair and an innocent expression. They were so besotted with Tessa that they hardly tasted the food she cooked! But then, when Tessa went back to the cabin on the hill, those same men came to women like her with other appetites.

But there was only one man for her now. It enraged Delilah that Lucky seemed as taken in by platinum hair and an innocent expression as the others!

Delilah glanced at the doorway and noticed that Harley Knox stood there boldly watching the platinum-haired wonder work her appeal. Her fury mounted. *He* was the cause of her careful plan's failure two weeks earlier. She had done her part in keeping Lucky out of the way at great personal expense, even going so far as to obtain a pill that would induce a temporary fever. Yet in doing his part, Harley had hired stupid men who had succumbed to the wiles of a worn-out French whore who had then managed to scuttle the entire plan.

Delilah's heavily kohled eyes glowed with threat. Harley had maintained his distance from both Lucky's tent and her since Clarice's death. He had obviously been afraid that someone would connect them to the abduction in some way, but it seemed he finally felt safe enough to show his face. And, if she were to judge from the look in his eyes tonight, his desire for the blonde witch had not lessened.

Delilah's ire exploded. What was it about that pale-haired woman that caused men to go to such lengths for her? But then, Harley's intentions were different. He wanted Tessa for the money he expected her to earn for him.

Delilah moved slowly across the crowded floor, determined to make Harley pay for all his mistakes. She arrived beside him before he noted her advance.

Startled, Harley whispered, "What do you think you're doing? Get away from me! I don't want anyone to see us together."

"Why, Harley, old friend? Is it because you managed to ruin my foolproof plan? Is it because the woman you want still does not fill a place in your house as you intended?"

"Shut up! Get away from me!"

"No, I don't think so."

"Then I'll leave," he said. "But I promise you that this won't be the last of our encounters."

Furious at his reply, Delilah waited until Harley had cleared the exit before walking briskly out behind him. Catching up with him in the shadows, she gripped his arm and turned him around to face her as she said through clenched teeth, "No, you're not going to get away that easily. My plan was perfect, but it was not entirely *foolproof,* and you hired two *fools* to implement it! It's your fault everything went wrong. It's your fault Tessa is still working in this tent, and I demand that you fix your mistakes!"

Mumbling under his breath, Harley pulled Delilah deeper into the shadows. Glancing around, satisfied at last that they could not be seen, Harley said warningly, "You take a risk in angering me further, Delilah. You do not seem to be thinking clearly at this moment."

"I'm thinking clearly, all right." Delilah's face flushed with heat. "And what I'm thinking is that you need to make up for your mistakes."

"I carried through just as planned."

"No, you didn't! You hired idiots to do the job!"

Harley smiled knowingly at Delilah's rage. "So, little Tessa has managed to snag your man away from you."

"No, she hasn't! Whatever he feels for her is temporary."

"And what he felt for you wasn't?"

"I kept him happy and content!"

"Obviously not content enough, which is one of the reasons why I didn't want you in my house."

"Your house was too good for me, is that it? But not for the likes of Clarice!"

"Clarice was beautiful and cultured at one time. You are *common*. You will always be *common*."

At his deliberate insult, Delilah sprang forward, barely missing Harley's cheek with her nails as she punched and kicked him with all her might. Her teeth clenched and her eyes wild, she did not see Harley raise his clenched fist until he struck her hard.

Stunned, Delilah stumbled backward, but Harley did not stop there. Dragging her deeper into the shadows, he pounded her again and again, propping her upright against a tree as blood flowed from her nose and mouth, and her hair fell into her blackened eyes. He pummeled her body relentlessly, and when her body doubled over from repeated blows to her ribs, he kicked her again and again.

His rage gradually subsiding, Harley paused and straightened his clothing. Standing over her, he whispered, "I hope you have learned a lesson, my dear Delilah, because if you should dare to approach me again, you will not survive."

Turning, Harley left Delilah lying on the ground gasping for air through a throat filled with blood. Feeling no regrets, he smiled. He had taught the whore a lesson that she had badly needed to learn. He did not look back.

"Tell me now what's bothering you."

Tessa glanced at Lucky where he sat beside her on the wagon seat. They had started back toward the cabin, and the trail was lit by twilight as the wagon moved steadily upward.

Tessa did not speak until Lucky urged, "Tell me what you meant about your being selfish."

Refusing to meet Lucky's stare, Tessa replied, "I suppose I was so concerned about what I needed to do in order to make myself feel like a person again that I didn't really care what it cost you." She frowned. "I know now that I was wrong. I've interfered with your life, and you've become quiet and withdrawn because of it."

Lucky raised his brows with surprise. "Is that how I appear, quiet and withdrawn?"

Tessa looked up. She hesitated a moment, but then said, "No, you don't appear that way to me. You appear strong and in charge of a difficult situation."

"A difficult situation?"

"All the trouble I've caused you since I arrived in San Francisco."

"What trouble is that?"

"I was sick, starving, and exhausted, and you found me a place to recuperate from my ordeal. You gave me work I could do, but as soon as I was finally starting to pay you back, I took in Clarice and sent my bill up higher. Then there was a kidnapping attempt, a death, the need for you to drive me back to the cabin each night, which means more time missed at the tables than you're accustomed to."

"I'll live through that. No one seems to be complaining, either."

"Some are."

"Some?"

Tessa frowned at her unconscious slip of the tongue. She didn't want to make trouble for Delilah.

Tessa revised that thought. No, if she were to be completely honest with herself, that wasn't true. Although she despised herself for it, she was *jealous* of Delilah. Each time she looked at the voluptuous woman, she could only think that Lucky had kissed Delilah's heavily rouged lips, that he had run his fingers through the long length of her brightly colored hair, that he had stroked the clear, white skin she exposed so seductively at the bodice of her dress, and had then—

Tessa refused to complete that thought as she raised suddenly moist eyes to Lucky. She said humbly, "I'm so sorry, Lucky."

Appearing disturbed by her sudden tears, Lucky allowed the reins to fall lax in his hands as he said softly, "Sorry about what, Tessa?"

"I'm so sorry to have disrupted your life."

"Tessa." Slipping his arms around her in what was intended as a reassuring embrace, Lucky drew her close. But the comfort he hoped to extend became more. He pulled back to whisper, "Don't you know I'd do anything for you and that you've brought something back into my life that's been missing for so many empty years. Don't you know, don't you know . . ."

His words trailing away as the horse plodded along the trail, Lucky covered her lips with his own, and a shot of pure joy rushed through him. Suddenly helpless against the emotion of the moment, he pressed his kiss deeper. He separated her lips to taste the sweet wonder of her mouth, moved to her darkly fringed eyelids, the delicate shell of her ear, the fragile line of her jaw before returning again to indulge himself in her lips.

Lucky drew her more tightly into his embrace. He mumbled loving words in a frenzy of tender kisses that only made him hunger for more. Tessa's arms slipped around his neck, her lips separating farther under his as she responded to his heated caress. She did not seem to understand that his need for her was so deep.

Lucky snapped back to reality when the wagon stopped at the cabin door. Drawing back from her with the realization that he had taken advantage of Tessa's vulnerability, Lucky whispered, "Now it's my turn to be sorry, Tessa. Please forgive me. I didn't meant to exploit the situation."

"Is that you, Tessa?" Lucky's penitent gaze snapped to Maggie's figure as she emerged from the cabin with the dogs at her heels. Maggie swallowed, appearing visibly upset as Lucky lifted Tessa down from the wagon.

"Is something wrong, Maggie?" Tessa asked.

"Yes, something is very wrong. I want to talk to you about it before I go."

"Go? Where?"

"To the diggings. I told Nugget that I'd go with him tomorrow when he rides out to be with Strike."

"To be with Strike?"

Maggie took a breath. "Strike is dying."

Lucky felt Tessa's shock at Maggie's pronouncement. He grasped her arm as she staggered and briefly closed her eyes. "I was about to say he looked well when he left, but I can't say that's true, because he didn't. He was too thin, his eyes too cloudy, and his color poor. I knew something was wrong."

"It's his heart. Nugget came to me because Strike told him that I had done a good thing in helping you and that I must be a good woman. Nugget knew how much it meant to Strike to have found a woman he respected. Nugget says he knows now that Strike went back to the diggings to die, and he figured I'd want to know because I was one of the last people Strike thought of before he left."

"But you didn't tell me Strike was here."

"Strike asked me not to. He didn't want you to think that he was checking up on you, even if he did want to know that you'd be well taken care of. We spoke for a while. I think he thought of you as the daughter he had lost, and of me as a woman he could trust. Honestly, I believe that the fondness of years was established in the short time Strike and I spent together in that sincere conversation. I know I've often thought about him with true affection in the days since."

"You're sure that Nugget is right about Strike's condition?"

"I'm sure. Nugget and Strike are good friends, and Strike stayed with Nugget while he was here. A fellow prospector who was passing by Strike's claim told Nugget that Strike was in bad shape."

Lucky shook his head bewilderedly. "I've considered Strike a friend over the years, but I didn't know he was sick."

"Don't berate yourself, Lucky," Maggie offered softly. "Strike did his best not to let anybody know."

Tessa's voice choked as she confessed, "There was something about Strike's honesty and generosity, and the way he looked at me, that reminded me of my father. Now it's like losing my father all over again." She asked unexpectedly, "When are you leaving?"

"Tomorrow morning."

"I'm going with you."

"No!"

Maggie's abrupt refusal startled Tessa. She shook her head as Maggie said almost apologetically, "I'll need someone to take care of my animals while I'm gone. You can do that, Tessa. You know the routine they're used to and the food they need."

"But—"

Maggie continued simply. "If you don't stay behind and take care of them, I can't go, and it's important for me to do this. I hope you can understand that I need to care for Strike in a way that I wasn't able to care for my Wally when he was dying because I was ill, too. I have looked back on those days with so many regrets, and this is a chance for me to make up for my inadequacies then, no matter how inescapable they were. I want to make Strike's last days comfortable and give him the attention he deserves. He has a goodness inside him that is so like my Wally that—"

Maggie's voice choked off and Tessa hastened to reassure her, "I understand how you feel, Maggie. Of course I'll do as you ask, but please don't think you're inadequate in any way. You've done so much for me."

"But you're well now, Lucky doesn't need me anymore, and he has taken over responsibility for you."

Speaking up at last, Lucky put in, "Maggie, I thought you knew how I felt. You're the mother I looked for and could never find. I'll always be grateful to you, and you'll always hold a special place in my heart."

Tessa asked abruptly, "When does Nugget expect to get here tomorrow?"

"At dawn. I've already packed what I'll need."

Tessa said gently, "Don't worry about anything while you're gone. I'll take care of things, but I will miss you."

Tessa's heartfelt words lingered on the evening air as Lucky ushered both women into the cabin.

Lucky was unusually silent as he played cards with an eye on his pocket watch. Tessa would arrive at the tent in a little more than an hour. The crowd awaiting her had grown larger as her reputation had spread, necessitating the addition of even more gaming tables, which meant greater profits. He now had a standing order for additional bottles of liquor each night, which swelled his profits even more. He was well aware that if he so chose, he could erect another tent especially so Tessa might hire help and be able to offer a greater variety of meals. But the truth, which he disliked admitting to himself, was that the idea of Tessa becoming independent of him in any way held little appeal. And her only goal in working there was to pay him back so that she might return to Iowa debt free.

But despite those truths, he could not contain his feelings any longer. No other woman held any appeal for him. Tessa was everything that he had unconsciously looked for, hoped for, wished for in a woman. Her sense of purpose was strong, yet she had come to understand the problems of the haphazard San Francisco society where they resided. She had made subtle adjustments in her thinking without compromising her ideals or her determination. She saw the strengths as well as the weaknesses of the people she met, and she actually enjoyed knowing the majority of them. She treated the prospectors as old friends and they had come to love her for it. She grew more beautiful, more appealing, more desirable to him every day, yet she still thought mainly of going home.

The only persons who appeared to resent her were the women in his employ, and he suspected he knew who had tainted their opinions of her. Yet he did not forget that they had all served him well.

Raising his head from the gaming table, he noted that those same women were not circulating through the crowd in their usual fashion, but had gathered instead in a corner of the tent in whispered conversation. He knew they did not know about Strike's condition, and that, unlike Tessa, they would not care even if they did. No, their discussion involved something that affected them directly.

Sensing a problem, Lucky spread his cards out on the table for all to see. He waited until he heard spontaneous groans before gathering up the pot and calling another dealer in to take his place as he stood up and declared, "I have something to do."

Lucky walked directly to the cluster of brightly painted women and said, "All right, what happened?"

Lily, a woman whose age was revealed on her round face but whom his customers appeared to enjoy for her dauntless personality, replied unhesitatingly, "Delilah isn't here."

Lucky shrugged and said, "She's probably just late."

"She's not late," Velda interjected. "She's never late. She's just not coming."

"Not after what happened to her," Marisa added, calling attention to herself. "She went outside and didn't come back last night. We noticed that she was gone, but we figured she was meeting somebody out there." She added with a shrug of her shoulders, "When she didn't come back, we figured she got involved and decided to stay until morning. She's done that before, so we weren't worried. But one of the fellas found her unconscious in the brush this morning when it was light enough to see. She wasn't in good shape."

Lucky's frown deepened as he questioned, "What happened?"

Marisa responded, "Somebody beat her up. The fella who found her took her to Doc Riker, but from what we heard, she couldn't identify who did it."

Lucky took a deep breath. First Tessa, and now Delilah. He asked hoarsely, "Where is she?"

"She's in her tent now, but she ain't moving much. None of us really liked her, but Delilah did her job, so I went to see her when I heard. She looks terrible, and I don't mind admitting that I'm scared. Somebody has something against the women here. It ain't safe for a poor, helpless woman no more."

Lucky declared, "You're safe as long as you're working here, so do your job. I'll take care of this."

He did not wait to see the women quickly disperse among the crowd as he walked out the exit.

Uncertain whether his chest was heaving from the exertion of the climb or from anxiety, Lucky approached Delilah's familiar tent a few minutes later and called out, "Delilah, it's me. Are you in there?"

The whimper from inside caused him to push aside the flap without delay. Delilah was lying prone on her cot. His eyes widened with shock at the sight of her. Her eyes were blackened, her nose appeared to be broken, her face was severely bruised, and her lips were swollen so badly that she could barely talk. She clutched her hand to her ribs and said, "G . . . go away. I don't want you to see me like this."

"What happened to you, Delilah?" Crouching down beside her cot, Lucky looked at her bloodied and almost unrecognizable face and said, "Who did this to you?"

"I don't know."

"You don't know?"

"He . . . he attacked me from behind."

"He?"

"It had to be a man. He was so strong."

Tears rolled down Delilah's battered cheeks and Lucky asked, "Who is taking care of you?"

"I can . . . take care of myself."

"You can walk down to the city to get yourself something to eat."

"N . . . not yet."

"You can handle your own cuts and bruises."

"No, but—"

Lucky said in a voice that tolerated no objections, "I'll make sure somebody takes care of you until you can." He hesitated and then added, "You don't have to worry about the money you'll lose until you're able to come back to work. I'll take care of things there, too."

Delilah batted her bruised and bloodshot eyes in a pathetic attempt to be seductive as she simpered, "You'd do that for me, Lucky?"

Instead of replying directly, Lucky added, "And I'll find out who did this to you, too."

"No. Don't."

Lucky's dark brows rose with surprise. "You don't want to find the person who did this to you?"

"I . . ." Delilah gulped. "I . . . I don't want you to waste your time. Nobody saw him because nobody found me until this morning. Just forget it. I will."

"Delilah."

"I want you to forget it!"

Lucky stood up at Delilah's agitated words. He responded softly, "Whatever you say. I have to get back, but I'll have someone come up to help you as soon as possible."

Delilah did not reply, merely closed her eyes. Lucky knew he would not forget the sight of her as he pushed aside the tent flap and strode away.

Delilah wanted to scream! Opening her eyes at the sound of Lucky's departing footsteps, she wanted to rail and shout the name of the man who had beaten her so badly that she was now an object of pity to the man she had hoped to win.

Delilah closed her eyes at the pain that stabbed through her body with each breath. She knew she looked bad and that several of her ribs were broken. Doc Riker had said she was lucky her ribs hadn't pierced a lung or she wouldn't have survived. She almost wished she hadn't if she couldn't count on regaining her looks. She knew she could still make her way as long as she had a pleasant face and figure. But how would she win

Lucky now that she was no longer any competition for the platinum-haired witch?

With a feeling of desperation, Delilah knew that it was not really Tessa who had stolen Lucky from her. Rather, Harley Knox was responsible for changing her from a desirable lover into a lingering liability in Lucky's eyes.

She had told Lucky to forget the attack and had said she would, but she had lied. She had no intention of forgetting. Her memory was long, and her determination was strong despite her present physical debilities. She would get her revenge on Harley Knox, but she needed to be able to stand on her own two feet and regain some of her mobility first. When she did, she would make sure Harley realized that incurring her wrath had been the biggest mistake of his life.

As had become his custom when Tessa finished serving her customers, Lucky lifted her onto the seat to drive her home. But he was quiet and uncommunicative.

Tessa broke the uneasy silence between them by asking quietly, "What's in that box in the back of the wagon, Lucky?"

"Some of my things."

Uncertain, Tessa repeated, "Your things?"

Lucky turned toward her to say, "You didn't think I'd let you stay alone at night in that cabin now that Maggie's gone, especially after what happened to you, did you?"

"You mean the abduction?" Tessa shook her head. "But I'm safe up here. It's isolated."

"I know. And you're all alone without Maggie."

"Maggie's an old lady! She wasn't any protection if that's what you were thinking."

"Maggie knows how to shoot a shotgun and she'd use it if she had to. Everybody knows that. It won't do any good to argue with me. Especially after what happened to Delilah."

Tessa stiffened. "What happened? I didn't see her at the tent, but I never gave it much thought."

"I didn't tell you because I wanted to avoid frightening you, but somebody beat her to within an inch of her life. She doesn't know who and she doesn't know why. I sent Pedro's wife up to stay with her until she can care for herself, but that makes two attacks on the women in my tent. I've taken steps to make sure it doesn't happen again, but I can't give this man the chance he's been waiting for to try to abduct you again."

"Lucky—"

"Don't argue, Tessa. I've already sent two of my men to look over the cabin and remain outside until I'm free to take over for them at night. I'll be staying with you until Maggie returns."

Tessa's eyes widened. "But you'll be working most of the night!"

"I won't be working all night long. I'll be turning over my table to Harry part of the time."

"But the men are depending on you to be there," she objected, "not just some fellow you've hired."

"It won't be the first time that I've taken some time for myself. I'll rig up some kind of shelter that I can sleep in so I can send the men at the cabin home to get some rest."

"You'll be sleeping out in the open?"

"I've done that before, too."

"But you've earned the right to more."

"It's only temporary, and as far as my profits are concerned, I own the tent, so it doesn't really matter."

"But—"

"That's the way it's going to be."

Adamant, Lucky remained silent until they reached the darkened cabin.

Nodding to the two men who met them there, Tessa remained tight-jawed. It was obvious from his expression that any objection she might add would fall on deaf ears.

Without another word, he swung her down from the seat and went to work constructing a shelter outside her door.

The cloud that had covered the full moon had been blown off by the stiff sea breeze. Wakeful in her bed, Tessa had listened to the departures of the men who had kept watch outside her door. Zeke and Tony were middle aged and tight-lipped. She had known they wouldn't do any talking about the situation after Lucky arrived to take over for them. But Lucky's arrival and subsequent work outside the cabin in the middle of the night hadn't gone unnoted. The dogs had whimpered and cried until she had let them out to sleep beside him in the shelter he had rigged. She had peeked outside a short time later to see that the animals were snoring peacefully while Lucky twisted and turned in his make-shift shelter.

Lying in her bed, Tessa was just as restless.

The memory of Lucky's kiss the previous night replayed vividly in her mind, and Tessa flushed. She could not be sure if it was the recollection of Lucky's arms around her or her guilt at his sleeping outdoors that disturbed her most. She only knew that Lucky was sleeping on the hard ground while she slept on a cot in comfort.

Abruptly making up her mind, Tessa stood and wrapped the coverlet around her as she walked to the doorway. The dogs did not even bother to raise their heads when she called out into the darkness, "Lucky, are you still awake?"

No answer.

"Lucky?"

After a brief silence, she heard him reply, "I'm awake."

"Please come inside. I can't sleep with the thought of you trying to get comfortable on that hard ground."

"It's not cold out here."

Tessa shook her head. "You know what I mean."

"I'll stay where I am."

Suddenly angry, Tessa replied, "If you do, I'll sleep outside, too!"

When Lucky did not reply, Tessa wrapped herself tighter in her coverlet and started to pull the door closed behind her, only to hear a stirring in the direction where Lucky lay. He stepped into her view with his hair ruffled, his clothing wrinkled, and his expression dark as he said in a voice deep with warning, "This is a mistake. You know it and I know it."

Tessa's heart jumped a beat as he walked closer and his aura enclosed her. Maybe it was a mistake after all, even if the closer he came, the more right it felt. She swallowed and then stepped back to allow him to precede her into the cabin. She said shakily, "You can take Maggie's cot."

Lucky did not speak.

"Mine is in the corner."

Silence.

"Good night."

Tessa hurried to her cot and closed her eyes when she lay down. Her heart was pounding and an ache unlike any she had ever before experienced expanded deep inside her. She told herself that the kisses Lucky and she had shared before had been an aberration. He wasn't interested in a woman like her who could not offer him even half of what any of the women in his tent could. She was young and foolish, and despite the hardships she had endured, she was inexperienced.

Lucky was not. She would only disappoint him.

With those thoughts in mind, Tessa plugged her ears against all sound, turned on her side, and attempted to sleep.

Lucky twisted and turned as he listened for the sound of steady breathing that would indicate Tessa was asleep, but the only sound in the cabin was restless tossing and turning similar to his own. His mind fought his growing desire with the reasoning that Tessa was an innocent, and he was not; that she had no intention of remaining in San Francisco; that her sole goal was to earn enough money to go home without any debts. He admitted to himself that Tessa probably felt she owed him for his kindnesses. He told himself that the fondness she felt for him now would be forgotten the minute she was established back in Iowa; that to go home was what she really wanted, not him.

But what did *he* want?

He knew that answer only too well.

Tessa moved restlessly again, and Lucky could bear it no longer. Aware that truth was hard to avoid in the darkness of night, Lucky stood up and approached the cot where Tessa lay. He crouched beside her. Her face was visible in a slender beam of moonlight that lit the exquisite features that he longed to follow with his lips. Her unbound hair was spread across the pillow in a shower of silver and gold that he longed to stroke. Her eyes were closed and her lips parted, but he knew she was not sleeping. It would be so easy to cover her lips with his own, but instead, he whispered with his last shred of control, "Tell me to leave now, Tessa, and I will. I promise. Tell me you want nothing to do with me now or ever. I won't hold it against you. I promise you that, too. Tell me that you want me to walk out that door and never approach you again because you don't feel the same as I do right now, and that—"

Tessa's eyelids fluttered open. He saw the moisture of tears in the great gray eyes turned up to his as she slipped a delicate, trembling hand across his lips to stop him from speaking.

"What if I can't tell you all those things, Lucky, because they aren't true? What if I don't care whether you'll hold rejection against me because I don't want you to leave?"

"Tessa."

Tessa continued resolutely. "And what if I tell you that all I'm really sure of right now is that I want you to hold me close, to stay with me, to make me feel complete in a way that I know only you can make me feel? What then?"

Tessa gasped when Lucky hesitated only briefly before responding with the warmth of his kiss.

Lucky's strong body trembled as he separated Tessa's lips with his kiss. Her arms encircled his neck and all reasonable thought slipped away as he kissed her again and again. Lying beside her as he became reacquainted with the flavor of her mouth, her fluttering eyelids, the hidden intricacies of her ear, the slender slope of her jaw, he was uncertain when her faded nightgown slipped away to bare her smooth flesh to his gaze.

He caressed her with wordless wonder. He encircled the roseate tips of her small breasts with his tongue, not taking them in his mouth until her gasping and his own need drove him to suckle them wildly. She crushed him against her and his desire soared higher. He tasted her skin. He left not an inch of her untouched as he smoothed, caressed, titillated. Wild in his pursuits, he was nearly mad with wanting to consume her, with wanting to take her and make her his alone. His sense of wonder was so strong that he did not remember how long he worshipped her slenderness before sliding his passionate assault lovingly downward. Meeting the juncture of her thighs at last, he paused at the emotion throbbing deep inside him as he first looked upon the pale nest awaiting him. He lowered his head to taste it lovingly.

Tessa's mumbled protest was instantaneous. He raised his eyes to meet her troubled gaze and whispered, "This time is ours, Tessa. Whatever the future holds, whatever it can be, these moments belong to us alone." He saw the tears that unexpectedly trailed down her cheeks and he brushed them away as he continued hoarsely. "We belong to each other. You are mine to love without holding back. Do you understand that, Tessa? Don't ask me to limit what I want to give with all my heart."

Waiting only until her protests ceased, Lucky slid his tongue inside the delicate crease to pleasure her with the full breadth of his desire. He exalted at the sweetness of her as he stroked her gently with his kiss, delighting in her distinctive fragrance, breathing deeply of her scent. He kissed, smoothed, consumed, and then rejoiced and drank deeply of the pulsating nectar that surged forth when Tessa could no longer withhold the fervor he had induced.

Waiting only until her spontaneous spasms ceased, Lucky slid himself back atop her to whisper into her parted lips, "Tell me that you love me at this moment, Tessa. I need to hear the words."

Responding in a trembling voice, Tessa whispered, "I do love you, Lucky."

Near the end of his restraint, Lucky whispered, "Tell me that you need me right now as much as I need you—"

Unable to hold back any longer, Lucky thrust himself into the moist inner core awaiting him. He heard Tessa gasp and waited a moment, filling her even as he lay breathlessly motionless inside her. Moving slowly, he sank his thrusts more deeply, the rhythm of his lovemaking growing more urgent until Tessa rose to join his thrusts with a spontaneity that took them to the brink.

His final thrust carried them over the precipice, sending them spiraling to the colorful ecstasy of full release.

Silence reigned as they lay spent in each other's arms.

The first to move, Lucky withdrew himself from Tessa's moist warmth and slid down onto the cot beside her. He kissed her lips lightly and smoothed back the few wisps of light hair that clung to her damp forehead as he whispered, "I love you, Tessa."

Lucky kissed her again, but a strange sadness assaulted him as he wondered how long their love would last.

He kissed her more deeply then, reveling in the moment and aware that this time together was worth whatever heartbreak might follow.

Tessa awakened as dawn brightened the sky outside her window. She started at the unfamiliar warmth beside her, and then slid closer to Lucky. She drew the coverlet up over their naked bodies with brief modesty, and was then amused at her actions. She had shared an intimacy with Lucky unlike anything that she had dreamed was possible. He had made love to her over and again throughout the night. Yet when he had first approached her in the darkness, he had said that if she wanted him to, he would leave. She realized now that her greatest fear had been that he would.

Lucky's arms slipped around her to draw her into the curve of his body, and Tessa leaned back against his warmth. She felt his lips move against her hair while he stroked her intimately, stirring the heat inside her anew. Pressing back against him more tightly, she then turned abruptly to face him. She saw that his dark eyes were half-lidded and sensual, and the moment became suddenly bittersweet.

"These moments are ours alone, for as long as we want them to be."

She had no gift to give the man who had given her so much and whom she loved with all her heart, but Tessa made him a silent promise. The cost to her did not matter. Freedom was his with no regrets, whenever he wanted it.

Yet in the meantime she was tinder to the match and spark to flame, as the fire within them ignited once more.

Chapter Nine

Lucky climbed the hill toward Delilah's tent slowly. The truth was that he was wary about the visit, but he needed to check on her progress. He had sent Josephina to stay with her until she recuperated, and he had heard from Pedro, who rarely complained, that Delilah was a difficult patient for his wife. He had remained silent at that report, but he had not been surprised.

Lucky thought back to the first day that Delilah walked through the entrance of his tent. She had been a striking sight in a flamboyant gown that left little to a man's imagination. Her smile had been enticing, and her gaze welcoming. He had hired her, knowing at once what kind of woman she was. And in the midst of their intimacies, he had been fully aware that Delilah's expertise indicated she had had many men before him.

But that hadn't mattered. He had been satisfied that she did her job well. That included the time spent in his bed. He had known he could not ask for more from her.

Then he had met Tessa, and he'd been introduced to a very different kind of woman: determined in the face of difficulty, self-respecting despite adversity, possessing innocence that came from the soul, and an honesty that came from the heart. He had respected Tessa before he came to love her. He had wished her well before he had taken her as his own. He still wished her well, and despite his desire to do otherwise, he was willing to let her go in order for her to accomplish her goals.

Not so certain of that last, Lucky paused in front of Delilah's tent. He then called out, "Delilah, it's Lucky."

Delilah's voice called back with a noticeable lack of strength, "Come in, please."

Lucky pushed back the flap, but was unprepared for what he saw. Her nose was still grotesquely swollen, her eyes squinting, and her more obvious cuts and bruises were still jagged marks against her white complexion, but she was fully painted with thick makeup in an attempt to conceal her wounds. Yet her effort had succeeded only in making herself appear a caricature of what she once was. It was a pathetic picture.

Lucky glanced at the silent Josephina and noted the frustration she tried to hide. He then looked back at Delilah. "How are you feeling, Delilah?" he asked.

"Oh, I'm doing well. As you can see, I'll soon be back to myself again and able to work." She continued nervously. "I miss the tent, you know. The noise, the frivolity." She glanced up at the silent Josephina and said, "There's little here to stimulate my mind."

Josephina's matronly face expressed her resentment, and Lucky said, "I think you can consider yourself fortunate that Josephina came up here to help you recover."

Delilah replied tightly, "You pay her for her efforts, don't you? I didn't expect that she'd come up otherwise."

"Josephina has been neglecting other aspects of her life in order to help you."

"What other aspects—her washing, ironing, and cooking? I should think she'd be glad to get out of doing those things. Except that she has been cooking Mexican food for me, which I don't find appealing."

Lucky stiffened. "Would you rather have Josephina leave? I could arrange it, you know, but you'd be left alone here with only neighbors to help you, or maybe the women in the tent."

"No, I didn't mean that!" Seeming suddenly to realize the sullenness of her reply, Delilah made an attempt to smile brightly. The result was that her cut lips cracked and bled profusely. She raised a cloth to her mouth and said, "As you can see, I'm not quite ready to be left alone yet." She repeated as if to herself, "Not ready."

Unwilling to subject himself to Delilah's moods any longer, Lucky said, "Just let me know when you are. When you're ready, your job will be waiting for you." Feeling the necessity to add a white lie, he said, "Some of the men in the tent have been asking about you."

"Really?" Delilah raised her bruised chin. "You can tell them I'll be back in another week or so when the swelling goes down and I'm steady on my feet." She added, "Josephina can stay until then."

"If she chooses."

Delilah glanced at the silent older woman and said stiffly, "Of course she chooses, don't you, Josephina?"

Replying directly to Lucky, Josephina said softly, "Senor Lucky has been very good to my Pedro. I will stay as long as he says it is necessary."

Delilah's face flamed. Barely concealing her anger, she replied, "Well, that's your answer, Lucky. She's happy to stay."

Wondering how he had ever been attracted to Delilah, Lucky avoided a direct response by saying as he tipped his hat, "I have to go back to work now."

He breathed a sigh of relief when he closed the tent flap behind him. He had made the necessary visit. He hoped it would not be necessary too soon again.

Tessa paused when footsteps sounded outside her cabin door as the midday sun climbed higher in the brilliant blue of the sky. She picked up the shotgun lying nearby, pointed it, and put her finger on the trigger. She remembered that Lucky had told her to keep it close to her during the day while she cooked, although he did not believe anyone would try anything during daylight hours. When cautioning her to keep the gun by her side, however, he had added that she didn't need to be a good shot. She only had to point that kind of gun in the right direction. That was what she did as the door swung open.

Tessa sighed with relief when she identified her visitor.

"Put the gun down, darlin'. You're shaking so hard that you might just pull the trigger by mistake."

"Lucky."

Uncertain exactly which of them closed the distance between them, Tessa flung herself into Lucky's arms and surrendered to the warmth of his kiss. She separated her lips, allowing him to deepen it seductively, and to scoop her up into his arms and easily carry her to her cot, where he kissed her again and again.

Breathless at the touch of his hands at the buttons of her dress, Tessa felt a moment's panic. She glanced at the bright light shining through the windows and protested, "It's full daylight, Lucky."

Lucky paused. "You've never made love in the light of day before?"

"You know I haven't," she whispered.

A small smile hovered at his mouth as he loosened the first button and replied, "There's always a first time."

"But someone will see!"

"Who, Tessa?"

Tessa swallowed nervously. "At least let me lock the door."

Lucky let her go, but she had just slipped the bar across the door when she turned to feel the rise of Lucky's passion against her. It was hard and warm as his lips brushed her cheek and he whispered, "I suppose you've never had a man pin you to the door with his passion, either, huh?"

"No."

He looked down into the wide gray eyes peering up into his and said, "Like I said, there's always a first time."

Raising her skirt, Lucky stripped down Tessa's underdrawers and slid himself inside her. Covering her gasp with his lips, he sucked her breath deep inside him, allowing his kiss to deepen, his hands to move more freely, his body to throb more hotly against hers as he began to stroke deep inside her.

Tessa gasped again when his movements grew more rapid. She closed her eyes and encircled his broad back with her arms, clutching him even harder as he pressed her tight against the wooden door. The hard surface rocked with his movements, imparting a pleasure close to pain. She did not protest when he raised her legs to encircle his waist and fitted her flat against him so he might sink himself more deeply. Breathing hard with each surge, gasping at the depth of his penetration, Tessa wondered at the glory Lucky brought her with his body. She responded spontaneously when he fitted himself to her even more tightly and took her still higher. Breathless at the sensations he evoked, she gasped his name with a brief exclamation of wonder that echoed in the silence of the cabin. They climaxed simultaneously and the world came to a shuddering halt.

Still holding her close, seeming unwilling to separate from her, Lucky whispered against her hair as he strove to regain control. Finally drawing back, he raised a hand to her chin and kissed her again, his tongue brushing hers before he whispered, "I'm supposed to be working in my tent, but I had to come here to see you. I couldn't wait until evening."

Tessa asked in a shaky whisper, "Are you going so soon?"

"Do you want me to go?"

"No."

Lucky replied hoarsely as he lifted her up into his arms, "That's all I wanted to know."

Walking the few steps to her cot, he laid her down and said softly, "Wait a minute." He removed his jacket and then unbuttoned his shirt to bare the broad, muscular expanse of his chest, then threw it aside. He stripped off his boots and belt. Within minutes he had stepped out of his trousers and underdrawers and stood unabashedly naked in front of her. He paused, frowning, as she took in the full extent of his masculine form. Her gaze traveled the length of his body, noting his supremely muscular tone, the length of his long, muscled legs, and then paused at the erection so apparent despite their recent lovemaking. He whispered in response, "You do that to me, Tessa."

He then added with a small smile, "Now it's your turn."

Slowly, appearing to savor every moment, he undressed her. First loosening her makeshift bun, he allowed her hair to cascade over the pillow in a splash of gold. He paused to stroke it gently, and then went to the buttons left undone on the front of her dress. He cursed softly, silently vowing to purchase a garment for her that was not so difficult to undo as he finally stripped it from her shoulders and bared her to the waist. His hands trembling, he slid the dress the rest of the way down her long legs, taking her underdraws with it. He halted only briefly at the juncture of her thighs before tossing them and her oversized shoes into the corner. Standing back, he said softly, "I've never seen you naked in the sunlight. You're beautiful, Tessa. I want to keep this picture in my mind forever."

Tessa was unable to speak. In lieu of words, she simply held out her arms in silent invitation.

Suddenly flesh to flesh, heat to heat, mouth to mouth with her, Lucky joined her as the joy of love swelled once more.

Sated at last, but only briefly, Lucky whispered against her lips, "I love you, Tessa."

"I love you, too."

Lucky slipped onto the cot beside her and looked down at Tessa as her words reverberated on the silence of the cabin. With a silent ache inside, he wondered if she realized what she had said. He did. She had said she loved him. But would her love change anything?

Something was different about them, and Harley knew what it was.

He watched as Lucky brought Tessa and her daily offerings into the tent to the cheers of the prospectors waiting for her. He pretended to consider the cards in his hand in an effort to make his presence in Lucky's tent credible, but in truth, he couldn't care less about them. Whatever money he could possibly make gambling was a mere pittance compared to the sum that his house earned nightly.

He inwardly sneered. His women were hardworking. They had to be. They had seen what happened to Clarice when she opposed him, and it was a lesson well learned. They were in a strange country and they knew that the only place where they would receive respect was in the house constructed especially for them. He had actually gone out of his way to keep them comfortable, bringing in a madam from France so they would be totally comfortable confiding in her. They did not realize, however, that everything he did was calculated to pay off richly for himself, and that the French madam he had hired secretly passed their confidences along to him.

Harley barely withheld his amusement. Madame Helene LeFleur was so afraid of him that she reported everything to him and would do anything he asked. He knew, for instance, that Jacqueline, a striking titian-haired woman, had tired of humdrum sex and now looked for customers whose appetites demanded the unusual. He also knew that Madame LeFleur steered some of her more aggressive patrons Jacqueline's way, knowing that her tolerance was high and that her own lust would counter theirs. The rewards had been extremely gratifying.

He also knew that Marietta and Desiree, both wide-eyed brunettes, were less forward; but when the bedroom door closed behind them, their play was worth the price charged and more. He was aware that Madame was not opposed to offering both women at the same time to one man under special conditions, because she knew that they would enjoy that deviation from the norm.

Then there were Michelle, Colette, Darlene, Evangeline, Denise, and Simone, of course. They had all come over on the ship with the disgraced Clarice and had performed well. Yet the customers of his bordello still looked for more.

Clarice's bedroom remained empty and a daily reminder of one who had believed she was immune to the rules of the house. He intended to fill that bedroom with the new "princess" of his establishment, the jewel in its crown.

Harley stared at Tessa with hidden heat as she walked toward the tables where the line of prospectors had already formed. Her reputation grew with every day that passed, and the men all but worshipped her.

It was generally known that Maggie had left the city to tend to Strike while he was ill. Noel Richman, who resented Nugget's absence at the mercantile, had spread the news. It was also generally known that Lucky had hired two men to watch over Tessa's cabin so that she would have no surprises awaiting her as night fell.

Lucky's early departure from the tent when most of the men were otherwise occupied had stirred little comment, and Harley had the feeling that everyone accepted his absence without thought. Tessa was, indeed, a "princess" to every man, and every day made Harley more determined to possess her for his own purposes. He realized, however, that he would not be able to accomplish that task easily.

Harley watched with a tightening in his gut as Lucky observed Tessa's actions with a proprietary eye. Everything was the same, yet different. He guessed the difference meant that Tessa was no longer a virgin, yet he was unsure if that realization made him happy or sad. He would not be able to ask the great amount he had expected for Tessa's virginity. But the new reality meant that she would be completely his to instruct. It was his intention to enjoy the experiences they would have, but also to make sure that she paid dearly for acting as if she were too good for him and then taking up with a common gambler. Yes, her payment for that mistake in judgment would be steep, indeed.

He was impatient and time was his enemy, but it was necessary that he wait until caution became lax and the right opportunity presented itself. He could not suffer another failure. His only consolation was the fact that the "medication" Madame had bought for him was safely secured in his bordello, and he knew that it was just a matter of using the right amount to guarantee Tessa's acceptance of him. Afterward, when she was well indoctrinated, he would see to it that Tessa accepted as many men as he deemed profitable, because she would be his virtual slave.

That delicious thought cheered Harley until Tessa's gaze caught and held Lucky's with an emotion so deep that his enjoyment was eclipsed by it. He swore silently that Tessa would look at him that way one day. After she did, and when he had had enough of her, he would then scorn her.

He would scorn her, damn her, he would scorn her!

"I don't want any more water, Maggie."

Maggie looked at Strike Walker, her heart aching as she placed the cup down on the table nearby. Nugget and she had arrived at Strike's claim to find him lying on a crude cot in his cabin, breathless, hardly able to move, and alone. It had not mattered to him that her gray hair was clasped back in an untidy bun, that her lined face was weary, that the men's trousers and shirt she wore were stained from the trail, or that Nugget's condition was similarly unkempt. His wordless gratitude at seeing them both had been profound.

Having arrived late in the evening several days earlier, they had set about to do their best for him, and Nugget was now chopping firewood outside. Tall pine trees surrounded the simple cabin set down in a hollow. The log structure was so isolated and hidden by the hills surrounding it that the noise from the closest mining camp a few miles away was unheard. It appeared that Strike's claim was in the middle of country that had been ravaged by gold seekers, yet still remained beautiful. She could understand why Strike had returned again and again to this spot over the past years. It was his home.

Surprisingly, it appeared that Strike had stocked his shelves with plenty of food for the three of them even without the stores that Maggie and Nugget had brought with them. It was obvious, however, that Strike had barely managed to shelve his staple supplies of flour, lard, bacon, and salt before becoming ill. Few of the packages had been opened, and Strike had become even thinner and his skin grayer than when they'd last seen him.

The steady sound of Nugget's chopping echoed off the nearby hills. He had left Maggie alone to care for Strike, and she was glad. She wanted time with the old fellow, and there was so little time left.

Strike's eyes were bleary and half-lidded as he struggled to breathe. It obviously took more energy to eat than Strike felt was worth expending, but Maggie nevertheless persisted.

"Maggie," Strike gasped, "I'm not going to get better."

Maggie managed an understanding smile. To her, Strike was not a stranger that she had met only once before, and she knew he felt the same. She sensed that similar episodes in their pasts had knit them together with an unusual understanding. She felt instinctively that although Strike handled the weight of his sorrow with a smile and a good word for all, they recognized in each other a need to satisfy long ago pain.

Maggie replied softly, "I just want you to know that you're not alone."

"I know." Strike's voice softened. "I was alone for a long time. Nugget helped to ease that feeling while he was here, but life got too hard for him in this place, and he chose an easier way. I wish I could have done that, too, but I just couldn't."

Maggie nodded with understanding bright in her eyes as he continued. "I don't know how it all happened, Maggie, with my wife beside me one day, and dead the next. I blamed myself because I should have realized the danger in attempting to cross that wash, but the wave of water that flooded it came so fast and so deep that I barely survived myself. There was nothing I could do to save Cindy. It was all gone, Maggie, the wagon, my horses, and my wife. I felt my life was over. I didn't find Cindy's body until days later and I buried her in a spot where I was certain no one would find her but me."

Strike's bitter laughter was short. "I was wrong there, too, because when I visited her next time, the grave had been dug up and she was gone."

Maggie wiped away an errant tear.

"Don't cry. I resolved a time long ago to face whatever

life had left for me with a smile. I don't want to make you sad."

"It's just that I understand."

"I know you do. I know you recognize that things ain't always the way you want them to be, so when you find a person who's worthwhile, you do the best you can to make sure everything turns out right for them. That's the way I feel about Lucky and Tessa. They made me feel like they was good and strong inside and could rise above whatever happened to them. They made me feel like the world's a better place because of them being here. I had the feelin' that if Cindy's and my children had made it, they would've been like that. I made my feelings known as best I could, and I liked what you did for them both. You showed how much you cared, like my Cindy, and that's why your being here is important to me."

"I knew it would be."

"Nugget knew it, too. He's a nice fella and a good friend."

"I know."

His difficulty in breathing returned sharply and Strike managed a smile as he whispered with sudden urgency, "Call him in, will you?"

Not bothering to reply, Maggie went to the door and called, bringing Nugget quickly to Strike's side. Strike said weakly, "I just wanted to say thanks to both of you. There ain't many folks a man can call his friends. It's good to know—"

Strike's statement ended abruptly when his rheumy eyes went suddenly blank. His lips parted slightly with the last gurgle of life, and then there was silence. Seconds passed before Nugget slid his hand over Strike's vacant stare to close his eyes. His gaze was heavy with unshed tears while Maggie stared at Strike's still form.

"He's dead, Maggie."

Maggie nodded.

"He had what he wanted, his friends close to him when he died."

She nodded again.

"But I wish, I wish—"

Maggie stood up and smiled through her tears. "I wish I had more time with Strike and I'm thinking that you wish the same thing, too, Nugget. Yet it doesn't mean too much what we wish. Like you said, Strike had what he wanted at the end, and he also achieved a kind of absolution for something he couldn't help. Strangely enough, he somehow gave me peace, too, and I'm thinking that's part of the reason why he wanted me here. It's time now for us to finish it all for him like friends, with a decent, godly burial."

"Yes, ma'am."

Nugget stood up and Maggie added more quietly, "Thank you for bringing me here, Nugget."

Surprising her, Nugget stepped forward and hugged her tight. He said hoarsely, "I'm glad you came. It meant a lot to Strike, and it means a lot to me, too."

Maggie laid her weary head on Nugget's shoulder, unable to reply as her tears flowed.

Tessa finally admitted to herself that there was something she needed to do. The task had been lying heavily on her mind and now she was determined to do it as she climbed the nearby hill and walked toward the inhabited tents nearby.

Tessa's steps slowed. The sun was shining, and the ground was damp but rocky underfoot. She had finished cooking early, which surprised her, considering the time that Lucky and she had taken together earlier.

Tessa's smiled at the memory of waking in Lucky's strong arms that morning, of feeling his kiss on her lips. She had felt supreme contentment when his strong body joined hers. She would never forget the way his lips moved against her hair with loving words, or the way he looked at her when he stood up and prepared to dress. It was as if he was as reluctant as she to end their moments together.

Several days had passed since that fateful night when Lucky and she had first made love. With each day his appeal for her seemed to grow.

She loved the way his heavy, black hair slipped onto his forehead, almost demanding her touch. Then there was the way the coal black eyes under his thick lashes regarded her so sensually. She remembered distinctly the way her heart thumped when he turned his profile toward her and she glimpsed the strong nose and sharply chiseled cheekbones that made his appearance so distinctive. And his mouth. A chill ran down Tessa's spine at the memory of his smile and the thought of the things his mouth did to her when his tongue stroked her so intimately.

The power Lucky exuded had originally affected her more deeply than she liked. His high-handed attitude had bothered her, but she had learned that it was a manifestation of his concern for her welfare.

She had discovered that she loved to sate the silent hunger for her hidden behind his autocratic facade, and that hunger seemed consistently present. He had become her helpmate, her lover, her closest friend; and in a way, he had become her family. But she was aware of the heavy weight those words carried. Lucky had said he loved her. The intimacies between them had grown deeper and more fulfilling, but the pressures of life in the transient atmosphere of San Francisco seemed to get in the way. She loved Lucky. She no longer had any desire to return to Iowa. The life she had known there was a part of her past. She had been born anew on the trail west, and Lucky had been there to help her grow and accept the person she had become.

Having reached the top of the rise, Tessa looked at the cluster of tents that crowded the area. She knew the one she was looking for was among them, but she wasn't sure which one it was. She had been neglectful in ignoring the attack Delilah had suffered. She had only had one, disturbing conversation with the woman.

She now realized that the other woman mourned the place she had held in Lucky's heart. She could not hold that against her, and she needed to express her sympathy to Delilah, who had suffered at the hands of an unknown assailant just as she had. Especially since Delilah no longer knew the luxury of being held in Lucky's arms.

She hoped never to be in that position, where the emotion between Lucky and her was a thing of the past.

Stopping a boy who walked past, she asked, "Can you tell me which one of these tents belongs to Delilah, ahh . . . ?" Suddenly aware that she did not know Delilah's last name, Tessa went silent.

"Everybody knows where Delilah's tent is because she's so noisy. It's the last one in that row," the boy directed.

The boy scampered away as Tessa's frown darkened. Noisy. She could not help wondering if the noises coming from Delilah's tent originated from pain, or from another source entirely.

Tessa took a breath as she approached the tent. Outside, she asked hesitantly, "Delilah, are you in there?"

An almost unrecognizable voice responded, "Who is it?"

"It's me, Tessa White."

A harsh mumbling sounded inside the tent before the flap was pushed aside and a matronly Mexican woman left, frowning. Delilah then responded, "Come in, Tessa."

* * *

Delilah barely maintained the meager smile she could manage without cracking her bruised lips. She saw Tessa halt to stare at her in dismay. Delilah forced a laugh that she did not feel and said, "I suppose I don't look like myself, battered and bruised as I am, but you look lovely as usual."

Regaining her voice, Tessa smiled and responded, "I was lucky that the men who kidnapped me went out of their way not to mark me."

"It's likely they had other uses in mind for you."

"I suppose. I try not to give that possibility much thought. I was fortunate to have been rescued before anything could happen." Tessa went momentarily silent and then added, "Of course, my rescue came at the expense of someone's life."

"Yes, Clarice LeBlanc's life, I hear. But that wasn't much of a loss. She was on her way out anyway."

Tessa appeared startled by her response, and Delilah shrugged. "It's the truth, and I've never been one to mince words."

"I suppose some see it that way." Obviously anxious to change the subject, Tessa offered, "I came because we share a terrifying experience. While I managed to survive it unmarked, you've obviously suffered badly."

Delilah cooed, "I got the beating of my life, but I can say in a way that it was worth it. Lucky has been so good to me."

"Yes, that's his way."

"It's more than just his way." Delilah continued

deliberately. "Lucky and I were very close at one time. I think you know that this tent was intimately familiar to him—he woke up here in the morning more times than he could count." Noting that her words cut Tessa, Delilah went on. "The truth is that I was beginning to believe he had tired of me, but this particular difficulty has proved that I was so wrong."

"It has?"

"You don't think that I'd be able to afford a full-time maid to handle my difficulties alone, do you?" When Tessa frowned, Delilah added, "You saw her leave when you entered. Lucky pays her to take care of me and to keep to herself about what goes on here."

"What goes on here?"

"Lucky is a virile man, Tessa. He comes to see me regularly, and he doesn't come here for his health."

"But you're still suffering the result of a beating!"

"I'm not that sick that I don't like the pleasure of Lucky lying on top of me. It's worth any discomfort I might feel." She added, "Oh, and I want to thank you for whatever you did to take care of him for the short while that I couldn't. Lucky's a randy fella. He needed someone to fill in for me." Aware that Tessa looked taken aback, she continued with feigned acceptance. "I'm sorry if what I said hurts your sensibilities, but I'm realistic. He had to go somewhere, and the closest woman is usually the place a man goes when he's cut off from what he really wants. I'll be able to take care of all his needs in a little while. He knows that, and so do I, so I don't hold anything against the woman or women he visits in between."

Deriving a surge of enjoyment from Tessa's shocked expression, Delilah said, "I admit it bothers me that Lucky might still be visiting others while I'm not at my best, but I know the situation is only temporary. You can see that I've already started applying my makeup, which means it won't be long before I'm back completely. Then I'll resume my responsibilities. Lucky has assured me that everything will be exactly as it was before, which suits me fine."

Delilah noted the backward step Tessa took before saying, "Well, I came to ask if you needed any help."

Delilah replied offhandedly, "Of course I don't, dear. Whatever help I need is readily supplied, but I do appreciate your asking." Unwilling to allow Tessa a response that might push her tentative control over the edge, she said abruptly, "But the truth is that I'm still not at my best and I'd like to rest for a while if you don't mind."

"Of . . . of course."

Delilah added, "If Josephina is out there waiting, just tell her to come inside. I have some things for her to wash out for me."

"All right."

"Good-bye."

Noting Tessa's almost imperceptible stagger when she turned and raised the flap to leave, Delilah did her best not to laugh aloud. *Witch . . . thief . . . pretender! I have taken care of you!*

Delilah's chest heaved as she withheld the emotion raging through her. The simpering blonde witch came here to help her, did she? Well, she had set her straight, and if she had stretched the truth a bit in doing so, she did not care. If she didn't miss her guess, she knew what that *innocent* was thinking right now, and Lucky was the last person she would want to see.

The thought struck Delilah that Lucky might come to her for an explanation, but she could pretend innocence as easily as the blonde witch did. She would do what she needed to do in order to get him back, and when that happened, she wouldn't let go again.

Memory of the expression on Tessa's face made her laugh aloud. Lucky would have a hard time talking his way out of this one.

Josephina entered unexpectedly, and Delilah cursed aloud. She ordered, "I need you to rinse out my personal items. Do it quickly and get out of my sight. I wish to rest for a while."

"*Sí, senorita.*"

Delilah closed her eyes and reclined even farther on her cot. She needed to get well quickly. She had much to do and she was impatient to get it done.

Chapter Ten

It was nearing sunset when Nugget's wagon pulled up in front of Maggie's cabin at last. Smoke escaping from the chimney rose into the gradually darkening sky, and Maggie knew that Tessa was probably getting her meal ready to be transported down to Lucky's tent. The fact that life was going on consoled her.

The previous few days had passed as if in a dream that remained with her after she awakened. Nugget and she had buried Strike near the cabin he had called home, and Nugget had said he would see what he could do about having the claim that Strike had recently registered on that land transferred to his name. She had smiled at the realization that Nugget would not make that effort because he expected the stream beside the cabin to yield great deposits of gold, but because it had been the home of his friend, and it was his final resting place.

Maggie looked at Nugget as the horses drew to a halt in front of the cabin. She climbed down from the wagon before Nugget could help her and turned to face him. Tears were bright in her eyes as she said, "Thank you again. I will never forget that journey."

"Neither will I."

Surprising her for the second time, Nugget hugged her spontaneously and then climbed back into the wagon as she approached the front door. The wagon rattled back down the trail behind her, and Maggie knew Nugget had chosen not to talk to Tessa because his emotions were too raw. Again, she understood.

She was not looking forward to telling Tessa about Strike's demise. When Tessa came to the door, her expression sober, Maggie entered silently. Tears filled her eyes as she said simply, "Strike is gone."

Contrary to Maggie's expectation, Tessa did not react right away. Instead, she murmured, "Strike was one of the first to make me feel welcome here. I didn't want to lose him."

"Neither did I."

Tessa moved into Maggie's arms then and hugged her tight, her eyes remaining strangely dry. Closing her eyes wearily, Maggie accepted Tessa's consolation. She was unsure how much time had passed before they heard another wagon on the path to the cabin.

Maggie looked outside and said, "It's Lucky. He's probably coming to help transport your food to his tent."

Tessa nodded with a frown that caused Maggie to inquire softly, "Is anything wrong, Tessa?"

"No, nothing." She attempted a smile. "It hasn't been a good day for me, that's all."

Maggie nodded. She turned at the sound of the wagon coming to a halt outside the cabin. She braced herself for Lucky's entrance.

Lucky pushed open the door, the smile on his face fading when he spotted Maggie standing there. He said thickly, "Is it over, then?"

"Yes. Nugget and I buried Strike near the cabin he called home."

Lucky nodded. "The way it should be." Then covering the distance between the two women, he reached out to draw both of them into his embrace.

Something was wrong.

Lucky watched Tessa smile stiffly as she served the men in his tent their evening meal. He could not put his finger on what it was, but he sensed that she was upset by something beyond the bad news Maggie had brought home with her. He knew Tessa had become inordinately fond of Strike over the short course of their acquaintance. She said there was a special quality in the old prospector that she had come to revere. He knew how deeply the news of Strike's death had affected her, yet she seemed angry as well as grief-stricken.

Lucky saw Pedro glance again at Tessa as he worked steadily beside her. The difference in her was obvious to him, too. Neither Tessa nor he had mentioned Strike's death to anyone else. His grief was too fresh to put into words. The old man had become a friend who was more important to him than he had realized, and his death was another in long line of losses. He knew Tessa felt similarly about the old codger, and he had expected that once they were out of sight of the cabin, Tessa would collapse in his arms. But that hadn't happened, and the silence that had reigned between them once they were alone was so complete that he had not dared to breach it.

He found he missed their usual easy conversation during the ride. Tessa had confided in him as he was certain she had in no other, and he had done the same. He had cherished each whispered word she had uttered, each confidence she had revealed, every moment that brought them closer than before. He admitted to himself that his first thought upon seeing Maggie in the cabin was that Tessa and he would no longer enjoy the seclusion that Maggie's absence had afforded.

And then Maggie had said the words he dreaded to hear. Everything had changed at that moment, but to a degree that he did not understand.

Determined to put an end to the silence between them, Lucky strode toward the table where she was still standing and asked tightly, "Are you done here, Tessa?"

Her nod was his only response.

"Let's go, then."

Taking an empty pot in one hand and her arm in the other, Lucky did not hesitate as he drew her toward the door.

Something was wrong between Tessa and Lucky. Harley could see it, sense it. He could not explain it, but he was filled with a feeling of glee. He had been waiting for a rift between Tessa and Lucky. He would now watch the situation closely. It would be no problem to do so because he had established himself as a gambler in Lucky's tent over the past week, and Lucky turned no one away from his tables.

When he was ready, he would hire two more thugs. There were many men hungry for a fast dollar in this town. His plans for Tessa would not fall through this time because he would not be rushed into meeting someone else's agenda.

Harley inwardly snorted. He had made sure that Delilah suffered heavily for that first, mistaken plan. She would not bother him again.

Harley turned his cards down and stood wearily before making an excuse to walk to the tent exit. He watched from there as Lucky swung Tessa up onto the wagon seat, his expression as sober as hers as he started the wagon into motion.

Harley frowned after regarding them a few moments longer. On second thought, he would find the two men immediately. If he did not miss his guess, he should make his move right away.

Tessa looked steadfastly forward as the wagon rattled along the trail and a myriad of thoughts raced through her mind. The overland route to San Francisco had been fraught with losses she had never anticipated, but then she had met Lucky, Maggie, and Strike and their love had lessened those burdens.

Now Strike was gone, and she feared Lucky had never really been hers in the first place. Her usual self-confidence was assailed by doubt.

The silence stretched uncomfortably long between them, as Lucky negotiated the trail. Waiting only until they were no longer visible from the tent, Lucky drew the wagon to an unexpected halt and asked, "What's wrong, Tessa?" Startled from her thoughts, she turned toward Lucky as he pressed, "I know that Strike came to mean more to you than a mere friend, but I'm thinking that the shock of his death isn't all that's come between us."

Tessa looked up at Lucky. He was so handsome, so strong, so virile, and so very tender. He had overcome her inexperience with his gentleness, showing a need for her that she had grown to love. She had given to him selflessly and with a joy that she had never anticipated. He was everything she could ever want in a man, and her heart filled at the sight of him. Had she been a fool in believing that he could love a woman as common as she, a person who had arrived in San Francisco a "walker" and who had no prospects at all without him? Did he think of her as just another one of his women? Was she just a temporary challenge that would soon bore him? Would he revert to Delilah, or a woman like her, who could offer him greater variety in lovemaking than she could? Had he truly kept Delilah on the sidelines until she recuperated?

A single tear slipped down Tessa's cheek, and she brushed it away.

Dropping the reins at first sight of that tear, Lucky grasped Tessa's shoulders and turned her averted face toward him.

"Tell me what's wrong, Tessa. I need to know."

Tessa looked at Lucky silently. He deserved the truth. "I loved Strike, you know," she began slowly.

"I know, but you knew he was sick. We both expected Maggie's news. There's something else bothering you. I need to know what it is."

"It's just . . . it's just that two losses in one day are difficult."

"Two losses? If you're referring to Maggie's return cutting into our personal time together, it needn't."

"No." Tessa shook her head. "I . . . I went to visit Delilah today."

"Delilah?"

"I thought it was only right. She was attacked just as I was, even though she suffered a beating that I escaped."

Lucky did not respond and Tessa continued. "She told me how good you've been to her."

Uncertain where she was heading with that statement, Lucky frowned and said, "I felt I owed it to her. She's been a loyal employee."

Tessa persevered. "Delilah said you've taken care of her, that you hired a maid to sit with her, and that you provided her with everything she needs until she recuperates."

"That's right."

"Because she was a loyal employee?"

Lucky pulled back. He responded slowly, aware that he had to tell the truth. "I felt I owed her not only because she was a loyal employee, but because she was more than just an employee to me before you arrived in San Francisco."

"Because she was able to do things for you that I cannot."

"No, that's not true. I helped her because she was badly beaten and alone, and I know what it's like to be alone."

"Because she was temporarily unable to . . . to work for you."

"That's right if that's all you mean." Lucky stared at her. "But I don't think it is."

Tessa's voice was choked. "I need to know if you've visited Delilah at her tent since she was attacked, Lucky."

"Of course I have."

"You didn't tell me you went to see her."

"It was something I needed to do."

"Did you tell her that you were saving her spot for her?"

"Yes."

Forging ahead despite the pain she felt when Lucky confirmed everything that Delilah had said, Tessa pressed, "Just to be clear, did Delilah fill a part of your life that I filled while Maggie was gone?"

Lucky blinked. He took a breath. "In a way."

"Yes or no, Lucky."

"Yes, she did, but it was never the same between her and me as it is between us."

"Was I the one lacking, or was she?"

Suddenly angry, Lucky demanded, "What do you want me to say, Tessa? Do you want me to demean Delilah? Or do you want me to say that her expertise by far outstrips yours? Do you want me to tell you that she satisfied me fully in the past? Do you want me to tell you that I said the same things to her that I said to you when we lay in each other's arms?"

Unable to bear any more, Tessa put her hands over her ears and rasped, "Don't say anything else. Just take me back to the cabin."

"Tessa, you don't understand."

"I *do* understand, and that's the problem, Lucky." Her face flushed and her eyes bright, Tessa whispered, "I understand everything too well."

"Tessa, listen to me."

"I have to go back to the cabin now. Maggie is expecting me and she is grieving."

"Please listen."

"I don't think that's wise. I'm out of my element in San Francisco, Lucky. I belong in a place like Iowa, on a farm where life is simple and nothing is expected of a person beyond hard work and commitment."

"I want that, too, Tessa."

"I know. You want it all, and you'll probably get it. The only problem is that I can't be the one to give it to you." When Lucky was temporarily at a loss for a response, Tessa continued softly. "Please take me home now, Lucky."

"But—"

"Please."

Too stunned to think of an adequate response, Lucky slapped the reins on the horse's back. His mind raced in circles as he started the wagon up the trail again. When he was finished carrying her things inside, Tessa stood in the doorway, barring his entrance. "You can purchase those tickets back to Iowa for me tomorrow, Lucky. It's time for me to go home. I'll pay you back. I give you my word on that." She forced a smile as she added, "I tried, but San Francisco just doesn't fit me well enough to stay."

Tessa stepped back into the cabin and closed the door behind her. After standing motionless for long moments, Lucky left without a word. There seemed nothing left to say.

* * *

Delilah lay on the cot in her tent as night darkened around her. She turned the kerosene lamp up higher to shed more light. She was restless. She regretted some of the things she had said to Tessa earlier that afternoon because she sensed they might come back to haunt her. She knew she had stunned the young woman with the many half truths and outright lies she had uttered so nonchalantly. She had been temporarily happy to see the blonde witch turn pale with every sentence she spoke, but concerns had begun crossing her mind. What if Tessa told Lucky everything she'd said and Lucky became angry enough to revoke all his previous promises to her? Lucky had guaranteed her a job in his tent. Where would she go if he changed his mind and she didn't look good enough to get a respectable job after she healed? She was able to walk around now—barely— but she did not want anyone, most especially the men who had pressed for her favors, to see her the way she looked now. She kept Josephina as her servant so that the woman could shop for her and prepare her food, making it unnecessary for her to be seen until she was ready.

Those concerns grew greater as the night darkened. Most upsetting of all, however, was the possibility that retribution against the man who had stolen her only asset might slip away. She had been unable to devise a way to bring Harley down. She wanted him to suffer the way she had suffered, but he was wealthy and was respected for his success in a place where success was applauded and defeat was ignored. He had no family, no particular woman in his life that he kept closer to him than any other. The only things that were truly important to Harley were the sense of power that his money afforded him, the fear he commanded, and the wealth he had accumulated. All those things signified success in his mind.

She wanted to take those things away from him. She wanted to make him feel the frantic sense of loss that she felt! She wanted to see him reduced to what he so despised—commonness.

But how?

Delilah got up and limped to the opening of her tent to stare down at the city lights twinkling below her. The city had an almost fairy-tale quality at night when its many faults were hidden by darkness. No one would believe that San Francisco had sprung up from the ashes of a fire only recently and that—

Delilah's blackened eyes widened with sudden realization.

Fire.

Why hadn't she thought of it before? San Francisco was a tinderbox with piles of sawdust and other combustibles lying about everywhere. Trash was also piled high from the endless migration of men who abandoned their belongings on the streets rather than carry extra baggage with them to the gold fields. No one would give it a second thought if Harley's magnificent bordello succumbed to one of the many fires of mysterious origin that continually struck the city.

But Harley might rebuild his whorehouse with money that he had hidden. But where did he keep his money? She was positive he did not trust banks in the city. No one with any sense did. Would he conceal it where the Frenchwomen he had brought to his house might find it? No. The only other possible location was his personal quarters. She recalled that massive, marble staircase, the magnificent book-lined study, and the impressive foyer that he had rushed her through in order that no one would see a woman like her there.

Delilah knew what she must do. She would destroy both his lavish bordello and his impressive home. With the trappings of success gone, Harley Knox would then be as alone and desperate as she.

Exhilaration rushed through Delilah, lending her new strength. But she needed to accomplish everything quickly, before her own house of cards collapsed.

Delilah realized this very night would be ideal. She had sent Josephina home in order to be rid of her for a few hours. The stupid woman believed Delilah Pierce was too weak to do anything but rest while she was gone. After all, her patient was bedridden and unsteady on her feet. Josephina would tell anyone who asked that Delilah could not possibly have set fire to Harley Knox's establishments.

Delilah turned and walked toward the corner where the kerosene for her lamp was stored. Josephina had purchased a new supply just that morning. If the old woman noticed that the can was empty again, Delilah would just claim that she had spilled it. In her "weakened condition," she would be totally believable.

Delilah's heart pounded with excitement. She would need to wait until it was darker and everyone else on the hill was asleep. She would then steal down into the city and accomplish her task. Harley Knox's residence and business would be engulfed before anyone knew that she was gone.

Delilah laughed aloud. She had vowed that she would get her revenge if it were the last thing she ever did, and tonight was the night.

Lucky sat at his crowded card table in a tent that was alive with music and laughter, but his mind was not on the game. He glanced around him at the frivolity of the tent, at the fiddler and piano player in the corner who had arrived to play as loudly as possible, adding to the din of shouted guffaws, the slapping of cards, and the loud groans that often accompanied the outcome of a game. Yet he saw only the image of a fair-haired woman whose gaze had touched his heart, but whose warmth had gone suddenly cold. He did not comprehend how Tessa could have changed in an instant from the lover who had become his life, into a stranger.

The raucous sounds had become almost deafening as the evening progressed, but Tessa had left hours earlier and had not been subjected to the excesses that sometimes occurred in the tent. He was glad.

He loved her innocence and purity. He did not want the more sordid side of the tent's amusements to touch her in any way. He wanted to protect her from that. He cherished everything that she was and wanted her to be with him for the rest of his life. He had begun believing that Tessa felt the same. He had gone to the cabin that very evening with the hope that he could convince her they were meant to face the future together. He still wasn't sure what had gone wrong. He had been unable to deny any of the truths that Delilah had told Tessa, but his honesty seemed only to confirm something darker in her mind, something so dark that it had driven Tessa to decide to return to Iowa, debts and all.

"We're waiting, Lucky, and we're getting damned tired of it."

Lucky looked up at the frustrated prospector sitting across from him. He growled, "Hold your horses! I'm thinking."

"You mean you're dreaming! Come on. I don't have time to waste. I have to go back to the diggings tomorrow."

Casting his confusion aside, Lucky dealt the cards.

Delilah glanced outside her tent furtively. The night had grown darker, the tents around hers had gone still, and the sky had become overcast enough to allow her the anonymity she sought. Yet the outlandish shade of her hair was still bright enough to be seen and remembered.

Glancing around her with frustration, Delilah spied an oversized dress that Josephina had left behind. Smiling, she snatched it up and slipped it over her head. The garment was too large for her and the coarse cotton scratched her skin, but she knew she was unrecognizable and her discomfort was only temporary. She then picked up the shawl the maid had also left behind and slipped it over her brightly colored hair.

When her injured ribs caused her to hunch over, Delilah realized that her posture aided the disguise. No one would recognize her as the flamboyantly dressed, proud woman she had formerly been, because, Delilah realized with mounting horror, she was not that woman any longer.

Hatred was carved deeply into the lines of her face as Delilah picked up the heavy kerosene container. She tied the shawl around her head more tightly, and slipped out into the darkness.

"I heard what you said to Lucky, Tessa. You didn't mean it, did you?"

"I don't want to talk about it, Maggie."

The two of them were lying in their beds in the darkened cabin as Maggie said, "You know that it isn't wise to make a decision that will affect the rest of your life at a time of loss, don't you? Strike was only an acquaintance, but he touched your life. You and Lucky were two of the people he spoke about just before he died. He claimed that you two were—"

"Please, I don't want to talk about it."

"Tessa . . ."

Tessa looked at the dear woman whose concern for her was written on her aging face. "I know you're worried that I haven't made the right decision, but Lucky was happy and content with his life before I came. Now he isn't anymore. I was happy and content with my life when I was in Iowa, too, but I'm not anymore, either. The solution to those problems seems simple to me. I should go home. I should've gone home earlier, and if I hadn't been so stubborn, I would have."

"It wasn't stubbornness, Tessa. It was determination to stand on your own two feet after your losses. I respected you for that, and so did Lucky."

"He may respect me, but I don't think he really wants me."

"How do you know what he wants? I think he sees something in you that he doesn't see in anyone else."

Tessa's troubled expression deepened. "You're right, I don't really know what he wants. That's the problem."

"What about you, Tessa? What do *you* want?"

"Don't you see, Maggie? I want Lucky, but not unless he wants me, too."

Maggie sighed. She said unexpectedly, "We're just going around in circles here because we're tired. Sleep on it, Tessa. That can't do any harm, and tomorrow is a new day."

"A new day won't change how I feel."

"Go to sleep. Things always look brighter in the morning."

"Maggie—"

"Good night, Tessa."

Sadness enveloped Tessa as Maggie rolled over and fell asleep. She turned her head onto a pillow smelling of fresh air and sunshine. She remembered the loving moments that Lucky and she had spent there. She loved him, but the true test of her love was yet to come. Could she take those tickets tomorrow and allow Lucky the freedom that he seemed to want?

She knew the answer to that question.

The knowledge that she would soon be lying in this bed for the last time was more than she could bear, and Tessa closed her eyes.

Delilah walked slowly along the street in front of the elaborate bordello that Harley had constructed. The night had deepened, but there was more traffic outside the establishment than she had imagined. Expensively suited men were arriving and leaving regularly, preventing her approach. She had not considered that possibility. She had believed that most of the patrons of the establishment would already have arrived by that hour. It was obvious that she was wrong.

Caustic laughter escaped her throat when another of those expensively dressed men gave her a wide birth as she limped along the street. She looked like an old crone carrying a container that they did not bother to identify. As a matter of fact, they hardly acknowledged her existence.

So it had come to that.

Delilah's anger heightened. They would all regret their behavior soon.

She found what she was looking for when she noticed a small alleyway beside the house where supplies were delivered. Slipping into the shadows there, she opened the container and splashed the rear entrance liberally. She then reached into her pocket for a match, struck one, and threw it toward the door.

Laughing almost madly as the flames roared to life and quickly engulfed the rear of the building, she hurried again to the front of the house. She splashed more kerosene on the front steps, grateful that no one was on the street to witness her act as she tossed another match. She stepped back, waiting only until the entrance and roof of the bordello were alight with fire and the screams inside indicated panic. She then hurried, with her weakened leg throbbing, toward the street where Harley resided.

So intent on her purpose was she that Delilah did not look back to see that the flames soared higher with every persistent gust of wind. She paid no attention to the chaos that erupted as the blaze popped and swelled, as the wall of flames roared higher and sparks flew on swirling currents of air onto neighboring buildings, where the fire flared anew. She neither saw nor cared that desperate men and women emerged onto the street, their nightclothes singed and burned, as they fled to the hills in a mass exodus. Instead, she headed for the house that she remembered so well.

Delilah reached the street breathlessly, aware only that the heat surrounding her seemed to grow greater with each passing moment. It was getting more difficult to breathe, but even that thought was swept aside when she recalled her uncertainty in approaching Harley's house weeks earlier. She remembered his haughty manner when he pushed her up the stairs ahead of him and then glanced around to be certain no one had seen her enter. She would never forget her first impression of the elaborate interior of the home, or the way Harley pulled her roughly through the closest doorway so that no one would see her. Harley would regret each and every one of those moments when he stood over the burnt remains of the residence he was so proud of.

Delilah slipped to the rear entrance and splashed her dwindling supply of kerosene there. She tossed a match but did not wait to see the area burst into flame. She hurried to the front entrance, where she used up the remainder of the kerosene before tossing another match. Mesmerized by the flames that burst into play, she watched as the blaze consumed the building more rapidly than even she had imagined it could. Gleefully, she tossed another, then another match into the blaze and then stepped back to observe the house's demise. So entranced was she that she paid little attention to the stiff sea breeze that showered her with glowing cinders. Nor did she note the intense pillars of flame that were igniting nearby houses and jumping toward the plaza where the canvas tents glowed with merriment.

The storm of burning embers grew thicker. She felt the intense heat of the fires and stepped back again. As residents of the area shoved her relentlessly from side to side in their efforts to escape, she realized that everything around her was burning.

She saw that her only chance to escape the flames was a single route crowded with people and horses, made unmanageable by the falling debris.

She panicked. Picking up her empty container, she joined the anxious throng only to be jostled and pushed from side to side. She fell behind as those more steady on their feet surged forward.

The smoke thickened and the heat intensified. Coughing, her eyes tearing and her leg weakening, Delilah dropped the kerosene container and attempted to go on, but her injured leg would not cooperate.

Delilah looked around her. Was there no one who would help her? Was there no one who cared enough to rescue her?

Aware that her dire situation was of her own making, Delilah forced herself onward, only to have her leg collapse underneath her as a final exodus of people rushed through the heavy smoke and fiery cinders. She gasped when an ember ignited the shawl that concealed the bright color of her hair. She tossed it away.

It was too hot to breathe, and the smoke was too thick. The steady downpour of burning cinders continued to sear her skin as she struggled to regain her feet.

She stood up at last! Coughing and sputtering, she limped toward the narrow avenue that still remained open between the flames, and exhilaration swept her mind. She would make it, and she would win. Harley would never recover from his loss.

Coughing, still struggling for each breath, Delilah approached the narrowing escape route as quickly as her weak leg would allow. She did not see the last wooden structure on the street appear to billow as the flames devoured it. She paid no attention to the gust of wind that shook it with unexpected force. Nor was she warned by the groan of collapsing walls the moment before it crashed onto the street in a fiery shower, blocking the only route left open to her.

Delilah's battered eyes widened. Overcome by the heat, she fell to the ground. She cried out over the din of crackling flames and falling timbers, but no sound emerged from her throat as the fire she had set roared higher, and then consumed her.

Harley smelled smoke. He heard the explosion of sound the moment before the ceiling of Lucky's tent burst into flame. Because his table was near the exit, he was among the first to leave, but he stopped abruptly in the doorway. The city of San Francisco was aflame!

Panicking, he saw that his bordello, formerly one of

the most magnificent structures in the city, was on fire. He started toward it, consoling himself that everything within it could be replaced: the air of luxury, the imported furniture, even the Frenchwomen. The only thing that could not be replaced was the sum in the strongbox that he had concealed under the floorboards of his luxurious office there.

He needed to get it! He could not bear to start all over again.

Running toward the burning streets, battling the pushing and screaming residents who fled past, Harley forged on toward the raging fire. He coughed and sputtered, choking on the smoke-heavy air. He beat out fiery sparks that rained down onto his hair and clothing and emerged at last on the street where his bordello stood. Hardly able to bear the extreme heat, he halted abruptly and watched the edifice that had been his pride and joy collapse in an ocean of flame.

It was gone! All of it! He was too late!

Harley fell to his knees as the smoke thickened and flurries of burning particles seared his skin. Unable to bear the ever-increasing heat, he covered his face, but there was no relief. His eyes and throat burned unmercifully. He looked briefly behind him to see that the ocean of flame had spread, flooding the remaining area with rivulets of fire.

Comprehension of his situation came in a sudden rush. There was no way out this time. There was no escape from what was to be his end.

But . . . but he was certain he would have achieved all his dreams of power and glory if he had just had a little more time. He would even have been able to manipulate this last disaster to his advantage. He could have. He was sure of it. All he had needed was a little more time.

But he had no more time. The fire overtook him.

"Do you smell smoke?"

Those words had barely escaped Tessa's lips in the darkness of Maggie's cabin when she heard the unmistakable sounds of chaos coming closer. Jumping to her feet with Maggie close behind her, she flung open the door to see smoke-stained men and women in all manner of undress climbing the trail in their direction. She ran toward them, and then stopped still when she saw the night sky alight with the glare of fire.

The city was ablaze!

Grasping the arm of the nearest man who stumbled toward her, she gasped, "What happened?"

"I don't know." The man coughed and sputtered as he replied, "All's I know is that I was having a good time in a tent on the square when all of a sudden it burst into flame. I don't know how or when it all happened. Just that it did."

Horrified, Tessa stared down into San Francisco Plaza. She saw the tents were caught up in the blaze consuming the city. One of the tents exploded unexpectedly before her eyes and Tessa gasped. Aware that the smoked-blackened stranger was still speaking, she interrupted, "Lucky Monroe's tent . . . did everybody get out all right?"

"I don't know."

"That's where I came from." Another fellow stumbled onto the ground as he continued hoarsely. "It all happened so fast. One minute we was playing cards, and the next the tent was on fire."

"Did Lucky get out?"

The disoriented fellow shook his head. "I . . . I don't think so. The last I saw Lucky, he was heading back into the tent toward one of the women who had gone down under a pileup. I turned around to look for him when I got out, but that part of the tent had collapsed already, and the fire was coming so fast that I just followed everybody else up here."

Tessa had taken a few steps forward when Maggie grasped her arm to pull her back. "Where are you going?" she demanded.

"Down to Lucky's tent."

"It's too late! The fire's too hot. The tent is gone."

"I have to find Lucky."

"Tessa, if he can, he'll come up here."

Panicking, Tessa jerked her arm free. She heard Maggie calling her name behind her as she tripped and stumbled down the hill, moving against the steady stream of people heading up. She did not stop despite the thickening smoke and intensifying heat.

Struggling for each breath, she reached the area

where the last of the burning canvas structures flapped hotly in the unrelenting wind. She called out Lucky's name, but the sound went unheard in the clamor of crackling fire and crashing uprights. Walking deeper into the blinding smoke, she came at last to the place where Lucky's tent had stood. She staggered at the sight of the burning remains. She grasped the arm of a man wandering there and shouted, "Did you see Lucky get out?"

"No, ma'am." Apparently disoriented by the smoke, the man said, "I saw him go back in just before the tent fell. Which way do I go to safety, ma'am?"

"Follow the trail."

The fellow turned in the direction she indicated as Tessa sank to her knees. She covered her eyes, overwhelmed by the grief of knowing that Lucky had died believing that she would leave him. She cried hoarsely in broken apology, "I made a mistake. I should have fought for you, Lucky. I should have made you realize that I loved you enough to spend the rest of my life with you, and to make you happier than you had ever been."

Her tears falling freely as the heat intensified, Tessa felt a hand on her arm. Her head jerked upward at the sound of a familiar voice demanding, "What are you doing here, Tessa?"

Incredulous, she stared at Lucky's smoke-stained face as he said urgently, "Let's get out of here before it's too late."

Blinded by the smoke, Tessa allowed Lucky to pull her toward the trail. She climbed rapidly, barely managing to keep up with him, until he noticed when she stumbled for the second time that her feet were bare. Scooping her up, he carried her to a place of safety, where he sank to his knees. Holding her tight as others streamed past them, he looked into her tear-streaked face and said in a rasping voice, "I don't care what you think or what you heard that made you say the things you did, I'm not going to let you go, Tessa. Listen to me now, because I want you to hear what I say. I never loved anybody the way I love you. I never will. I'm not going to buy those tickets back to Iowa, even if you still want to return. I'm going to spend every minute I can convincing you how I feel—"

Tessa's kiss did not allow the remainder of that statement to be spoken. It was a brief kiss because of her shortness of breath, but it was full of meaning.

"I love you, Lucky. I realized tonight that I'll always love you. That's the way it is, and it'll never change."

Still gripping her in the tight circle of his arms, Lucky repeated hoarsely, "That's the way it is, all right, for both of us."

He drew her closer. There was nothing left to say as his mouth found hers.

Epilogue

Weeks had passed since the fire. Lucky curved his arm around Tessa as they watched San Francisco rebuild and the walls of his tent rose from the ashes. The gold rush continued unabated by the blaze that had all but consumed the city, and Lucky knew that San Francisco would continue to grow with it because the harbor was alive. The clear blue of the ocean was dotted with ships bringing in supplies for the rebuilding in progress, and construction materials were snapped up almost the moment they arrived.

The increasing influx of gold seekers appeared unaffected by the fire that had ravaged the city. From his vantage point, Lucky saw men from all stations of life descend on the city from ships that had recently docked. Each had his own destination in mind and his own dreams of gold-gilded glory. He knew that some would see defeat and that some would achieve great things in their quests. He also knew, however, that the former would be many while the latter would be few.

Lucky tightened his arm around Tessa. He had answered all her questions in the aftermath of the fire.

He had told her that he had used up most of his waning strength when he pushed aside the burning canvas that fell on him. He had barely managed to lift the woman he'd saved into the arms of one of the men making his way up the hill. He himself had remained beside his tent until he was relatively sure everyone had escaped.

The fact that so few fatalities had resulted from the fire was a minor miracle. Delilah's whereabouts remained one of the as-yet-unsolved mysteries. Although her tent was unaffected by the fire, she had disappeared. Some thought she had become frightened by the fire and had fled on the first wagon leaving the city. Some believed that she had become disoriented and had run into the burning city, instead of away from it. The disputes raged even as his own uncertainty remained. He knew only that he had done his best for her, and that he wished her well in spite of his recent doubts about her character.

Harley Knox was another of the missing. His determination to return to the burning city had been noted by many. Most of them believed that he had died attempting to save the cache of funds that he was rumored to have hidden in his brothel. Strangely enough considering the respect he'd commanded while alive, no on appeared to mourn him.

Another anomaly was that all the Frenchwomen from his bordello had departed. Some, including the older madam who had seemed relieved that her duties in Harley's house were over, had returned to France. Others had sailed for different American cities.

Lucky tightened his arm around Tessa as his love for her surged through him. As for himself, the rising tent was temporary and meant to be replaced at a later time with a more permanent structure. In the interim, he had decided to attach a section where breakfast and supper could be cooked and served with additional help that Tessa would hire. Tessa had expressed concern for the prospectors that continued to pour into the city, and he had welcomed the idea of providing extra meals.

As for Tessa and himself, well, that was another matter entirely.

Lucky lowered his head to kiss Tessa's warm lips as she leaned up against him. He knew that he would never grow immune to the gaze of her wide, gray eyes, to the perfection of her delicate features, or to the sheen of platinum hair that would eventually go gray along with his after a lifetime spent together. He had great plans for that lifetime, which included a family and friends in this new San Francisco, and years spent in each others' arms.

Because he loved Tessa.

Because she was now his wife.

Because she was expecting their first child.

Because they had already decided that Maggie would make a great grandmother and Nugget a great grandfather for the child when it was born in the cabin that he had built for his growing family—a cabin also meant to be replaced by a more permanent structure at some time in the future.

Lucky dipped his head again to taste Tessa's lips. He was happier than he had ever been, and was looking forward to the future in which he had a greater stake than ever before.

Because Tessa had made his life complete in every way.

Because she lay in his bed each night, close, loving, forever his.

Because he knew he would never tire of a woman who answered all his needs so completely.

Suddenly sobering, Lucky looked down at Tessa. He asked unexpectedly, "Are you really happy, Tessa?"

Appearing initially startled by the question, Tessa replied with a question of her own, "Are you still uncertain?" Not waiting for him to respond, she continued. "In the event you are, I'll answer that question once and for all. You're all I'll ever want, Lucky. You've made all my dreams come true. I'm not talking about the dreams of gold that originally brought my parents and me out here. I'm referring to dreams of finding a man who is honest and true, who will protect me with every bit of strength he possesses, and who will love me as much as I love him. That's the way I feel. That will never change, and yes, I am happy."

Lucky took a breath. He stared wordlessly down at Tessa while realizing that she had voiced everything he could ever hope to say with that simple statement. He clutched her closer as the hammering and sawing of construction grew louder and their tent rose before their eyes like a phoenix from the ashes. Whatever came their way, he and Tessa would share it together.

That was the most important thing.

And there was nothing more to say.

✂ ❏ **YES!**

Sign me up for the Historical Romance Book Club and send my FREE BOOKS! If I choose to stay in the club, I will pay only $8.50* each month, a savings of $6.48!

NAME: _____

ADDRESS: _____

TELEPHONE: _____

EMAIL: _____

❏ I want to pay by credit card.

❏ **VISA**   ❏ **MasterCard**   ❏ **DISCOVER**

ACCOUNT #: _____

EXPIRATION DATE: _____

SIGNATURE: _____

Mail this page along with $2.00 shipping and handling to:
Historical Romance Book Club
PO Box 6640
Wayne, PA 19087
Or fax (must include credit card information) to:
610-995-9274

You can also sign up online at **www.dorchesterpub.com**.
*Plus $2.00 for shipping. Offer open to residents of the U.S. and Canada only.
Canadian residents please call 1-800-481-9191 for pricing information.
If under 18, a parent or guardian must sign. Terms, prices and conditions subject to change. Subscription subject to acceptance. Dorchester Publishing reserves the right to reject any order or cancel any subscription.